Debutantes in Paris

*Three friends, three dashing heroes,
one life-changing trip!*

Three best friends from Miss Grantley's School for
Young Ladies, Diana, Emily and Lady Alexandra,
are excited to finally be free of school, family and
society's expectations as they head off
for a summer of adventure in Paris!

They each have plans for their futures—and they
don't include marriage anytime soon. But meeting
three dashing gentlemen in the most romantic city in
the world soon puts paid to the best-laid plans...

Read Diana's story in

Secrets of a Wallflower

Read Lady Alexandra's story in

The Governess's Convenient Marriage

Read Emily's story in

Miss Fortescue's Protector in Paris

All available now

AMANDA McCABE

Miss Fortescue's Protector in Paris

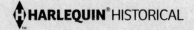

Recycling programs
for this product may
not exist in your area.

ISBN-13: 978-1-335-63511-2

Miss Fortescue's Protector in Paris

Printed in U.S.A.

Amanda McCabe wrote her first romance at the age of sixteen—a vast epic, starring all her friends as the characters, written secretly during algebra class. She's never since used algebra, but her books have been nominated for many awards, including a RITA® Award, an RT Reviewers' Choice Best Book Award, a Booksellers' Best Award, a National Readers' Choice Award and a HOLT Medallion. She lives in Oklahoma with her husband, one dog and one cat.

Books by Amanda McCabe

Harlequin Historical
and Harlequin Historical *Undone!* ebook

Betrayed by His Kiss
The Demure Miss Manning
The Queen's Christmas Summons

Debutantes in Paris

Secrets of a Wallflower
The Governess's Convenient Marriage
Miss Fortescue's Protector in Paris

Bancrofts of Barton Park

The Runaway Countess
Running from Scandal
Running into Temptation (Undone!)
The Wallflower's Mistletoe Wedding

Visit the Author Profile page
at Harlequin.com for more titles.

Prologue

Miss Grantley's School for Young Ladies—1888

It seemed like an ordinary day. Not *completely* ordinary, of course—it was the day families came to visit at Miss Grantley's School for Young Ladies. Lessons were suspended and games of tennis and croquet were played on the wide green lawns, tea served in shady groves, while teachers were dispatched to answer parents' anxious questions about their daughters' progress.

The red-brick Georgian mansion that housed the school gleamed in the bright spring sunshine, as if the weather was specially ordered for the day, and girls streamed in and out in their fluttering white dresses. Laughter was light and musical on the warm breeze.

Emily Fortescue twirled her tennis racket as she took in the whole pretty scene. It was her last spring at Miss Grantley's. In only a few weeks, she and her friends would graduate and scatter out into the world to find their destinies. She knew what surely awaited her best chums, Lady Alexandra Mannerly and Diana Martin—

marriage to a suitable gentleman, a place in society. For Alex, the daughter of a duke and the goddaughter of the Princess of Wales herself, a high place indeed was expected, despite her shy reservations. She was beautiful and connected. Diana, too, came from a respectable family, with her father retired from the India station, and could be expected to find someone of similar stature, a life helping her husband in his career, even though she truly wanted to be a writer.

But what lay ahead for Emily?

She held up her hand to shade her eyes from the sun. She studied the families who were gathered around the tea tables, who strolled the garden paths, mothers arm in arm with daughters, fathers peppering the teachers with questions. But her own father, her only family, was not there. He seldom was.

Not that she blamed him, she thought with a sigh. Albert Fortescue had a business to run, a business that grew larger and more complex every year. Ever since Emily's mother died when Emily was only a toddler, her father had been determined to give his only daughter a good life. He had expanded a small wine distribution and import-export company into a very lucrative concern, with many different departments and accounts all over Europe.

His hard work had given them a large house on Cadogan Square, Emily's education at Miss Grantley's, travels abroad and lovely clothes. And she had far more freedom than most of her friends. She was not hemmed in by chaperons, except for those dictated by the school, and had few expectations heaped upon her beyond doing well in her studies. Her father talked of her helping him in the company and that would surely suit her well. Being a delicate, retiring fine lady would be suffocating.

But, just once in a while, she wished her father could just—be with her. Come to a families' day at Miss Grantley's, look at her schoolwork, sit with her in the shade. Or, even more achingly, she wished her mother could be there, elegant in a fashionable feathered hat and pearls, comfortingly rose-scented like the other mothers, taking Emily's arm as they strolled through the gardens. Smiling, giving her advice, listening to Emily's doubts about the future.

But then again—her mother might not have been like the sweet, understanding, light-hearted being Emily held in her imagination. She might have been more like the Duchess of Waverton.

Emily watched as Alex's mother gave her one more lecture before climbing into the glossy black carriage with its ducal crest on the door and finally leaving Miss Grantley's. Alex looked pale against her sky-blue dress, her hands twisting in her skirt as she nodded at whatever the Duchess was saying. It was no doubt a stern list of proper behaviour for a duke's daughter.

Yes, Emily thought. Maybe she was lucky after all. Her future was an open question, whatever she wanted to make of it. Alex's was set.

'Poor Alex,' she heard a voice say behind her, low and slightly rough, a hint of suppressed laughter hidden in its depths. 'I always thank my lucky stars the Duchess is my aunt, and not my mother.'

Emily smiled. *Christopher Blakely.* Alex's cousin

always livened up the school when he came to visit. Handsome, funny, light-hearted, always up for a game of tennis or a quick quarrel about whatever issues of the day happened to strike like a match between them. Yes, they always argued, but Emily had to admit it was fun.

She turned to look at him and was almost knocked over by her dazzlement. He really was ridiculously good looking; it was no wonder all the girls at the school were in love with him. Tall, slim, golden-haired like an Apollo, with vivid blue eyes and a perfect blade of a nose, sharp cheekbones, always moving with a quick, loose grace that matched the careless, yet somehow always elegant, way he dressed. She had heard such gossip about the trouble he got into in town and she quite believed it all.

'Do you escape the famous Waverton lectures, then?' she asked.

'Of course not. Anyone in my aunt's orbit is fair game for lectures on the proper way to live and I have much to correct,' he said with a grin, a flash of white teeth and sunshine that made her smile, too. 'She and my mother are like two peas in a pod. Organising lives is their reason for being.'

'And what do they tell you that you should do?' She thought of the whispered tales, of his trouble at Oxford, how he was almost sent down; the gambling and late nights in London.

'The usual things. Find useful work, get married. But not too soon. And only to the most suitable girl. Cease my rackety ways and finish my degree.'

Emily laughed. It was hard to picture Chris married to a 'suitable' pale, aristocratic girl, going to an office every day in a grey suit. He seemed to have been born too late. He should have been an Elizabethan explorer, not a Victorian aristocrat. 'And do they tell your brother that, too?'

Chris glanced at his brother William who was talking to Emily's friend Diana near the house. Will looked so different from Chris, dark and solemn, always so perfect. 'Of course not. Will is always serious and responsible. It's hard to live up to his good name at Oxford, I can tell you. He knows what he wants out of life. He does what he should do.'

Emily was suddenly caught by something in Chris's tone, something strangely wistful and sad. She had never heard that from him before. 'And you don't know what you want to do?'

'Certainly not. What normal young man of my age does? Will is unnaturally solemn. It will get him into trouble some day. I intend to take my time deciding on things. Exploring the world.'

Emily sighed. 'At least you *have* the time. I feel like mine is running out.'

Chris tilted his head back, his eyes narrowed as he studied her. He looked puzzled. 'What do you mean? You're still in school.'

'But ladies can't *try* things, can't take their time to decide who they are. We have to find someone to marry immediately and then our lives are set. No more exploring. No more—deciding.'

'Oh, Emily. You're so pretty, you'll have no worries there. You'll find a very good husband and have a very good sort of life.'

He thought her *pretty*? Emily studied him carefully,

feeling a little flustered, a little pleased and a little exasperated that he had missed her point. She almost
laughed. She saw he was trying to help, to be kind, but
he didn't understand. Perhaps he couldn't. Perhaps no
man could. 'What if being married isn't what I want to
do? Not the only thing, anyway.'

He frowned. 'What else would you want?'

Emily felt a jolt of exasperation flash through her.
'Oh—I don't know!' she cried, frustrated. She thought
of Diana and how she wanted to write; Alex, and her
sweetness and kindness to others. They all had so much
to offer the world and no one seemed to want it. They
only seemed to want women to set up nurseries and go
over menus.

She remembered when she was younger and her father would take her to the office with him. When he
worked, she would sit at a desk in the corner and look
at the ledgers. She liked seeing how the accounts lined
up, liked seeing the list of imported goods and imagining where they would go. She liked the way it all
made sense.

'Maybe I want to run a business, like my father,' she
said. 'Or travel the world! Or invent things or raise ter-
rier puppies. The point is, I don't know yet. And I don't
have time to find out, as you do. Men are still young
blades at twenty-five, while women are growing old
and useless.'

He still looked adorably, maddeningly, puzzled. 'But
you're a lady. Good at running a household, surely.
Where would society be without that? Good at raising
children, helping charities...'

Emily threw up her hands, the tennis racket she still held tumbling to the ground. 'You just don't understand, Christopher! It's like speaking a different language— men and women will never decipher each other.' She stalked away, down the pathway that led through quiet, shady stands of trees to the ornamental pond. It was usually a walk that soothed her, made her feel peaceful in nature, but today its beauty only made her feel more unsettled.

She dropped on to a wrought-iron bench near the edge of the pond and stared out at the rowboats that dotted the water. It looked like a French painting, all dappled light and hazy figures in white lazing in the warm afternoon.

She heard the rustle of footsteps and Chris sat down carefully beside her. She glanced up at him and he gave her a sweet, placating smile that surely melted hearts all the way from Oxford to the Scottish border.

'Do you really think that is all a lady can do?' she asked, feeling so sad. 'Marry and do charity work?'

He glanced out at the pond for a quiet moment, as if thinking over her words. 'It seems to be what most of the ladies *I* know want to do,' he said. His smile turned mischievous. 'Except for ladies who aren't really ladies, of course.'

Emily had to laugh. 'Actresses and chorus girls? Women who work in cafés?'

'And what do you know about that?'

'Not nearly as much as you do, I'm sure. But maybe *I* should be an actress.'

'You wouldn't be the fun sort.' He studied her closely,

until she wanted to squirm. 'You would be some terribly serious Shakespearean tragedienne, or maybe you would sing grand Italian opera. The sort that makes me fall asleep.'

Emily shook her head. 'I can't carry a tune at all, I'm afraid. I got tossed out of music class. And I can't memorise a poem to save my life. I am the despair of our literature teachers.' She felt a pang that there was something she could not, after all, excel at, when other classes came so easily. 'I guess it must be marriage for me after all.'

She felt a gentle touch on her hand, and, startled, she glanced down to see Chris's fingers over hers. His touch was warm, tingling, delightful. She looked up at him to see his cut-glass handsome face was serious, watchful, even more beautiful than ever. For just that one instant, she thought he might actually *see* her.

'Some bloke will be so lucky, Em,' he said softly. 'And he had better work bloody hard to make you happy.'

Emily didn't even notice the cursing, she was too lost in his eyes. Like drowning in endless blue. She felt like someone in one of the novels Diana loved so much, caught in moments that felt out of time, sparkling, delicate, perfect. His expression changed as he looked at her, darkened.

She was drawn closer to him, unable to turn away, as if invisible, unbreakable bonds tied them together. As if in a hazy, warm dream, she felt Chris's arms come around her, drawing her so close nothing could come between them. Emily found herself longing to seize the moment, to make it her own and never forget it.

She looped her arms around his neck and closed her eyes, inhaling the warm scent of him, of fresh air, clean linen, faint lemony cologne, of Chris himself. It made her feel dizzy, giddy, like too much champagne.

She gently touched his cheek. He moaned a low, hoarse sound, and his lips claimed hers at last. She met his kiss with everything she had, all the emotion locked away inside her. It wasn't a gentle kiss, as surely first kisses usually were, but one filled with heat, desperation, need. She wanted it to go on and on for ever.

A burst of laughter nearby broke into Emily's dream and she pulled back from Chris's embrace, hot and cold all at the same time. Flustered and panicked, and full of a strange, bursting—joy. Had she just *kissed* Chris Blakely? Where had such a fantastical thing come from?

She stared up at him in astonishment. He looked just as shocked as she did, a dull red flush over his sharp cheekbones. His eyes closed and he shook his head, an appalled expression spreading over his face.

Appalled? At the thought of kissing her? Had she been that bad at it? Emily suddenly felt so disgusted with herself.

'Em,' he said, his voice tight and strangled, so unlike his usual joking self. 'I'm so very sorry. What a rotten thing...'

Emily wanted to hear no more. She couldn't stand that something which had been, only a moment before, strange and wondrous and almost beautiful, had become something *rotten* to him. She jumped to her feet and backed away, trying not to scrub at her lips with her hand, to erase the memory of his touch. To try to erase those awful feelings.

Surely those London chorus girls he knew would never be such ninnies over a mere kiss. 'Don't think anything of it,' she said, trying to laugh. To her own ears, she sounded high-pitched and frantic, like an ingénue on the melodrama stage. 'How silly we are today! I must be getting back to the school.'

He stood up beside her, his hair tousled, his eyes wide. He held out his hand. 'Emily, please...'

Her own eyes were starting to film over, making the sparkling water of the pond hazy, and she would rather throw herself into its depths before she let him see her cry. Before she would let *anyone* see her cry.

She whirled around and ran back down the path, ignoring the sound of her name as Chris called after her. She scrubbed furiously at her eyes and pasted a fierce smile on her lips. No one could suspect what a fool she had been.

Diana and Alex ran towards her as she came closer to the house. They both looked a little worried and Emily knew she couldn't fool them entirely as to her emotional turmoil. They were her best friends and a smiling façade couldn't quite conceal her thoughts from them.

But neither would they ever pry. All three of them would wait patiently until one had a confidence to share.

Emily knew this was one confidence she would *never* share, even with her friends.

'Are you quite well, Em?' Diana asked. 'Your cheeks are very pink.'

'Perfectly well,' Emily answered, giving her hand a careless wave. 'I've just been sitting in the sun too long.'

Alex held out a straw boater hat. 'You did forget your hat again.'

'Oh, drat it. I certainly don't need another lecture from Miss Grantley about freckles.' Emily took the hat and pinned it on her dishevelled hair, glad the wide brim could hide part of her face. Her expression.

'Maybe we should go inside, find some cool lemonade?' Diana said.

'Or maybe we should take you to the nurse?' Alex asked, her tone full of her usual quiet worry. Alex always wanted to take care of everyone. 'Too much sun can be dangerous.'

'Of course I don't need to see the nurse, I'm perfectly all right,' Emily answered. She scooped up her tennis racket from where she had dropped it in the grass. 'Let's just have a game before we have to go in to tea!'

Alex and Diana exchanged another long glance, before they nodded. 'Maybe Millie or Elizabeth could join us,' Diana said.

Emily took a deep breath and made a couple of fierce practice swings with her racket. She imagined they were landing right on Chris Blakely's golden, handsome head…

Chris was very much afraid that, when he looked back on this one instant years later, he would see his life divided into 'before' and 'after'. Before Emily Fortescue and after.

He stood in the shadows of a grove of trees at the

edge of the sun-splashed green tennis lawn and watched her play with her friends. She leaped into the air, her white skirts billowing around her, her racket wielded like a young Athena charging into battle. Her chestnut hair, red and gold and amber in the sunlight, was tumbling from its pins and she was laughing.

Her face, sharp-chiselled and angular as a cat, was usually so serious, so deep in thought and watchful, as if she saw deep into people's thoughts and read their deepest secrets—and didn't quite approve. But when she laughed, she was utterly transformed. The rich, merry, uninhibited sound of it would draw anyone closer. Like a siren.

But sirens drove men to their deaths with unfulfilled longings. They pulled men in even as they shoved them away. Chris feared that was definitely the case with Emily.

He raked his hands through his hair, leaving the overlong blonde strands he was always meant to trim properly standing on end—another disappointment to his parents. But he couldn't dislodge the memory of that kiss.

That kiss.

What had he been thinking? Had he gone sun-mad in that moment? But he knew the truth. He had *not* been thinking. Just as his father always shouted at him, Chris never thought about what he was doing. Yet kissing Emily was hardly like missing his tutor's lecture to go for a lark on the river or drinking at the Dog and Hare. Kissing Emily was…

Was the stupidest thing he had ever done. And the

most wonderful. For just that one moment, when their lips touched and he tasted the tart sweetness of lemonade, felt the lithe grace of her under his touch, it was like breaking free and soaring. Like the drunken, sparkling magic of a Bonfire Night. Like he was just where he should be.

Only for a moment. Then it all crashed down again. This wasn't a chorus girl, no matter what wild ambitions she proclaimed. Not a tart at the Dog and Hare. It was *Emily*. Emily Fortescue. His cousin's friend. A young lady of education and wealth. Being involved with her would mean promises, expectations. *Serious* promises. And he was no good at serious.

Not that she would have him even if he was. She was far too good for him and everyone knew it.

He watched her now, laughing in the sunlight. She had picked up the ball from where it fell by the net and was casually tossing it high and catching it again as she chatted with her friends. Graceful, easy, her mobile, sensual mouth smiling. Her hair like autumn leaves, shimmering, heavy, enticing a man to pull it free from its pins and see how long and luxurious it was. Feeling it under his touch. She was so enticing, beautiful and smart and serious…

And he was someone in danger of being sent down from Oxford unless he mended his careless ways and started behaving like a Blakely, according to his parents. He was someone who excelled at making parties merrier and not much else. Emily was clever, beautiful, smart enough to run her father's business one day, if she wanted. Smart enough to marry anyone she liked.

His cousin Alex said Emily was sure to even expand her father's already lucrative business and become an even more wealthy heiress one day.

He could certainly believe it, after how angry she became when he suggested marriage was her best option, a lady's only choice.

Yet if she *didn't* marry, he thought ruefully, it would be quite a waste. What a kisser she was. It made him wonder what else she would be brilliant at, in the privacy of a bedchamber…

Chris shook his head hard to dislodge a sudden image of Emily Fortescue dressed only in a thin silk chemise, laughing amid a billow of white pillows, her glorious chestnut hair spread mermaid-like around her. He had no business thinking about her that way.

And when they were together, they always seemed to argue. She was definitely not for the likes of him and he was not for her. Maybe they would have fun in the bedroom, if that wild kiss was any indication, but they would quarrel each other to death everywhere else. She was too strong-minded, too gloriously goddess-like, for everyday use.

And he was sure he would never quite measure up to her.

Yet, oh, she was so beautiful. He watched as she gracefully drew her arm back to serve, the long, lean line of her body. How had he never realised that before? Oh, he had always known she was pretty, that was impossible to miss. But she was actually incomparable.

'What are you doing lurking out here, Chris?' he heard his brother William say.

He glanced back to see Will walking towards him along the pathway between the trees, his brother's dark suit and dark hair blending into the shadows. He looked impeccable, responsible, the always-serious one. 'Just hiding for a moment before I plunge into all that Miss Grantley's schoolness, I suppose. I have a newfound allergy to academia, even if this isn't quite Oxford.'

Will gave a wry chuckle. 'I'm rather surprised you showed up at all. It doesn't seem like your sort of scene.'

Chris glanced at Emily again, her white skirts a blur as she dashed along the net. Her laughter floated back to him on the breeze. 'Lemonade and deportment lessons? No, thank you. But I thought Alex might appreciate someone here besides the Duchess.'

Will smiled. 'Yes. Poor, sweet Alex.' He, too, studied the tennis game and for one awful instant Chris wondered if he, too, admired Emily. But then he realised Will watched Diana Martin, her hair a bright red in the light, waving her racket in mock-threat at Emily. Will's smile seemed uncharacteristically—soft in that moment.

Interesting.

Will turned away from the sun-dappled scene and aimed his piercing blue gaze at Chris. Much like Emily, Will had an uncanny ability to see too much. Even when they were children, Chris could never pull off pranks on Will. And now Will had left university with a First in the Classics and worked for the Foreign Office, respectable and perfect.

'Are you sure nothing is amiss, Chris?' Will asked.

Chris shook his head, making himself give his trademark careless grin. It always seemed to throw everyone off. 'Amiss? Whatever could be amiss on such a bright, sunny day, far away from any work at all?'

'Yes,' Will said quietly. *Quiet* with him was always a dangerous sign. When Will got quiet, it meant he was thinking even more than usual. 'You want everyone to think all your days are bright and sunny, don't you, Brother?'

Chris turned away. 'Why should they not be? We are young, the world is open to us. Pretty girls, a drink at the pub tonight, maybe a horse race tomorrow...'

'And that's all there is?'

'Of course it's not,' Chris said, feeling a strange anger rise up in him. Life *should* be more, should have some purpose. That was easy for someone like Will to say, or Emily. They seemed brimming with purpose, with serious minds that led them towards something greater. Chris searched for it, but where was it? So, he played the pleasure-seeker, the clown, the trickster.

He looked towards the tennis lawn. The game was over and Emily had put on her hat and was hurrying towards the house, arm in arm with Alex and Diana, the three of them giggling together as if they hadn't a care in the world. As if the world hadn't been rocked with a kiss.

'But that's what life is for now,' Chris concluded. 'As to the future, who can say? Father declares I'm fitted for nothing. Maybe he's right.'

Will frowned. 'When has Father been right about anything?' he said. 'Listen, Chris, you'll be done at

Oxford soon. Why don't you come talk to them at the Foreign Office? I can arrange an appointment time.'

'And work with you?' Chris thought of how he would come off next to Will and shook his head. 'They wouldn't take me. And I'd die of boredom there after a day at a desk, thinking about infinitely boring people at infinitely boring foreign courts.'

Will laughed, a rare, rich sound. 'Not every job there is as tedious as formal diplomacy, Chris. There is a lot there that would suit you very well indeed. And I'll be leaving for India soon; they need more men at the London office. You should think about it, anyway. Father will start making noises again about the church and Mother will find you an heiress to marry if you don't head them off with a different plan.'

Chris grinned. Both of those were tacks their parents had taken with him many times. Both sounded like the depths of wretchedness. Maybe Will had a point. If he had a different job in mind, there could be no vicarages in his future. 'We'll see.'

'Good, do think about it. Now, should we go in? Surely it's time for tea and no one could ever fault Miss Grantley's for their excellent cook.'

'True. I've been thinking about those raspberry tarts all day.' Chris followed Will towards the arbour where maids were setting up the tea service and he was glad the day was almost done. But he could swear he heard the echo of Emily's laughter following him at every step.

Chapter One

London—spring 1891

Christopher Blakely was sure his eyes were crossing from the mounds of paperwork. He had been making his way through them for hours and still the piles of documents loomed high. This was by far his least favourite part of the job.

He pushed the papers away and sat back in his chair with a laugh. Surely he would be more useful at a party somewhere, drinking and laughing, drawing people in—and learning their secrets. Wasn't that why the Foreign Office had hired him in the first place, after his useless years at university? His light-hearted ways, his charm, his genuine interest in people and their strange ways. Such charm drew people close, invited their confidences, in a way that cool professionalism, such as that possessed by his brother Will couldn't hope to accomplish. At least not as quickly as Chris, with his dimpled smiles and endless bottles of wine, the way he seemed born to read people and situations and adjust his reactions accordingly, could achieve.

He sighed as he plucked the document off the top of the pile—a report from an operative in Berlin, where trouble always seemed to be brewing. Even though the Kaiser was Queen Victoria's own grandson, he was a troublemaker of endless ambition and jealousy. It was certainly difficult work, there on the ground in the embassies, a tightrope of keeping secrets while ferreting out everyone else's, especially in etiquette-ridden places like Berlin. Yet Chris found he rather envied those men. They were respected, known. His own work, once so exciting, now seemed rather—dim.

The parties, the laughter that hid so much behind the bright masks, the satisfaction of drawing out hidden dangers and using that information to help his country— it had been everything to him. It was all he could have wanted, using his own gifts to do some good, gifts so different from Will's, from what his parents had always demanded. It gave him a deep fulfilment. Pleasure, even.

But he was not as young as he once was. Chris ruefully ran his hand through his hair and wondered when its golden colour would turn iron-grey. When his 'light-hearted rogue' act would no longer be useful. It was already dull to himself.

He glanced at a photograph in its silver frame, set on the edge of the desk as if to remind him that he *did* have a family, that he owed something to other people. Will and Diana Martin on their wedding day more than a year ago, all elegant morning coat and white satin, all joyful smiles. Even after all these months, the soft way they looked at each other, those secret smiles only for themselves, were still just as tender as they had been on that day.

It made Chris smile to think of them. And it made him feel discomfited. Nothing like that was on the horizon for him. He had become *too* good at his work. His reputation as a rake put him beyond serious marital consideration, even if he had wanted to marry. Society mamas let him dance with their daughters and flirted with him themselves, but he knew they did not see him as a good prospect. They only saw what he chose to show them.

Even if he *did* marry, he could never really be honest with a wife, could never be his true self. He wouldn't put a person he cared about in a perilous position, not when his work included all manner of people and situations. Risking his own safety and reputation was one thing; he couldn't do such a thing to a lady. Even if there was one out there who would have him.

Against his will, an image appeared in his mind as he thought of a lady he *could* care about—an image that came up too often sometimes. Emily Fortescue.

He saw her as she was at Di and Will's wedding, her pale blue silk gown like the sky itself, her laughter as she caught the bouquet. Emily, with her sharply edged intelligence, her hazel eyes that always saw too much, her lips that tasted so sweet under his. So irresistible. She made him want to spill all his secrets to her, to tell her everything, and that was dangerous indeed.

Chris glanced again at the wedding image. Will and Di were Emily's friends, too. Diana was practically her sister. He could never offer Emily, who meant so much to so many people, the kind of marriage she deserved; neither could he trifle with her. Not that he could imagine *anyone* trifling with Emily's affections at all. She was too intelligent, too independent, and she had made it clear she did not intend to marry.

So, Emily Fortescue was the only lady he could imagine marrying—and the last lady he ever could. It was a prison of his own making and one he could never back out of now. His work depended on it; too many people depended on it, even if they would never know it.

He pushed away memories of Emily, as he so often had to do, and reached for the pile of papers again. Even the problems of Berlin were less complicated than romance.

Luckily, a knock at the door interrupted the tedious task. 'Come in,' he called in relief.

It was Laura, Lady Smythe-Tomas, another of the office's secret agents and one of their most successful. A beautiful, redheaded young widow, she had a rare sense of style, a deep, husky laugh and royal connections to the Marlborough House Set. She and Chris had worked together often before and he always enjoyed her company, even if they were far too similar to ever be romantically involved. It was too bad; he wouldn't have to hide his work from her.

'Christopher, darling, are you ready for...?' She paused in adjusting her kid evening gloves and sapphire-blue gown, her luminous green eyes narrowed as she took in his shirtsleeves and tousled hair. 'I see you are not. Are we going to be fashionably late?'

'Late for—what?' Then Chris suddenly remembered. A gambling party at a very secret, very exclusive club, one which high-ranking German and Russian diplomats favoured.

Laura laughed and perched on the edge of his desk. 'Too engrossed in all those fascinating reports, I see. Well, there is plenty of time. It's better if we give them time to find the claret, then they're easier to talk to. And we must appear to be carelessly late fribbles, anyway, yes?'

'Fribbles we must be.' Chris went to the wardrobe in the corner where he kept his extra evening clothes for just such emergencies. He glanced back at Laura, who was sorting through her beaded reticule and humming a little waltz to herself. She had been widowed for many years, left almost penniless by her titled older husband. Was she ever lonely? Did she ever regret the work? 'Laura…'

'Yes, darling?' she answered, tucking a strand of dark red hair into her beaded bandeau.

'Have you never considered marrying again?'

She gave a startled laugh. 'Why, Chris! Are you proposing to me?' She laughed even harder when he was afraid he looked rather alarmed. 'Oh, don't look so frightened. I know very well you are not. If there is anyone who is *less* the marrying sort than I am, it's you.' She slid off the desk and planted her gloved hands on her hips. 'Why? Have you met someone and are having second thoughts about this work?'

'No, not at all. I was just—just thinking about Will, I suppose.'

'Oh, William.' Laura waved her hand. 'He is different. He works above-board at an embassy, he must have a spouse. One would just get in the way of our kind of work. You know that.'

'Of course I know that.' He had always known that, that being rakish was part of the importance of what he did. It was only lately that he felt himself changing, changing in ways he did not understand. 'But have you not ever felt, I don't know—felt alone?'

'Oh, Chris, darling.' She gave him a concerned frown and stepped forward to press his hand. 'I confess I do. My marriage was not all it should have been, but still it was nice to know someone was there if I stumbled. But I am so much better off now and so are you. We are too good at our work to give it up.'

Chris nodded. He did know the score, he always had. He just had to shake away those wistful feelings and get on with what he was so good at doing.

'Tonight's party should be just the thing to chase the glooms away!' Laura said, handing him his silk cravat. 'Just think of all the lovely ladies who will be there, ready and eager for you to sweep them off their feet and learn all their little secrets…'

Chapter Two

*E*mily was running...running down the same endless dark alleyway lined with towering bales of cloth stretching so tall and so out of sight that she was sure they reached up into the sky that was always night. She couldn't even see the starlight, only splashes of hazy, haloed gaslight that came from unseen lamps. She heard voices, but they came from so far away they only seemed like an echo of mocking laughter.

But the footsteps behind her were very clear. Slow, stately, unrelenting. Not hurried at all, not a panicked run like hers, but always moving closer.

Her lungs ached, her breath was strangled in her throat. Her hair tumbled into her eyes, blinding her.

She tried to run faster, but the alley was now choked with cobwebs, wrapping around her ankles, pulling her back. Making her trip. The footsteps grew louder and she fell, toppling towards the ground. He would surely catch her now and she was helpless, cornered like a fox pursued by baying hounds.

She was falling...

'No!' Emily cried, sitting straight up. For an instant she was sure the cobwebs had trapped her, holding her limbs immobile. Then she realised it was only the blanket, tangled around her. She was on her bedroom *chaise*, where she had gone for an afternoon rest, safe in her own chamber.

It was only that nightmare again.

With a cry of frustration, Emily pulled the blanket free and tossed it on the green-and-white-flowered carpet. She lay back on the tufted velvet cushions and closed her eyes.

For a time, after the *event*, the dream had plagued her almost every night when she tried to sleep. It had got so bad, she would just stay up every night and go over all the business ledgers in her father's library. Her hard work, and begging pleas, had finally convinced her father to let her stop with her social Season and go into business full-time with him. With work, lots of work, the nightmare stopped and she almost forgot that one stupid event.

But it seemed it didn't want to be forgotten. Not entirely.

She had been a foolish girl, thinking a man like Gregory Hamilton—handsome, highly connected, known for being something of a rake—would be truly interested in her. Yet it had been her first Season, fresh out of school, and she had wanted to dance and flirt, to laugh. Then he'd got her out on the terrace at that ball and she'd realised how foolish she really *had* been.

She had got away then and Gregory had gone away

to Ceylon. Work had made her forget that cold fear, but still the dream came sometimes.

It was the last time she would ever be foolish over a man, Emily had always vowed, and she kept that promise to herself now. She'd had lots of suitors, some of them just as handsome and rich as Gregory had been, all of them quite dull. None of them could tempt her. She threw herself into her work, into making her father's business even more successful than before.

Except whenever she saw Chris Blakely. When he came near, her vows to be sensible seemed to just fly out the window. They quarrelled every time they met, the last time at Alex's wedding to Malcolm Gordston, and then Lady Rippon's garden party. Chris was quite hopeless, given up as a wastrel by everyone. But when he kissed her...

'No more,' she cried, kicking at the blanket.

'Miss Emily,' she heard her maid Mary call out, as Mary knocked at the door. 'Are you quite all right? Edna thought she heard you cry out while she was dusting down the corridor.'

'Oh, yes, Mary, I'm fine,' she answered, reaching for the dropped blanket. 'It was just a bad dream. I must have fallen asleep.'

Mary hurried in, Emily's dinner gown of blue silk and chiffon draped over her arm. Emily glanced at the half-curtained window and saw that the light was dark amber now, almost evening. Her father would be expecting her soon for their shared meal.

'I'm sorry, I didn't mean to sleep so long,' Emily said, trying to smooth her rumpled hair.

Mary laid out the dress on Emily's green-brocade-draped four-poster bed and searched the wardrobe for the matching shoes. 'It's no wonder, Miss Emily. You were gone before breakfast this morning.'

'I had to check that the Gordston's shipment was ready to go,' Emily said. Alex's husband, the owner of two, soon to be three, very successful department stores, was one of their best business partners.

She sat down at her dressing table and reached for her silver-backed hairbrush. She tried to pull out the knots in her thick, chestnut hair, but it was hopeless.

'Here, let me do that, Miss Emily,' Mary said, taking the brush with a tsk. 'You'll have no hair left if you keep on like that. And then what would we pin your hats to?'

Emily laughed, some of the tension of her dream dissipating. She thought of the rows and rows of hats that sat on their own shelf in the dressing room, feathers and bows and fruit on straw and velvet and silk. It was part of her job now to be always super-stylish, to advertise the latest fashions, and she had to admit it was a part of her job she rather enjoyed. 'True. I leave myself in your capable hands, Mary, as usual. Is my father already downstairs?'

'He's in his library, I think, Miss Emily.'

Where he always was when he was at home in Cadogan Square. 'Working, no doubt.'

Mary tsked again as she swirled Emily's hair into an elaborate coil at the nape of her neck and secured it with tortoiseshell combs. She handed Emily a pair of aquamarine earrings. 'You both work much too hard.'

'What else is there to do?' Emily murmured as she

slid the jewels on to her earlobes. She thought of what her friends did: Alex with her charity work in Paris as she helped Malcolm run his stores, and Diana writing her magazine articles in Vienna, where she hosted diplomatic receptions for her husband Will. They were busy all the time, too, doing useful things. Emily had to do the same. One day, her work would no longer be hers to do and she would have to find something new. She rather longed for what Diana and Alex had, but such longings did no good. Work was what she had.

Mary frowned disapprovingly, making Emily laugh. Mary had been with the Fortescue household for years, starting as a tweeny when Emily's mother was still alive, and Emily knew she had *opinions* about how they should run their lives. Mary always thought Emily should follow her friends' examples and marry. Emily knew her father felt the same way, though he rarely said so. He would love to see her settled with a good husband, a son-in-law to help carry on his work.

But Emily knew that was impossible. After Gregory Hamilton and his cold hands on that terrace, she couldn't face intimacy with another man—except for Chris Blakely, who was impossible for entirely different reasons. And she could never give up her work.

'For now, I suppose, Miss Emily,' Mary said. She helped Emily out of her brocade dressing gown and into her dinner dress. 'Is there anything else you need?'

Emily reached for her gloves. 'Not now, Mary, thank you. After dinner, I'll need to change into a tweed suit, though, something sturdy. I'll be off to the meeting of the Women's Franchise League.'

* * *

By the time Emily hurried downstairs, her father was waiting in the drawing room, a pre-dinner sherry in hand, reading through the day's newspapers. The financial pages, no doubt, Emily thought as she crossed the room to kiss his cheek. After a day visiting suppliers, checking accounts and lunching with clients, Albert Fortescue liked to know what his rivals were doing.

Emily glanced over her father's shoulder as the butler handed her a cut-crystal glass of the ruby-red liquor. She saw an advertisement, a full half-page, for Gordston's Department Stores of Paris, London and now Brighton.

'I'm very glad to see Gordston's is doing so well,' she said. 'I see he is carrying the latest hats from Madame Fronde's! Anything about the expansion of the Paris store?'

'Not here, but I was looking over the café accounts; we are at beyond capacity there every day. It was an excellent idea of yours to go into such a venture with Mr Gordston, Emily. We will be opening one in the London store any time now, I am sure.'

Emily gave a satisfied smile, remembering the hard work of setting up the elegant café in the Paris store. 'I am certainly glad to hear it. It was a stroke of genius on our parts, I must say, for both us and Malcolm. Ladies can shop even longer if they're properly fortified for the day. Not to mention having a place to meet their friends for a cosy chat, without you men and your dreadful cigars stinking it all to bits.'

Her father laughed and folded his newspapers as he sat back in his armchair. Emily was a bit worried he was looking thinner than usual, his moustache show-ing traces of silver in the chestnut, and she wondered if Mary was right that work was not everything. Maybe her father could use a holiday, to Cannes or Portofino, some place warm. She did worry about his health and she knew that this caused many of his worries for *her*, for who would take care of her one day.

'It was a brilliant idea,' he said. 'Cafés in department stores, it's sure to catch on. In fact, that is something of what I wanted to talk to you about, my dear.'

'The cafés?'

'Paris. I had a note from Mr Gordston asking if we could have a meeting soon, to talk about the possible expansion.'

'Really? I thought the Gordstons were not in the city now. My last letter from Alex was from their country chateau outside Versailles.' She smiled to think of Alex and how happy she was now with her department-store millionaire husband, adored and pampered, just as she deserved. Emily rather envied her.

'Yes, it seems they don't plan to make it back to England any time very soon and I am so caught up in that business with the new spice company out of Ma-dras. I was thinking you could go to Paris in my place. You did such a grand job last year.'

Go back to Paris? Where she'd last seen Chris? Last did such a foolish thing and kissed him in the maze at Lady Rippon's garden party? Emily turned away as she felt her cheeks turn hot.

Her first instinct was to say no. Paris had such an intoxicating effect on her. But Gordston's business *was* very important. And she had heard that Chris was still gadding about the Continent somewhere, doing who knew what. Perhaps he was in Austria with Will and Diana. She would surely not even see him in Paris again.

The butler announced dinner before she could answer and she took her father's arm to make their way towards the dining room. She glimpsed her mother's portrait, as she did every night, hanging near the doorway. Maude Fortescue smiled down at her husband and daughter serenely, always young, always perfect. How Emily wished she could ask her advice now!

But she could not. She never could. Growing up without a mother had made her keep her own counsel, find her advice in books and from her friends. That couldn't change now. But Alex and Diana's marriages, the way they did something different from most of the women in their world, made her wonder if there could be a way for her, too. Probably not. Will and Malcolm were unique husbands.

The dining room was a grand space, meant for entertaining and impressing business associates. With a long, polished mahogany table lined with blue-and-white-striped satin chairs, the silk-papered walls lined with valuable Old Masters, the sideboard gleaming with silver, it spoke quietly of her father's success and good taste. But with only herself and her father at dinner, it seemed full of shadows, echoing, empty.

But two places were arranged at one end of the vast table, a cosy oasis of candlelight glowing on the Wedgwood porcelain, the heavy old silver. Their own cosy world, made just for themselves. What would she do one day when there was only one place laid at her table?

'How lovely it is to get to spend the evening with my beautiful daughter,' her father said as the footman ladled out the salmon bisque. 'It is much too rare. You've become quite the social butterfly lately!'

Emily laughed. Parties were one way to outrun herself, to be sure. 'You are the one who always taught me the value of connections, Father. I'm finding future customers wherever I go. You are no slouch in that direction, either. Were you not at the Criterion with Lady Musgrave's party last week? I am sure I read about it in the paper.'

Albert's cheeks flushed just a bit above his silvering whiskers and Emily wondered if there was more to the contact with Lady Musgrave than a visit to the theatre and a restaurant. She certainly *was* a handsome lady, widowed and energetic and cultured. Maybe that was the sort of rest her father needed? A new companion? Where would Emily's place be, then? Yet she would love her father to find a friend.

'You are quite right, my dear,' he said. 'Connections are all. And Lady Musgrave does serve the best wine in town, her cellar is beyond excellent. I should see about selling her a few cases.'

Emily laughed. 'See? Always working. But, yes, it *is* very nice to have a dinner to ourselves.'

The footman brought in the fish course, a trout in lemon sauce. 'Perhaps a hand of piquet after?'

'I have to go out after dinner.'

Her father chuckled. 'Another dance?'

'Not at all. A meeting of the Women's Franchise League.'

His laughter turned to a doubtful frown. 'Not Mrs Hurst's group?'

'Yes, of course, Father. She is the president of the League. You know I go every month. It's most fascinating and her speakers always have such excellent arguments to make.'

'Emily, I do wish you would not associate with people of such radical and dangerous ideas,' he scolded. 'It's dangerous.'

Emily sighed. They had indeed had such conversations before. She knew her father did not think her or any other educated woman incapable of voting; she knew he had supported the measure quite wholeheartedly when women householders were given the vote in local elections and two were even voted on to the London County Council in 1889. But he disliked tales of riots and arrests at meetings of union leaders and worried such things could happen with the League, as well. It was one of the reasons he was always trying to find a good husband for her, a son-in-law to take care of her and keep her away from such 'radical' interests.

But Emily liked what she heard at the meetings, liked not being dismissed for her brains and ambition. She had to believe her mother would have agreed, as well.

'Oh, Father, I know you do not believe women making their own decisions for their own lives to be *radical*,' she said. 'Have I not done a fine job with you in the business? Have I not a brain and ideas, useful things to offer the world, just like anyone else?'

Her father gave her a gentle smile. 'I could not have done without you these last few years, Emily, and you know that is true. You're a natural at the business, my own daughter, but you are your mother's daughter, as well. I'm afraid I have not reminded you of that often enough.'

'Oh, Father,' Emily said softly. 'I do think of Mama so often. But whatever do you mean?'

'I mean, you have her kind heart as well as her beauty. You should have your own family to appreciate that.' It was an argument he made often and one she knew came from his heart.

Emily stared down hard at her plate, trying to swallow past the knot in her throat. Trying not to think about why she had vowed not to marry. 'You know I don't wish to wed anyone. Not right now, anyway.'

'I know you have *said* that. And it's quite true I know of no man worthy of my lovely daughter. But there must be someone, someone strong and intelligent and kind, who could possibly come into the business with us.' He reached out and gently touched her hand. 'I'm not a young man, Emily. I want to leave everything in capable hands—and not leave you alone.'

'Oh, Father.' Emily covered his hand with her own, trying not to cry. 'You needn't worry about the business, or about me. I am not alone. I have friends.'

'Friends like Mrs Hurst and her group?'

'Yes. And like Diana Blakely and Alexandra Gordston. I am quite well, just as I am, Father. I promise.'

'Just keep an open mind, Emily. That's all I ask. Meet new people. Consider the future.'

Emily gave him a reassuring smile, though she didn't feel at all steady herself. 'I will, I promise. If you will consider taking a holiday yourself.'

'A holiday? Why on earth would I do such a thing?' he scoffed.

'Maybe go to the seaside. Read books. Go for walks.' She smiled at him. 'Maybe Lady Musgrave might enjoy a holiday, as well? You two could go on wine tastings. I do hear Burgundy is lovely this time of year.'

'Minx,' Albert said with a laugh. 'Maybe a holiday isn't such a bad idea after all. But let's talk about you and Paris…'

When Emily left the house after dinner, changed from her silk gown to a tweed walking suit and small felt hat, and journeyed towards the hall where Mrs Hurst and the League met in Pimlico, it had been decided she *would* go to Paris to see to the Gordston business and her father would take a holiday as soon as she returned. Emily tried to tell herself that it was only a short visit to Paris and Chris was sure to be gone from there. She wasn't quite sure if the idea was reassuring, or disappointing. Whenever she thought of Paris, she thought of Chris and the kiss they had shared there the last time they were together in the city. The kiss that made her feel so very much it was frightening.

She took her father's carriage through the city streets, crowded with people making their way to theatres and supper parties, but then sent the coachman away once they arrived at the hall, much to his dutiful chagrin. She promised she would find a ride home from one of the other ladies' carriages, but she didn't mention that they would probably go to a coffee house first to talk about suffrage issues. She waited on the pavement until the carriage had rolled out of sight. Then she hoisted the ledgers she kept as the League's treasurer into her arms and made her way inside.

The League's headquarters didn't look like anything remarkable or radical at all from the outside. A plain brick building, narrow and tall, identical to its neighbours, shutters drawn over the windows. There was no sign by the black-painted door, but a small brass bell. Ever since the League's president, Mrs Hurst, had published a pamphlet titled *Is Marriage A Failure?*, they had been forced to move a couple of times.

Emily gave the bell three short rings and, after a moment, there was the patter of footsteps, the click of locks and the door swung open. To Emily's surprise, it was Mrs Hurst herself who stood there.

Short, plump, greying brown hair in a knot atop her head, dressed in a plain shirtwaist and sensible dark blue skirt, no one would take Mrs Hurst for a radical, either. She smiled and reached out to take some of the ledgers. 'Oh, my dear Miss Fortescue! You are the first to arrive. Do come in. You can help me set up.'

Emily followed her up a narrow flight of stairs and into a small room with a low platform set at one end, faced by rows of chairs. Mrs Hurst handed her a stack of papers to place on each chair, with an article of issues to cover at the meeting: going over the financials, groups sent to seek volunteers in other cities, a roster of speakers at other meetings.

'I'm sure you have all the figures to present during the budget talks,' Mrs Hurst said, bustling around setting up more chairs.

'Oh, yes, of course. We've come out rather ahead last month, I'm glad to say.'

'All because of your hard work, Miss Fortescue! You are quite the most efficient treasurer we have ever had. If you were Minister of the Exchequer, I am sure every problem of the Empire would be quite solved!'

'I'm afraid I'm not such a whiz as all that,' Emily said with a sigh. The accounts had never been the most interesting part of business to her, but they were none the less essential. She made her way down the rows, leaving the agendas at each place. 'I'm not sure we have such a rosy picture for the rest of the quarter, though, unless we can hit on an idea for another fundraiser.'

'It never is especially rosy,' Mrs Hurst said, laughing. 'But I might have a plan to change that, if you're willing to help.'

'Of course I am,' Emily answered, intrigued.

'I was at the Pankhursts' At Home in Russell Square last week. Have you been there?'

'No, but I should dearly like to meet them,' Emily said. She had heard of Richard Pankhurst, a Liberal M.P., and his wife, who were interested in many causes such as suffrage, and the fascinating people they attracted to their drawing room for evenings of music, refreshments and radical conversation.

'Oh, you simply must! Richard and Emmeline are the most astonishing people, so open-minded and full of ideas, and simply everyone goes there. I saw

Grant Allen last week and that Italian anarchist, Ma-
latesta. Mrs Stanton-Blatch is visiting from America
next month. Well, I also met a woman called Madame
Renard, who runs an organisation much like our own
in Paris. They have faced problems similar to ours,
I fear—having the funds to do our work, attracting
women of every social station. But she has a few intriguing ideas for raising funds.'

'What sort of ideas?'

'It's a gentleman from Germany she knows, an Herr
Friedland. Much associated with the court of Emperor
Frederick and his wife, our own Princess Royal still af-
fectionately known as Crown Princess Vicky, of course.
The royal couple were very interested in new ideas, in
following the English liberalism of the Empress Dowager's father, much unlike the rest of the German royals,
and the Empress Dowager still is interested. Herr Friedland says he can act as liaison with her to set up a sort of
roundabout fund for organisations like ours. The Empress
Dowager wants to show her support to do so publicly.'

'Really?' Emily was intrigued, but rather dubious.
The support of people like the Princess Royal would be
very valuable indeed, even if it had to be discreet, but
how could this man be trusted? So many men would do
anything at all to make sure women never had the vote,
never had any power. And she knew Germany was a
very different place from England. 'How can we verify
his credentials, if it all must be so quiet?'

'Well, that is where you can come in, my dear Miss
Fortescue,' Mrs Hurst said, practically clapping her
hands with enthusiasm. 'Madame Renard is to meet

with Herr Friedland in Paris and has invited us to send someone to take part, to learn how we can all benefit. I cannot go, but I know the matter can be in no more capable hands than *yours*.'

'Paris?' Emily said, astonished. A visit to the city coming up twice in one day—it must be a sign she was meant to be there. 'I am meant to go there soon anyway, on business for my father, but I don't know…'

'Excellent! Then it is meant to be, I'm sure,' Mrs Hurst cried happily. 'With enough financing, we can spread our operations to every corner of England at last and ensure freedom to every woman. I will have Madame Renard send you the particulars.'

Before she could ask any more questions, though, the bell rang again and Mrs Hurst dashed down the stairs to let in the others. Emily heard the burst of laughter as the women clattered up the steps and she knew she couldn't focus now on anything but the important business at hand.

Chapter Three

The streets were quieter than Emily expected when she left her friends at the meeting, and she couldn't glimpse any hansoms. She glanced at the watch pinned to her tweed lapel and realised it was later than she usually was. But the city was not completely deserted. She still saw a few carriages leaving late, post-theatre suppers, some lingering diners in cafés. So she decided to walk for a time until a hansom came by, a few minutes to clear her head.

After a League meeting, she always felt filled with energy, fizzing away so she could hardly rest. The rightness of what they were working for filled her with such a sense of purpose, of being right where she should be, that it felt as if she was floating in another world entirely from the real one of parties and appointments.

It was just like that when she was absorbed in her work. Or like those moments hidden in the thick green maze with Chris, his lips on hers, all else vanished…

'No!' she muttered aloud, stabbing at the pavement

with the tip of her umbrella. She wouldn't think about Christopher Blakely now, not tonight. It was only the idea of being in Paris again that brought him back to her so vividly. Paris had been a magical place and time, so beautiful and sparkling, and Chris had been such a part of it. Just as beautiful and sparkling as the Champs-Élysées itself, lit up at night, and just as illusory.

Yet she couldn't help but wonder—what *was* he doing now? Did he ever think about her at all?

'Don't be silly,' she told herself. Of course Chris didn't think of her. He was too busy doing his Chris-like things: gambling clubs and horse races, theatres. He never had serious thought and he was all wrong for her.

But, oh, he *was* fun. Handsome and merry, so unlike her own serious self. Yes, she did rather miss him now. Blast him.

Emily heard an echo behind her, a slow, steady sound like a footfall on the paving stones, and she suddenly realised how quiet everything had become. While she was daydreaming, she had turned from the busier lanes of restaurants and hotels to a silent residential street. She stopped and glanced over her shoulder, but could see nothing but shadows in the pale light that fell from a few windows. The echo of footsteps stopped.

A memory flashed through her mind, of Gregory Hamilton and that deserted terrace, of the claustrophobic feeling of not being able to get away. She thought of the strange letters that had recently started to arrive at her house, notes she couldn't explain, but had dismissed as the ramblings of an overzealous mystery suitor. She shivered and felt the hairs on her arm prickle a bit.

She spun back around, feeling foolish, and hurried ahead, as fast as she dared. The footsteps started again, also moving faster, and as she turned a corner a hand suddenly seized her arm, appearing from the darkness.

She was suddenly caught in her own nightmare, the cobwebs closing around her feet, tripping her as she tried to flee in the darkness.

Using her weight, Emily whirled around towards her attacker instead of trying to pull away. She drew back the hand that held her umbrella and lashed out with it at the shadowy figure.

He just looked like a phantom in the night, featureless, pale, terrifyingly tall and swathed in a black coat, a hat tugged low on his brow to conceal his face. But the iron grip on her arm was all too real.

She screamed and lashed out again with her umbrella. He muttered a low, rough curse and tried to grab her other arm as she landed a lucky blow to his skull. She screamed again, desperately, and tried to bring her boot-heel down on his foot.

A window somewhere along the street opened and someone called, 'Here, what's this about? Leave off or I'll call on the constables, right now!'

As if startled, her attacker suddenly released her and fell back a step. Emily broke away and started running, as fast as she could. It had been a long time since her days of chasing tennis balls and rowing on the pond at Miss Grantley's, but she could still move like the wind when she needed to. She didn't stop until she somehow reached her own front door and she pounded her fists on it frantically.

She stumbled inside when the butler opened it and only then did she feel the ache in her struggling lungs, the pain in her legs. He stared at her in astonishment as she collapsed on the nearest chair.

'Miss Emily,' he said. 'Whatever is the matter? Are you ill?'

Emily shook her head, gasping too hard to say anything. She wanted to beg him not to alert her father, but it was too late. Albert had already appeared at the top of the stairs in his dressing gown, his face creased with worry.

'Emily,' he cried, hurrying down to her side. Mary appeared behind him, her face shocked. 'Fetch a doctor right away!'

'No, I don't need a doctor,' Emily managed to say hoarsely. 'I just had a bit of a fright, that's all.'

'Oh, Miss Emily, was it him? The letter writer?' Mary gasped. 'I knew he would show up!'

'Him?' Emily's father said sharply.

Emily shot Mary a reproachful glance, but she didn't blame the maid, not really. When Emily had confided in Mary about the notes, they had both determined it was probably just an overzealous suitor. Emily had begged Mary not to say anything, not to worry her father, and surely the letters would stop soon enough. Mary had agreed, but had they been very wrong after all?

'I'll just fetch a brandy, Miss Emily,' Mary said, and she and the butler hurried away.

Albert sat beside Emily and gently took her hand. She felt steadier already, being in her own home with her father, and anger was beginning to replace the fear.

'Emily, what does Mary mean? Was someone pestering you tonight? Someone you have had problems with before?'

Emily shook her head. 'Someone *was* following me, I think, and I did receive one or two letters recently— very, um, affectionate letters. From someone nameless. But I am sure they are not connected.'

Albert looked shocked, his face turning red. 'I never should have let you go alone to that blasted meeting! If only your mother were here. She would have known what to do.'

Emily held tightly to his hand. 'It has nothing to do with the meeting, Father, I'm sure of it. It happened long after I left the hall. I was just being silly, distracted by a daydream. I will always take the carriage from now on, I promise.'

Mary returned with a glass of brandy and Emily took a bracing gulp of the amber liquid, glad of its steadying warmth.

'Well, Paris is out of the question now,' her father said.

'Oh, no, Father,' Emily argued. 'We can't let one strange incident get in the way of our business. I swear to you, I will be much more careful in the future.' And the letter-writer, and that night's follower, if they were indeed one and the same, could never be allowed to interfere in what really mattered: her work.

Her father looked as if he very much wanted to argue with her, but he just shook his head and patted her hand. 'We will talk about it tomorrow, my dear. You look exhausted. Let Mary take you up to bed now. You need some rest.'

Emily nodded. She *was* exhausted, but she feared she wouldn't find quiet sleep that night. She let Mary lead her up to her chamber, brush her hair and help her into her nightdress. The maid stayed beside her, reading from a book of poetry, as Emily climbed into bed. She closed her eyes and for a moment the fearful image of the dark alley wasn't there at all. Instead she saw a sunny French garden, Chris's teasing smile as he kissed her in that garden maze, and she was able to drift into slumber.

Albert Fortescue glanced through the darkened doorway at his peacefully sleeping daughter. In her slumber, she looked younger, serene, all the cares of the day, her endless energy, still for the moment. It reminded him of when she was a little girl and he would read her a bedtime fairy story, tuck her in before he went off to a dinner party or the theatre. Those quiet, precious moments, gone much too quickly.

But what wasn't gone, what would never be gone, was his need to protect her. To keep her safe. He had promised Emily's mother, as she lay dying, that their daughter would always be safe. Now he feared he was failing in that vow.

He remembered with an anguished pang the frightened look on her face earlier and the anger that anyone would dare treat her like that. *His* Emily, his precious girl!

Albert knew he had not raised her as most girls were.

But how could he have done differently? He had been on his own for most of their life together. Emily had no mother, no aunt, no grandmother to guide her. Perhaps he should have married again, given her a stepmother, but the business took all his time. They had seemed to do well, the two of them, and his Emily was so smart, so full of energy, so independent. She was a true assistant in his work.

Yet he was not as young as he had once been. He could feel his own strength flagging and one day, perhaps much sooner than he could have wished, he would have to cease working so much. It was time to organise, once and for all, things he had put off for too long.

Emily needed a protector, someone to stand by her side in life. A husband who could give her a secure place in society, give her a family so she would never be alone and perhaps take over the reins of his business once he could no longer do it. She needed someone—before it was too late. The danger she'd run into that night only proved that to him.

Albert sighed and ran a hand over his face as weariness and worry washed over him. How to convince Emily of this urgency? Every time he thought he had found a proper suitor for her, his darling, headstrong girl turned her nose up at them! She always had an argument against them and he would never want to see her with someone she could not love. Someone she could love as he had once so loved her mother.

Surely, though, there was a man out there who would be worthy of his intelligent, kind-hearted daughter? A man they could both trust?

Emily sighed in her sleep and Albert hurried to tuck the blankets closer around her, just as he had done when she was a child. 'Don't worry, my dearest,' he whispered. 'I will find a way to make it right…'

Chapter Four

'And Lord Henry Haite-Withers is getting married! I'm quite sure you remember him, Christopher, he is the son of my dear friend the Marchioness of Barnsworthy,' Beatrice Blakely said, her voice touched with barely concealed reproach. She gestured to the butler to bring in dinner's next course as she told Chris of every bit of marital gossip.

Was it only the fish course? Chris could have sworn they should be on the fruit and cheese at least. He felt as if he had been sitting there in the gloomy parental dining room for two days.

It was ever thus with his monthly obligatory family dinners. The dining room was a cavernous space decorated in the dark greens and burgundies of the style of his mother's youth, back when the Queen was a young mother and not grandmother of an Empire. Every corner was stuffed with tables of bibelots, porcelain figurines, old silver, vases of peacock feathers, and the dining table was laden with gilded bowls of fruit and flowers. It was draped in green damask, lined with rows of gold-rimmed crystal and platters, even when it was only he and his parents dining. It was all dark, airless, lifeless.

Yet the decor was only the outward representation of the unspoken emotions that always hung heavy in the air. His parents had not spoken a word to each other in years, if they could possibly help it, and when they did it was only for his father to send barely veiled barbs at his mother and his mother to ignore them and chatter on to no one in particular about gossip. It had been thus for nearly as long as Chris could remember. Leaving for school, even with its cold baths and canings, had been a blessing.

Matters seemed to have got even worse since Will left for his diplomatic postings abroad and married Diana Martin. Chris adored Di, she was the perfect sister-in-law, and had brought such laughter to his solemn brother's life. Yet Chris still couldn't fathom how Will had been able to take the matrimonial plunge in the first place. Not with such an example of connubial disharmony before them every day of their lives.

Chris took a deep gulp of his wine. 'Is he indeed? Old Harry... Who has he tricked into taking him on, then?'

'Oh, Christopher...' His mother sighed. 'Lord Henry is quite respectable now, running his father's estate in Devonshire. His fiancée is Miss Golens, a very pretty girl, I think. Perhaps you remember her from last Season? Mrs Golens, her mother, is very charming and she and I had rather hoped you might hit it off with her yourself. She really is very sweet.' She sighed again and picked at her trout amandine. 'But, alas, I think every good debutante from last Season is now spoken for.'

Chris's father, who had said barely three words since the wretched meal began, shot his wife a thunderous glance. 'How many times do I have to tell you, Beatrice? Christopher is hopeless. He will never make a respectable marriage, never settle into any useful work at all. You should direct your energies elsewhere.'

'Oh, one must never give up hope,' Beatrice murmured.

Chris, ever mindful of the careless façade he had to maintain, gave his mother a wide grin and drained his wineglass. He gestured to the footman for a refill. 'I've been working ever so hard, Father. I go to the office for, oh, at least three hours every afternoon. It gets terribly in the way of what's really important.'

His father's face darkened. 'Your brother got you that job and you should be grateful to him! He has better things to worry about than his ne'er-do-well sibling, with his postings in Vienna and now Paris, a wife to take care of...'

'And I'm sure a nursery to set up soon,' his wife said hopefully, but her husband ignored her.

'You should try to make William proud, not embarrass him—embarrass all of us—at every turn. If you botch up this position, it could ruin his chances for advancement,' Chris's father went on. He brought his fist down on the table, rattling the copious silver and china, making Chris's mother cringe. 'What other pursuits could be so important as bringing honour to your family name?'

'Oh, you know,' Chris said with an airy wave of his hand. It was always thus when he was with his family. They could know nothing of what his work was like, so they always disapproved of him. Always thought he would never fit in. 'There was a prize fought on Hampstead Heath last week. Couldn't miss that, could I? It was Big Jim Barnes, I won a mint. And the races. Ascot is coming up, isn't it?'

His mother gasped and his father turned purple behind his silver beard. 'I will hear no more of such things in my house! And how can you afford such nonsense anyway? After that Nixson investment business last year...'

'I didn't lose a farthing in that business,' Chris said and indeed he hadn't. The Nixson business had all been a set-up through his work to catch a spy, but his parents couldn't know that. To them he was just their disappointing son.

'Only because your brother saved you yet again.' His father turned away with a huff of disgust and silence reigned in the dining room again.

Chris finished his fresh glass of wine, secretly pouring most of it into a potted fern, and thought of his brother with a sharp pang of jealousy that Will was far away in Vienna. He had letters from him and Di every week, as they had to keep in touch for work as well as affection, and Chris couldn't help but be a bit envious of how happy they were together. How seldom they had to see the elder Blakelys.

It was with the greatest of relief that he could finally escape at the end of the meal, like a man walking out of the gates of Holloway after a long sentence. His mother followed him to the hall, where she stood silently beside him as they waited for the butler to fetch his hat.

'You know, Christopher,' she whispered, laying a birdlike hand on his arm. 'I do think Miss Golens has a younger sister. Not quite as pretty, perhaps, but still...'

'Mother,' he said. 'No respectable lady would have me. You know that. My reputation is irredeemably rackety, I'm afraid.' And that was exactly what had come to nag at his own mind lately, seeing how happy Will and Di were, knowing that could not be his. But that was his world and he would work with it. He just couldn't tell that to his mother.

'No man is truly irredeemable,' she said. Then her face clouded, as if she remembered her husband. 'Usually. You are so handsome and with your new place at the Foreign Office—I am sure if you worked hard...'

'Go off to India like Will, you mean? Then come back to astonish society with my newfound sobriety?'

'It wouldn't hurt. Many fortunes are made in India,' she said hopefully.

The butler came back with Chris's coat and hat, and Chris gave his mother a quick kiss on her cheek. 'Don't worry about me, Mother, please. Just take care of yourself. I'll see you soon.'

To his surprise, she caught his arm as he turned to leave. 'Where are you off to now, Christopher?'

He was going back to the office to face a new mountain of paperwork, but he couldn't tell her that, of course. No chink could ever show in his carefully constructed mask. He gave her a bright grin. 'Now, a chap should never say such things to his mother.'

He gave her one more kiss and set off into the night. It was the hour most of London was bent on merriment— or mischief. He saw carriages flashing past, pale faces and bright jewels in their windows as the riders set off to the theatre or a ball. A group of men, already staggering and laughing, moved in a blur just down the street. But, despite what he wanted everyone to believe, Chris was intent on neither. He found a hansom and directed the driver to a near-deserted office building in a respect- able, but not terribly elegant, part of town.

During the day, it bustled with business, crowds of men in their black bowler hats and carrying furled um- brellas hurrying on terribly important errands. At night, it was silent.

The foyer of the building was empty, the reception desk dark, but chinks of light flashed under a few door- ways. Chris made his way up the stairs to his own room on the top floor and lit the lamp. The glow fell on a couple of chairs, a cabinet, a large desk covered with neat piles of papers.

He hung up his coat and hat, and only when he sat down and reached for the folder on top of the stack did he let his mask drop. He had to pay attention now and get his work finished. He had to be sombre, responsi- ble Chris now.

Suddenly an image flashed through his mind. Emily Fortescue's face, the French sun shining on her chestnut hair, her lips pink from their kiss. A kiss he should *never* have stolen, but the temptation had been overwhelming as he saw her laughing there, running lost through the maze. The intoxicating sweetness of her taste, the way she'd felt in his arms. The way he'd never wanted to let her go.

No other woman in his life had ever been able to make him feel quite like Emily did, as if he was driven half-mad by her.

Then he remembered the terrible disappointment on her face as they parted that day in Paris. The sense that something had ended before its time and he didn't know how to fix it. Chris had become accustomed to such looks on people's faces—he had seen them all his life. But the glimpse of that same look on Emily's face had pierced him like an arrow and he had never quite been able to forget it. It drove him forward even more in his work, even though she would never know about it.

Chris sucked in a deep breath and pushed the memory of Emily away. She could never be his and it was no use remembering her now. He took out a sheaf of papers and started reading. Soon he was lost entirely in the work.

As the clock down the corridor tolled one, a knock sounded at his door. Chris was startled. No one ever disturbed anyone else's work at such an hour. Worried it might be an emergency, he pushed his papers back into their folder and called, 'Yes, come in.'

To his surprise, it was Lord Ellersmere, head of the office. 'Ah, Mr Blakely. I'm glad to see you're here this evening. Something has come up today and I think you might be just the man for the job.'

'Me, Lord Ellersmere?' Chris said, puzzled. He hadn't been sent on a foreign assignment since the Nixson business in France and he wondered what was happening now.

'Oh, yes.' Ellersmere sat down across from the desk, looking immaculate in a dark suit despite the late hour. He had been working for the Foreign Office for many years and nothing ever seemed to ruffle him. 'After your excellent work on the Eastern Star and then the Nixson business, you do seem to be just the one we need.'

Chris smiled wryly at the memory of those jobs, both in France. They had both required a great deal of subtlety, of subterfuge, and he had enjoyed them rather a lot. But his smile faded when he remembered Emily's contempt when she'd found him on the street, 'drunk' and flat broke, during the Star operation. 'The man to play the buffoon?'

Ellersmere chuckled. 'We are very lucky you decided to work for us instead of going onstage at the Lyceum. Your skills are invaluable, and rare among our sort. But I'm not sure buffoonery is needed so much this time, though one never knows in this line of work.'

Chris was intrigued. 'What is it?'

Ellersmere sighed. 'Trouble with the Germans again, I fear. Have you ever heard of a man called Herr Friedland, or maybe a Madame Renard?'

Chris mentally scanned through all the case paperwork he had just been reading. 'I don't think so.'

'Well, Friedland may not be his real name, we aren't quite sure yet. One of our people in Berlin, someone quite high up with the Crown Princess, has got word of some strange new scheme among some of the—wilder sort there.'

Chris sat back in his chair, fascinated. There was always trouble with the Germans, of course, the elderly Bismarck, the bellicose Kaiser and Queen Victoria's liberal-minded daughter Princess Vicky always creating a stir. 'Involving a Madame Renard?'

'A French radical, yes, and a friend of a woman called Mrs Hurst. Perhaps you've heard of her? She's a regular at the Pankhursts' At Homes. They're always involved in all manner of doings there.'

'Oh, yes. I believe she is president of something called the Women's Franchise League. Makes a nuisance of herself at Hyde Park Corner sometimes, but I don't remember hearing of anything really nefarious there.'

'Neither do we, though certainly radical elements like that always bear watching.' Ellersmere chuckled. 'Whatever would happen next if women got the vote? Female M.P.s? Preposterous.'

Chris wasn't so sure about that. Women often seemed to him rather more sensible than most men. Laura Smythe-Tomas was one of their best agents; Emily ran her father's business; Diana wrote articles. 'Some women can already vote locally, of course, and sit on school boards. It seems to go rather well.'

Ellersmere frowned. 'That is quite a different matter to what this Mrs Hurst and her ilk seem to want. We've heard she is setting up meetings with Madame Renard and Herr Friedland in Paris. What on earth could they be scheming about with the Germans? Our contact in Berlin thinks it is a fraud of some sort, one which could come to involve the Crown Princess. We cannot allow that to happen. We have enough to do diverting the scandals of the Prince of Wales, we don't need one with his elder sister, as well. Not that the Princess has ever given us a moment's trouble in herself.'

'And how can I help? I hardly think I could infiltrate the League. I'm a good actor, as you said, but not good enough to pass as a *Mrs* Blakely.' Nor was there likely to be a real Mrs Blakely by his side any time soon.

'We just need you to go to Paris and make friends with this Friedland person. Make him think you are sympathetic to German interests and want to promote their friendship with Britain. Maybe romance Madame Renard a little. You know the sort of thing. Whatever it takes to find out what they're up to.'

Chris seemed haunted by Paris tonight, by old memories there. By the magic of Emily herself in Paris. 'You want me to go to France?'

'Yes.' Ellersmere sat back, a confiding expression on his face. 'You know, Blakely, we have been very impressed indeed lately by your work. You have uncovered information that was invaluable. A position is soon to be open in St Petersburg which will need a— lighter touch.'

'St Petersburg?' Chris said, astonished. It usually took years for a man to gain a posting at such an important court. And it was a notorious tangle of complications. 'You need a jester in Russia?'

Ellersmere laughed. 'Hardly. It is an important post,

private secretary to the Vice Ambassador, with much room for advancement if all goes well. You know, Blakely, when I was young, before I met Lady Ellersmere, I often took on tasks similar to yours. It was all most exciting. But we all grow older; we all must move forward, make changes when the time is right. A fascinating place, Russia, most challenging. You might enjoy it, even if the duties might seem a bit duller than your current work at first.' His smile faded into sternness. 'Provided this Paris operation goes off well.'

'Indeed,' Chris murmured, his thoughts racing. A real position, a high secretarial post? For *him*? One where he could be himself again at long last, find out what he could become once the mask was off. It sounded fascinating. It sounded like work he could grow into, now that weariness had set in at his rakish role. Could it be possible?

Ellersmere sat forward, his hands clasped. 'I know I need not tell *you*, of all people, the great need for secrecy in this matter, Blakely. Paris needs a frivolous touch right now, shall we say.'

Chris nodded. He did, indeed, know how to be frivolous. He thought of Emily again, that disappointed look on her face, and a surge of energy for this new job filled him. 'Then, yes. I think I am exactly your man.'

Chapter Five

The Poseidon Club wasn't too busy yet when Chris arrived the next evening, which was just the way he liked it. A few moments just to sit by the fire, have a cognac brought to him by the wonderfully silent, wonderfully understanding staff, pretend to read a newspaper and just be alone for once. No one expecting him to be full of jovial chatter about the latest horse race, the prettiest new dancer at Drury Lane, some new mischievous scheme.

For a few moments, he could just—be. Be quiet, be still, be himself. The Poseidon, where he had long been a member, was a haven, at least early in the evening, before the crowds arrived to drink and play cards.

But maybe it would not be such a haven tonight. As Chris paused in the doorway to the library, handing his overcoat to the attendant, he studied the dark-panelled, leather-upholstered room. It was the usual gathering at such an hour—a foursome of older gentlemen who had served together in the army in India and met every day for a hand of piquet by the windows. The Duke of

Amberley, escaping his social-butterfly Duchess in a bottle of brandy, a couple of people reading the papers. He could hear the click of a game in the adjoining billiards room.

And Mr Albert Fortescue, slowly turning over the pages of the *Express*, a distracted frown on his face. Chris knew Emily's father was a member, yet he was very seldom seen at the club, being so busy with his business affairs. Chris was startled to see him there that day, as if his earlier memories of Emily had conjured him up in the library. He had not seen the Fortescues for a while. Now Emily seemed to be in his thoughts wherever he turned.

It made him feel strangely discomfited. Mr Fortescue glanced up and gave Chris a polite nod. He didn't seem to know any of Chris's past with Emily, or any of his wild thoughts now. Chris nodded back, and hurried to his usual armchair by the fire, which was not burning on a warm night. An attendant appeared with his usual cognac and newspapers.

'A double today, Mr Blakely,' the man murmured. 'If you'll forgive me saying so, you look as if you can use it.'

Chris laughed. 'I can indeed, Ralph. You are a mind reader.'

Left alone again, Chris took a deep gulp of the spirit and stared into the empty marble grate. It had been damp day, the grey sky a reflection of his own swirling mood. He hadn't been able to concentrate on the day's work at the office, his thoughts on the Paris business, on a possible future in St Petersburg.

He also hadn't been able to shake away those memories of Emily. He didn't know why she haunted him now. Any other woman would have faded by this time. But she lingered, like the sweet scent of her French perfume. He so often worked to prove himself to her, though she would never, could never, know that.

He knew he had to take that Paris assignment, and then Russia, if he was lucky enough to have it come his way. Maybe it could mean the end of the way he had been living for so long, the end of the secrets, the acting. Ellersmere was right—it had once been exciting, now it felt tiring. Maybe he could even begin to hope for a life such as William had, respect, a family, a wife. Things he longed for when he saw their happiness, but which he dared not want for himself.

Chris frowned, trying to imagine what such a life might be like. He had been so caught up for so long in his own work that he wasn't even sure what a 'normal' life should be. He had certainly never seen it with his own parents. Even William and Diana, clearly deeply in love to all who saw them together, were hardly conventional. They moved from royal court to royal court for Will's career, with Diana doing her writing.

Chris almost laughed to think of himself ensconced in cosy domesticity, a town house in Mayfair, draped in fringed curtains and decorated with nice landscapes and silver-framed photos, smelling of beeswax polish and lavender. A plump, smiling, pretty wife playing at her piano, making sure Cook had the roast on the dinner table at the right hour. No, he couldn't face *that*. But what Will and Di had, a partnership…

That he could just almost imagine. Almost even want.

He suddenly pictured Emily sitting across from him at a desk, going over her own business ledgers as he read her invitations from Russian nobility, deciding on which they should accept. She looked up at him, laughing as he put on a haughty Grand Duke accent, her hazel eyes shining...

'Blast it all!' he muttered, tossing down the unread newspapers as if he could erase his thoughts just as easily. Even if he *did* marry, it couldn't be to Emily Fortescue. She was too independent, too outspoken, too—too everything.

And marriage was not for the likes of him.

A sudden raucous burst of laughter reminded him he was not alone and he glanced up at the gilded clock on the mantel, surprised it was later than he had realised. He had been too wrapped up in his own thoughts, too unobservant, and that was a dangerous thing to be in his line of work. Even in his own club.

An attendant was just drawing the heavy green-velvet curtains at the windows, shutting out the gathering evening, and several new groups were crowding into the library. One of them was Freddy Anstruther, one of the primary troublemakers at the club since his bosom friend, the even worse Gregory Hamilton, had gone abroad. Freddy was leading a few of his equally disreputable friends, all of them the worse for drink. Freddy's cravat was loose, his dark hair tousled, his eyes reddened.

He even had a woman with him, his arm around the waist of her emerald-green satin gown, her hair an im-

probable shade of red. It was strictly against club rules
for ladies to be there, but Freddy Anstruther was never
one to care. Chris looked forward to the day Freddy
would be drummed out of the Poseidon.

And yet, he was supposed to be just like the Freddys
of the world. Everyone thought he *was* like that, just
as careless, just as reckless. He suddenly felt a pang of
disgust at himself, at the way his work made him behave sometimes, the deceptions he carried.

'Blakely!' Freddy cried, his voice and breath telling
the tale of all the gin bottles he had already been hit-
ting that evening. 'We haven't seen you in far too long,
man. Come have some wine with us, we're going on
to the Gaiety later.' Freddy's friends clamoured their
agreement.

Chris wanted nothing more than to refuse, to be left
to his own brooding thoughts again, but a sudden reti-
cence on his part might excite unwanted speculation.

He gave a careless grin and pushed himself up from
his chair to go join the rowdy party. He noticed Mr Fortescue was still there, quietly writing letters now, seem-
ing to take no notice of the loud newcomers.

Chris followed them to the card tables set near the
window, watching as Freddy cut a new deck and more
wine was fetched.

'And you must know Millie, sensation of the Lemon
Alley Theatre,' Freddy said, reaching out to drag the
redhead closer. He pressed a damp kiss on her rouged
cheek and she leaned away, a disgusted look on her
face. No doubt Freddy smelled like a distillery. 'Be
nice to my old friend Blakely, Millie love. It's like I've

told you before—if you're nice to my friends, I can be nice to you…'

Millie tried to pull away, but Freddy's grip tightened. 'I have to leave for the theatre soon,' she said desperately.

'They can't pay you as much as I can, now can they, you silly tart,' Freddy said with a dismissive snort. He dragged her even closer, trying to kiss her again, and she pulled away. Freddy laughed and kissed her anyway. She struggled to get out of his grip, but he just held on to her tighter.

Chris knew he was supposed to be like Freddy, a careless man about town to whom actresses were a penny a dozen, but not even for the sake of his work would he stand to see a woman treated that way. He shoved back his chair and grabbed Freddy's free arm in a bruising grip. He pushed the man away from Millie, who stumbled back on her high heels. Freddy looked astonished, quickly followed by drunken fury.

'Leave her alone,' Chris said quietly, intently. 'Be a gentleman.' He shoved Freddy away.

'Now, see here, Blakely,' Freddy sputtered. 'If you want your own tart, you can go out and find one. I bought and paid for this one.'

'You haven't paid me a farthing,' Millie spat. 'And if you had, I'd throw it right back in your face, you drunken lout!'

'You…you common little whore!' Freddy lunged for her, but Chris was faster. He landed a punch on the man's jaw and a fight broke out like wildfire in the club's library. Millie ran away sobbing, and Chris was forced to shove Freddy into a table to get the drunk off him. The wood splintered, silencing Freddy's followers, and attendants appeared to haul them to their feet.

'You will have to pay for the damage, Mr Anstruther,' one of them said, dragging the protesting Freddy away. 'And I'm afraid you are behind on your club dues, as well, which means you are no longer welcome at the Poseidon…'

'I am sorry, Mr Blakely,' Ralph said, helping Chris to an armchair and brushing off his coat sleeve. Silence reigned once again in the library. 'Such things usually do not happen here at the Poseidon. Men like Mr Anstruther should find more suitable memberships.'

'I quite agree,' Chris muttered. He suddenly realised his punching hand was sore and flexed his fingers. 'The boxing ring, maybe.' He took the cold compress another attendant brought him and held it to his aching jaw. It had been a long time since he found himself in such a melee. It didn't feel entirely terrible, but rather something of a relief to let his emotions out that way. To be useful to someone. 'Sorry for all the trouble, Ralph.'

'Not at all, Mr Blakely. I rather suspect Mr Anstruther has long had it coming. Let me fetch you some more cognac.'

Chris nodded and studied the now-silent room. Everyone was studiously ignoring him, pretending nothing amiss had happened at all, and he hoped that meant what happened at the club truly stayed at the club. He didn't need more disappointed looks from his mother. But Mr Fortescue was watching him, a thoughtful frown on his face. He gave Chris a nod and came closer.

'That was very well done of you, Mr Blakely,' Fortescue said, sitting down across from Chris.

Chris looked away. This was *Emily's* father, after all, who had just watched him brawling as though he was in a common pub. He knew what people thought of him, what he *made* them think of him, but he hated to know Emily must feel that way, too. 'Well done for breaking up a peaceful evening at the club, you mean?'

Mr Fortescue studied Chris closely. He did remind Chris of Emily, the same all-seeing hazel eyes, the same thoughtful expression. 'Well done in defending that poor girl from a bully like Anstruther. I've noticed you have a knack for defending those weaker in the world, Mr Blakely. Never an unkind word for servants or beggar children. Always chivalrous with all ladies. You are quite unusual.'

Chris was startled. He was so accustomed to being so careful all the time, to always hiding behind his mask. How had Albert Fortescue seen beyond it, even for a moment?

'I hate men who mistreat women, or anyone weaker than themselves,' he said. Ralph poured out two more glasses of cognac and Chris gulped his down. 'They are just cowards.'

Fortescue held up his glass in a toast. 'Exactly so, Mr Blakely. You know, I think you might just be the sort of chap I am looking for.'

Chris had already heard that, at work. But what could Fortescue be looking for that Chris might have. 'Indeed?'

'Yes. I hear you rather enjoy Paris.'

Paris again. If Chris had been a spiritual sort of man, he would wonder if it was a sign. 'It is, shall we say, full of fine diversions.'

'So you might not be averse to a short visit there?'

'Maybe you're looking for someone who really knows his French wines, then, Mr Fortescue? For your imports business.'

Fortescue laughed. 'I do have a great many such experts on my staff, Mr Blakely, but none I can trust with a particularly sensitive bit of important business indeed.'

'What might that be?'

Mr Fortescue turned his glass in his hand, a thoughtful expression on his face. 'It has to do with my daughter Emily. I believe you know her? Your cousin Lady Alexandra was her school friend.'

Chris stomach tightened at the sound of her name. Emily, Emily—she was always so close, yet so far away. 'I know Miss Fortescue, yes. A most—independent spirit.'

Mr Fortescue smiled tenderly. 'Yes, she is truly that. Most independent, just as her mother was. I couldn't run my business without her, but something is concerning me.'

'About your daughter?' Chris asked, worried. Was she ill? Hurt? He longed to go to her, but knew he dared not.

'Yes.' Fortescue sighed. He suddenly looked tired. 'I know I have indulged her too much, let her have her own way. How could I not? I was a parent alone and she has always been so smart, so capable. Yet I worry now her confidence might make her too easy a prey.'

Had someone hurt Emily, possibly as Anstruther had tried to hurt Millie? A surge of anger broke through Chris and he started to rise from his chair. 'Has someone like Freddy Anstruther been pestering her, too?'

'Not Mr Anstruther, no. But she has been followed home after her work with the Women's Franchise League and she's received some rather disquieting letters, which I've only just learned about.' His expression tightened. 'And she was knocked down in the street by an unknown assailant.'

Chris's anger flamed even higher. It was all he could do not to run out and find Emily immediately. Take her in his arms as he longed to do. 'It sounds as if your daughter requires hired guards.'

Fortescue shook his head. 'She would never stand for such a thing. I would never put it past her to run away from any guards set upon her in such an obvious fashion. That's where someone like *you* could help me.'

'Me?' Chris said, puzzled.

'Of course. She already knows you; you attend many of the same events. She wouldn't be surprised to see you there, now and again.'

Chris wasn't too sure about that. But then again, Emily's father knew nothing about their quarrels—or their kisses. If he did, he would demand Chris stay far away from her, which was what he should do. But Fortescue's news that Emily had been followed and attacked had him very worried. 'You want me to spy on your daughter?'

'Not at all! Merely keep an eye on her.' Fortescue tossed back his wine. 'She is going to Paris, you see, on a business errand, and she won't be put off the trip. I have tried to dissuade her, but short of locking her in her room she won't be turned away. Her work is important to her and I have no desire to be her jailer. I love her more than my own life. But I must keep her safe.'

Chris wanted nothing but to do that, too. But how could he trust himself with her? 'So, I should follow her to Paris?'

'It should only take a few days. Just see where she goes, make sure no one is watching her, that she is not harassed.' Fortescue's eyes narrowed. 'I can pay you generously for your time, Mr Blakely. One does hear that your family is not quite so open-handed as they once were about allowances.'

That was just what Chris wanted people to think— that he was too irresponsible to be approved of, even by his own family. Still, the words stung a bit. Was that what Emily thought, too? 'I am no pauper, Mr Fortescue. I don't need your money. And I am not a spy.' Not on his friends, anyway. And especially not with Emily.

'I am sorry I insulted you,' Fortescue said. 'It was not my intention. I am just very concerned about my daughter. And you seem like a man who could keep her safe. Who knows how to treat ladies.'

Chris was also concerned about Emily. Much more than he wished he could be.

'I will think about it,' he said grudgingly. 'Send me the particulars of your daughter's journey, Mr Fortescue, and I will let you know my answer.'

A look of profound relief swept over Mr Fortescue's face. 'Thank you, Mr Blakely. You will certainly have my deepest gratitude, and any favour I might give you in the future, it would be yours. Come by the house and see her yourself. I am sure we can find a way to work things out.'

Chris nodded, but he knew he could never do such a thing for favours or money. Only for Emily. And that was what scared him. He pushed back his chair and left the club without another word.

Out on the pavement, Millie waited, her red hair and bright green dress a beacon in the gathering, foggy night.

'Oh, Mr Blakely!' she called, grabbing his arm. 'You were ever so brave in there, saving me like that. Just like a knight in a play! Sir Lancelot or something.'

Chris knew he was very, very far from some Arthurian knight, slaying dragons and rescuing damsels. He was only someone who told lies for a career. He had to do what he had to do.

'It was nothing,' he said. 'Freddy Anstruther is a bully, I would stay away from him if I were you.'

'Oh, yes, you're quite right.' Millie pressed closer to him and gave him a rouged smile. Her tuberose perfume was heavy and cheap, the satin of her gown shiny and bursting at the seams of her impressive bosom. Completely unlike Emily Fortescue, with her intelligent, serious eyes, her elegance, her stern disdain.

He suddenly wanted nothing more than to forget Emily, to forget his worry over her, his disgust for himself, everything. Even agreeing to help her father deceive Emily made him feel discomfited. He only wanted to forget it all.

'Come on then, my dear,' he said, letting Millie loop her arm through his. 'Let's go have some supper, shall we? Then I will escort you to your theatre and you can tell me all about your role there...'

Albert Fortescue was sure he had just seen the answer to his wishes.

Christopher Blakely. Who would have thought it? The man's reputation in society was not the best; he was adored by the ladies, but not a prospect for marriage for their daughters. Charming, friendly, energetic, but rakish. Yet Albert had glimpsed another side to the man, one that rather reminded him of Emily herself. Kind and strong, the first to rush to defend someone. Someone with secrets behind their eyes. Albert decided to make enquiries about Blakely, try to learn more about him. The real him.

Albert tapped his fingers on his papers, his mind racing as it often did at business plans. But this could possibly be the most important scheme of his life. Blakely would surely agree to keep a protective eye on Emily in Paris. Albert could tell the man cared about her. Could he be persuaded to do even more?

An idea was slowly, carefully taking form in his businessman's sharp mind...

Chapter Six

Emily watched in her dressing table mirror as Mary curled her hair for that night's party. The Marchioness of Lyon's ball was always one of the great events of the Season, and for the Fortescues to secure an invitation was a great prize. She knew she had to look her best, to be at her sharpest wits at every moment, yet she found herself to be distracted.

All the recent drama was making her feel nervous, jumpy, not on her best business game. She had to find a way to push it away.

'What do you think, Miss Emily?' Mary asked. 'The pearl bandeau or the diamond aigret?'

Emily glanced at her reflection, studying the thick chestnut waves Mary had so carefully curled and pinned into an elaborate coiffure. 'Which do you think, Mary?'

'To go with the gown?' Mary gestured at that night's creation, white satin and Brussels lace with cascades of pearl beading from Worth. 'The aigret, I think.'

'The aigret it is, then.' Emily shook away the last

hazy vestiges of worry and tried to concentrate only on what she had to do in that moment. Put on perfume; find her white satin shoes. She opened her jewel case and took out her mother's pearl necklace, searching for the matching earrings.

She held them up to the light, the diamond clasps in the shape of fleur-de-lis sparkling. They'd once been her favourite gems, yet she hadn't worn them in a while.

And suddenly she remembered *when* she last wore them. Her familiar London bedroom faded away and she was back in a sun-splashed French garden, racing between the tall green hedge walls of a maze as she heard the echo of chatter from the faraway party...

She stifled her giggles as she ran over the gravel pathways, trying to move as quietly as she could on her velvet shoes. She knew very well she should not be there, not with him. Being with him was always trouble. But Rippon's party was so dull, the maze so fun and her head was buzzing delightfully with champagne.

'I can hear you, Emily,' Christopher called from beyond the green wall to her left. He sounded full of laughter, giddy just as she was.

'But you can't find me,' she sang in return. She turned a corner and found herself at a dead end, a cosy nook with a wrought-iron bench and a burbling fountain, topped with a plump little marble cherub that seemed to laugh along with her.

She spun around, and found Christopher right behind her, his golden hair tousled in the light, laughing.

'I've caught you now,' he declared and his arms swept around her. He lifted her off her feet, spinning

her around and around until the turquoise sky above them tilted and spun.

Emily couldn't stop laughing. Her sides ached with it, her mind was a blur. It was always thus with Chris. She always wanted to either strangle him—or never let him go. No one could make her forget herself, forget all her responsibilities, as he could.

And that made him so dangerous.

'Oh, do put me down, Chris, or I'll be sick,' she gasped.

He stopped spinning, but still held her off the ground. His arms were strong, hard, his shoulders broad under her hands, and he smelled of some delicious lemony cologne of sun and fresh air. Delicious.

'Very well, but only if you pay a forfeit, seeing that I am the winner of our little game of tag,' he said.

Emily frowned at him warily. 'What sort of forfeit?'

'Hmm. How about a ribbon from your hat? Just like a jousting knight of old, given a favour for the tournament by his lady fair.'

Emily laughed and smacked his shoulder. 'You are hardly Ivanhoe, Christopher Blakely!'

'No, I am merely a useless wastrel,' he answered. He put her down at last and she stumbled over to collapse on the chaise. *'Good for neither Queen, country, nor my family, according to my parents.'*

'It doesn't have to be that way, you know,' Emily said. She knew he wanted everyone to think that; maybe it kept him from finding his responsibilities. But she had seen his sharp intelligence flashing under the smile in his blue eyes, the hardness and strength he wanted to hide.

He sat down beside her on the chaise *and took out a silver flask from his pocket. He offered it to her and she took a sip of the warming brandy even as she knew she shouldn't. The combination of the sunshine, champagne and Chris himself made her feel quite wonderfully reckless. Quite unlike herself.*

'What do you think I should do, then?' he asked, taking a swallow of the wine.

'Oh, I don't know. You don't seem like the army sort and definitely not the church. The City? Banking, maybe, or imports, like my father.'

Chris shrugged. 'My mother's constant idea is that I should marry an heiress.'

Emily was surprised at the sharp pang those words gave her. 'Any particular one?'

'Any heiress would do, I suppose. There are so many Americans about these days. I do tell Mama that I have no title to barter, but she seems to think an English accent and some good, English fair hair and blue eyes ought to do it.'

Emily studied him, all golden in the warm light. Like a Greek god. 'She might have a point.'

Chris leaned back on the cushions of the chaise*. 'But what sort of life would that be? I'd make a wretched husband, not thoughtful at all.'*

'I know what you mean,' Emily answered with a sigh. 'I would be a wretched wife.'

'You, Em?' he said, his expression startled. 'You would be stupendous! You're smart, pretty, clever.'

He thought her pretty? Clever? Emily tried to not grin like an idiot and looked away, flustered. 'Most men don't want clever wives. And I do like my work very much. I would hate to give it up to do—what? Arrange flowers all day? Go to more parties like this one?'

Chris sighed. 'We are at an impasse, then, aren't we, Em? It looks like neither of us can go either forward or back.'

Suddenly wistful, Emily reached up to her hat, an elaborate confection of white straw and pale pink feathers and striped bows, just purchased at Gordston's department store after Alex married Malcolm Gordston. She pulled off one of the ribbons and held it out to him.

'There is always jousting,' she said, 'if no other career works out for you.'

He took the ribbon between his fingers and looked down at it with a crooked smile. 'Only if you are there to cheer me on.'

Emily impulsively laid her hand over his, feeling the warmth of his skin against hers, the slight roughness of his fingertips. There, in that moment, she forgot the hurt of that strange encounter at her school, of his rejection after the kiss that had turned her world upside down. That all seemed so far away.

'I shall always cheer you on, Chris,' she said. 'I know you'll find your way, just as you found your way through this maze.'

'Oh, Em.' His face darkened, grew serious, intent, just before his lips claimed hers, and just like the first time they kissed she forgot everything else. Everything but the wonderful way he made her feel, the sense that they were the only people in the world.

Emily pushed him away, suddenly frightened. Not of him, but of herself. Of losing herself in the power of his presence. In her emotions.

She jumped to her feet and ran out of the maze, hardly knowing which corner to turn, where she was going, what she was doing. She only knew she had to run far, far away from her feelings...

'What do you think, Miss Emily?' Mary asked, pulling Emily out of that sunny day in France, back to her own bedroom. Her own life, without Chris in it.

She blinked hard, pushing away the past. Pushing away her own foolishness. She slipped on her earrings and glanced in the mirror, hardly seeing herself. She could only notice how flushed her cheeks were. 'Perfect, Mary, as usual. You are an absolute gem.'

Lady Lyon's ball was, as it was every year, a blasted nuisance to get to, Emily realised as her carriage inched forward. There was a long line of equipages waiting to reach the grand portal of the Lyon house, one of the grandest mansions in London. The place was lit up like Bonfire Night, glittering and sparkling at every window, and the whole house was packed with guests. It would surely be just the same once she was inside, people wall to wall like a tin of smoked fish.

Emily sighed as she adjusted her kid gloves. She could jump down from the carriage and walk to the house in a fraction of the time, but striding down the street would hardly be the ladylike thing to do. She just had to be patient.

But patience was never her strong suit.

She glanced out the carriage window and wondered who else was waiting to get into the ball. Who she needed to speak to for the business. She had also heard rumours that Lady Lyon herself was rather interested in women's suffrage. Maybe there would be a moment to mention Mrs Hurst's organisation to her? Donations were always sorely needed.

The carriage at last drew to a halt at the front doors. Emily made one more check of her coiffure before she let the footman help her alight and left her white-brocade cape with the maid. Once she was able to make her way out of the hall, she saw she had been correct in her worries—they were all packed like fish in a tin. But what a glorious, luxurious tin!

The gilded horseshoe staircase that led up to the bedroom was lined with swags and wreaths of white roses and lilies tied with gold bows, the scent heavy and heady when mixed with all those ladies' perfumes. Their gowns were a kaleidoscope of bright silks and satins, luxurious velvets, delicate lace, plumes and jewels nodding in upswept hair, diamond necklaces glittering. Emily studied the lady in front her, whose gown was of a patterned dark blue damask embroidered with silver, rich and almost alive with flash and movement. She wished Diana was there to see it, she would surely want to write about it for her fashion articles.

The double doors to the ballroom at the top of the stairs were wide open, the Marchioness poised there to greet their guests, a Grecian goddess in a draped gold-satin gown. 'My dear Miss Fortescue, I am so glad you could come,' she cried, holding out her hand to Emily. 'We absolutely must make a moment to talk later.'

'Of course, Lady Lyon,' Emily answered, hoping it would be about the League. She tumbled into the ball-room and took a glass of champagne from a footman's tray as she surveyed the crowd, looking for a familiar face. The long, rectangular room, lined on one side with glass terrace doors and on the other side with a gallery of Gainsborough portraits and Old Master landscapes, was done in the most fashionable shades of pale green, gold and ivory, draped with more white flowers. An or-chestra played from some hidden gallery high above, a Strauss polka playing as couples made their way to the polished parquet dance floor.

It was indeed a ripe place for business contacts, but Emily found she rather missed quiet gardens instead. Lazy moments. Fascinating company, his golden hair gleaming in the sun…

She sighed, pushing away the memory again. She made her way further into the sparkling crowd, answer-ing greetings from friends, laughing and chatting, pre-tending she hadn't a care in the world. It was all part of the job.

Suddenly she glimpsed a lady seated on one of the small gilt chairs lining the wall, a small, thin figure in dark copper-coloured satin, faded blonde hair twisted up in an unfashionable chignon. *Mrs Blakely*, Emily thought with a jolt of surprise. Chris's mother. What was she doing there, at the most crowded, most fashion-able ball of the Season? Mrs Blakely was known to be rather shy and had seldom been seen in society since her sister, the Duchess of Waverton, Alexandra's mother, had gone to live on the Continent in social disgrace.

Did that mean Christopher was there, too? Waiting in the crowd to surprise her, to startle her into dropping her social mask? The last she had heard he was in Italy somewhere, or maybe Switzerland, she wasn't sure. She glanced around quickly, but couldn't see his tall figure, his bright hair. Mrs Blakely seemed to be alone.

Emily took two more glasses of champagne and went to sit down beside Mrs Blakely. She had always felt rather sorry for the woman, even if she *did* think Chris should marry an heiress.

'Mrs Blakely,' she said, offering one of the glasses. 'What a lovely surprise to see you here tonight.'

Mrs Blakely gave her a faint smile. 'Miss Fortescue. How long it has been.'

'Yes, indeed. I hope this means we will see more of you in society now?'

'Perhaps, yes.' She took a sip of the wine, her lips pursing. 'I heard Miss Percival was to be here tonight. I have had such a desire to meet her. I haven't seen her yet, though.'

'Miss Percival?' Emily remembered hearing stories about the beautiful redhead, a meatpacking heiress from America, and suddenly realised why Mrs Blakely was there. Still heiress hunting. Surely Chris would have to give in to her soon.

'Yes, the lady from—where was it? Pittsburgh?' Mrs Blakely cringed. 'What sort of name is that for a village, I do wonder? But they say she is quite pretty.'

Pretty enough to advertise soap, which only added to her millions. 'So I've heard.'

Mrs Blakely's frown turned thoughtful. 'She would have to be pretty for it to work.'

'Mama. I brought you some lemon squash, but I see you already have a drink.' It was the voice Emily had been dreading—or maybe secretly hoping against hope to hear? It was just the same, deep and low and dark, but touched at the edges with laughter that could never entirely be suppressed.

She glanced over her shoulder to see it was indeed Chris, large as life, twice as handsome as she even re-membered, dressed in impeccable black and white eve-ning clothes, but with his hair still tousled.

She longed to shrink into her chair, to vanish into the pale green walls. She felt her cheeks burn and had no idea what to say to him, how to treat him.

'Thank you, Christopher,' Mrs Blakely said, remind-ing Emily that there were people, many other people, all around, and she couldn't run in front of them. 'Miss Fortescue has been kind enough to keep me company.'

Christopher shook his head hard, as if he, too, needed to organise his thoughts. 'So I see. Perhaps she would also be kind enough to grant me a dance? I think a waltz is next,' he said roughly.

Emily opened her mouth to refuse, but he gave her such a surprisingly pleading look she found she couldn't say no. Not even for her own peace of mind. 'Thank you, Christopher, I would enjoy that.' She put her glass down on a table beside his abandoned lemon squash and stood up to take his hand. Even through their gloves, his touch was warm, rough.

'But, Christopher, Miss Percival...' his mother protested weakly.

'She hasn't yet arrived, has she, Mama?' Chris said with a laugh. He tugged on Emily's hand and led her on to the dance floor among the other couples.

Even there, surrounded by so many people, it felt like they were entirely alone. She could see only him, his turquoise eyes, his crooked smile. He smelled of that warm scent of lemons that reminded her of the French garden and their kiss.

She swallowed hard and tried to smile. 'So your mother is still heiress-shopping, is she?'

Chris groaned. 'I fear so. I thought surely she had given all that up, seen me for the hopeless case I am. It turns out Mama is a sneaky one, though. I should have had my suspicions when she insisted I escort her here tonight. She hasn't been to a ball in ages. I thought she just wanted to get away from my father.'

'They do say Miss Percival is charming. Pretty, too.' A suitable wife for him? She didn't like the queasy feeling such a thought gave her.

'Then she is too good for the likes of me, wouldn't you say?' His arm tightened around her waist, bringing her a hair closer than was absolutely correct, and spun her into the figures of the dance. It made her want to laugh, despite the uncomfortable idea of Chris marrying the pretty American. 'My opinions of a career as husband haven't changed.'

He had always said he would never marry and none

of his behaviour in recent years seemed to contradict that. She knew the feeling well. 'Then what have you been doing with yourself lately, Chris?' Emily asked breathlessly. 'I thought I heard you had gone abroad.'

'Really? No, not at all. I've just been doing a little of this, a little of that. Will got me a bit of a desk job at the Foreign Office, pushing pencils about. It fills the time until the next card game.'

'What sort of desk job?' Emily had a hard time picturing it.

'Counting papers, things like that. Stamping things.' He spun her in a wide, giddy circle, laughing when she protested. 'But you must be as busy as usual, Em?'

'Yes. Father's café collaboration with Gordston's has been such a success, he's looking to expand.'

'And suffrage meetings, too, I hear,' he said tightly.

Surprised, Emily studied him closer. He looked rather serious suddenly. 'Sometimes. I'm surprised you know about the League. Do you not agree that working for justice for my own sex is something important, something I should be doing?'

'I think I have never met anyone as determined and intense as you, Emily. But I also worry that you don't see the potential danger in what you're doing sometimes.'

Emily shivered as she remembered those following footsteps, the hard hand on her arm. 'I can take care of myself, Chris.'

'But you shouldn't have to. You deserve so much— well, more.'

'More?' More—what? Laughter? Sunshine? A different life? She could barely imagine such things, except with him. And that was impossible.

The movements of the dance had brought them to one of the open terrace doors and Chris spun her through them out into the night. The terrace was quiet, shadowed, a few couples murmuring quietly to each other behind the banks of potted palms that lined the marble floor, or sitting much too close to each other on the iron sofas and chairs. The music was just an echo there, making the whole scene dreamlike.

Chris led her to the edge of the stairs that went down into the dark garden and she followed, somehow unable to turn back. 'Em,' he said and she was immediately worried by the serious tone in his voice. Chris was almost never *serious*. 'You would tell me if there was something wrong? Anything you were—worried about?'

Emily was puzzled. 'Worried?'

'I just mean, I hope you know you can trust me. That I am your friend.'

Her *friend*. Only that. Once, for only a few wild moments, she had thought he might be more than that. Chris always seemed to bring out things in her she hadn't even known were there. A daring freedom, the sense that she could dash ahead and leap into the unknown, with him beside her. But her usual sensible self knew that couldn't be. She would lose herself and probably him, too. They were just too different.

But surely having Chris as her friend was no small thing. She studied him in the faint light from the ballroom, his face carved into harsh, austere lines by the shadows. His bright blue eyes watching her so closely.

She could tell him things she couldn't tell anyone else and surely he would understand. He had done so much that was scandalous in his own life and she had never seen him judge others. Her father, and Diana and Alex, would worry so much. Perhaps Chris would, too, in his Chris way, but maybe he could also help. Give her advice. Keeping the worry inside herself was sure to make her burst.

'It's true that I've been doing some work for the Women's Franchise League,' she said.

'That sounds perfectly suited for you, Em.'

'You're not shocked?' She had to admit *she* was rather shocked. So many men thought a woman who wanted to vote must be insane. But then again, Chris had always been one of the most accepting people she knew.

'That *you* would be in favour of votes for women? Certainly not. I would imagine you would be the first to the barricades.'

'It's very important work, especially for women who come after us. They deserve every opportunity to make the most of their lives.'

'But is something worrying you about this League? You seem a bit uncertain.' He looked at her closely. Too closely.

Emily glanced away. 'Not about the cause, of course, but—well, I wonder if perhaps someone is not happy with our work.'

'I would think a great many people wouldn't like it at all.' He frowned. 'Has something happened? Someone threatened you in some way?'

Emily closed her eyes and shuddered as she remembered that dark street. 'Someone followed me home from a meeting. I managed to get away, but I confess I was rather shaken by it all.'

Chris reached out and took hold of her arms, his hands warm and strong on the bare skin above her gloves. That serious look was on him again. 'Em. You mustn't walk home alone from these meetings, or any-where else. I certainly know it won't do any good to ask you not to go, but I beg you to be careful.'

'I *am* careful! I usually take the carriage at night and I watch what is happening around me.' She shook her head. 'I feel so foolish, as if I was distracted that night. I just can't help but wonder if I was the target, or if it was really the League itself.'

'Oh, Emily. Let me teach you some boxing stances, or swordplay, or—well, anything. Or let me go with you to these meetings.'

Emily had to laugh at the image of Chris lurking at the back of the room during League meetings, glaring at all the ladies. 'You would be much too distracting. But I will happily learn how to punch someone and break their nose if need be.' And she was glad he be-lieved in her, with no question or hesitation. It was too comfortable, too right to be talking to him. Just like the Chris of old times.

He drew her closer to him, wrapping his arms around her. She suddenly felt so safe, so certain. She never could decide how Chris, a man who lived his life so carelessly, could make her feel that way.

'Em,' he said softly. 'You mean so much to so many people. You must take care of yourself.'

She tilted back her head and studied him in the moonlight. He looked older, somehow, with his golden hair turned silver, his face so serious and stark. 'I could say the same about you.'

'Me?' he said, his eyes widening as if she had surprised him. 'No one relies on me as they do you. They all know I am utterly scatty.'

Emily shook her head, suddenly realising something important—Chris had so many layers he could hide beneath. 'You do underestimate yourself, as always.'

'Oh, yes? So what are some of my sterling qualities, then?' he said with a careless laugh.

'You are a good friend, for one. Trustworthy. Understanding.' And it was true, he was all those things. Even if he was also careless and rakish.

'I am sure my family would disagree with you. I am not trustworthy at all.'

'Then they are fools and you should never listen to them. Just as I never listen to people who decry female suffrage. We should never give credence to people who only want to limit us. Put us in their boxes.'

He gave her a startled glance. 'Em, you are really the most extraordinary person.'

He thought her *extraordinary*? She felt a warm glow to realise it and she didn't want to think too much about why that could be. 'And don't forget that.' She wrapped her gloved hands into the velvet lapels of his coat as if she could shake some sense into him. She felt the strength of him under her touch, the heat of his skin through velvet and linen, and she suddenly couldn't breathe. She peeked up at him to see him staring down at her as if he was just as stunned.

'Em…' he said hoarsely.

She shook her head, words vanishing from her mind. She didn't know what would happen next, but she had never known such a raw sense of longing. She closed her eyes and felt his lips brush hers, as if in question. She couldn't protest and his lips grew bolder. As always when she was with him, the world vanished in a rush of glorious sensations. She wrapped her arms around his neck and she was surrounded by him: his taste, his scent, his warmth. She felt his hand on her bare upper back and she shivered, wanting more.

She heard a laugh from nearby and it was like crashing back to earth after floating on a cloud. She stumbled back from him and shook her head when he opened his mouth to speak. She couldn't bear to hear his apologies, not now.

'I—I must have needed that,' she gasped, trying to laugh. 'I have to go.'

'Emily…' he called, but she whirled around and ran back towards the terrace doors, back to the safety of the music and crowds. She smoothed her hair, her skirt, and hoped she didn't look too dazed and scandalous. That she could make herself be the usual sensible Emily again.

'Miss Fortescue,' she heard someone say and she knew she couldn't run and hide now. She pasted a bright smile on her lips and hoped she didn't look quite so flushed and frantic. Looked as if her world had not just tilted and cracked.

She turned to see James Hertford standing there, impeccably correct and handsome in his black evening suit, his dark hair glossy in the ballroom lights. He was friends with Gregory Hamilton, or had been when those excruciatingly embarrassing events happened, but James had always been kind to her. He'd asked her to dance at balls, sat with her at teas, was always most polite, albeit a tad bit dull. And there he was now, smiling at her, a beacon of the ordinary world, yet she always felt so odd around him.

'Mr Hertford,' she said politely. 'How charming to see you again.'

'And you, Miss Fortescue.' His eyes, a rich, sweet hazel, seemed to glow as he smiled down at her. 'I have been hoping to call at your home, but you seem to be terribly busy lately.'

Emily remembered the flowers he had left a few times, pretty arrangements of white roses and lilies. 'Yes, there has been a great deal of work to see to. My father is expanding his business.'

He frowned. 'A lovely lady like yourself should never be forced to concern herself with such things.'

Emily had heard such things far too often and as always it gave her a pang of irritation. She pushed it away, though, and just kept smiling, as she often did. 'I enjoy it. I do hate being bored.'

'Well, I hope you are not too bored this evening.'

Emily thought of the kiss on the terrace and her cheeks felt hot. She waved her fan in front of her face, hoping to hide the blush. 'How could I be bored? With such lovely music.'

'We should take advantage of it, then. Would you care to dance?'

Emily glanced at the dance floor, where another waltz was starting amid the kaleidoscope of silks and satins. She looked back at the terrace doors, but there was no Chris there. 'I should like that, thank you.'

James offered her his arm and she let him lead her into the figures of the dance. They twirled and turned in time to the music, a wonderful, distracting swirl. Even though his touch didn't make her feel as Chris did, James was a skilful dancer and he soon had her laughing at his exuberant spins.

'Miss Fortescue,' he said softly. 'You do look most lovely this evening.'

Emily swallowed uncomfortably, trying not to fidget. 'Thank you, Mr Hertford, you are terribly kind.'

'Not kind, just honest. You *are* lovely and sweet. You deserve to have everything a lady requires in life, a home, a family, proper concerns. It's wrong for you to work thus. Surely your father sees that.'

Emily's laughter faded as she looked into his eyes. He seemed so very earnest, so sure of his words. Most men were when it came to what ladies 'ought' to do. Perhaps he was one of those '*parfit* knight' sorts, who thought she needed rescuing? She felt suddenly unsure and looked back down to keep from tripping on her train. 'That is a sweet thing to say, Mr Hertford, but I assure you I am doing exactly what I wish in my life. Now, what do you think will be served at supper? I am hoping for ice cream, myself.'

They turned again and she caught a glimpse of

Chris's bright hair in the crowd. She couldn't quite breathe, she wanted to run away and at the same time run *to* him. It was maddening.

Then she saw his companion. Lady Smythe-Tomas, one of the great 'professional beauties' of the Season. She leaned close to him, the green plumes in her auburn hair brushing his shoulder as she touched his arm and whispered something into his ear. He laughed and Emily felt quite deflated. As if all the air and light had gone out of the room.

I don't care who he talks to, the rogue, she thought fiercely. But she knew she was lying to herself. She had to forget him—and fast.

'My heavens, Christopher, but you do look even more at sixes and sevens than usual,' Lady Smythe-Tomas said with a laugh. She tugged his cravat straight. 'Do you have no valet?'

Chris had thought he had composed himself after the terrace and felt terribly uncertain now. Could everyone see it on his face, the rage of desire and fear that swirled inside of him when it came to Emily? 'Perhaps I would if Ellersmere paid me what I'm worth.'

She laughed louder, like a peal of silvery bells. 'Oh, my dear, none of us are paid what we're worth. We do it for love of the game, yes? Where did you run off to for so long?'

'Just needed a breath of air.'

'Mmm-hmm. We all need *that* once in a while. Do walk with me for a while and tell me all about it. I love the romantic tales of others.'

'I'm afraid I'll disappoint you, then. No romantic tales at all. No time for them.' He remembered Emily's kisses on the bench at Miss Grantley's, the maze in France. And just now, in the garden. The most golden moments of his life. But they were not the real world.

'I am quite sure that's not true. But walk with me anyway, we can gossip about everyone else's scandalous affairs.'

He nodded and offered her his arm, leading her on a winding path through the gilded chaperons' chairs, the refreshment tables, half-listening to her whispered gossip about the couples they passed. He studied the dancers and caught a glimpse of Emily's diamond headdress as she waltzed past with James Hertford. Her cheeks were rather pink, but she was smiling and nodding with him, as if their kiss had meant nothing at all to her.

He looked away sharply, trying to concentrate on Lady Smythe-Tomas's words, but it was no use.

When he didn't see Emily for weeks or months, he could almost tell himself he had forgotten her. But he never could, not really. She was too vivid, too bright— too *Emily* to forget. He shouldn't have kissed her again, shouldn't have reminded himself of how sweet she tasted.

'Have you ever heard of the Women's Franchise League?' he asked Lady Smythe-Tomas.

She broke off in mid-gossip, looking startled. 'I am a member. Why?'

Chris knew he couldn't tell her about Emily's confidences. Even he deserved to keep secrets sometimes and Emily was someone he could never betray. 'Is it a reputable organisation?'

'That depends on what you consider reputable. As I said, *I* am a member, so not entirely. But the cause is just and they are smart and organised. What have you heard?'

Chris watched Emily dancing and concern was all he could think about. Was it because of this League that she was being followed, or something else entirely? He didn't like it at all.

'Nothing that need concern us yet, I think,' he told Lady Smythe-Tomas. 'Just be careful about what goes on with this League.'

'Oh, believe me,' she murmured, 'I am always careful. I would advise you to be the same.'

'Would you care to take a turn on the terrace, Miss Fortescue?' James Hertford asked Emily. He tried not to sound too eager, but he feared he had failed. Time was running out for him, and he needed to close in on his goal—soon.

He had received another letter from his creditors, one filled with barely veiled threats. Their patience was wearing thin; soon, none of his excuses, his promises, would hold them off any longer. He was constantly looking over his shoulder now, hearing that ticking of the clock that spelled his ruin. Emily Fortescue, as maddening as she was, was his last resort.

He looked down at her as he led her off the dance floor. She *was* pretty, there was that at least. He would never be ashamed to call her his wife. She was also styl-

ish, at ease in society despite her business-world background. Surely she would be a good hostess. She was
much too independent, too clever for her own good,
yet that would change once she belonged to a man and
knew her true place.

The important thing, the only thing really, was that
she was rich. She could save him. If only she would
listen, damn her! He had tried so many things. He had
been gentlemanly, defending her from that lout Hamilton. He had tried fear, making her see that she needed
protection when wandering the city. He had been her
friend. Maybe courtship would work. A ridiculous, old-
fashioned wooing, as in those novels ladies like her
seemed to enjoy. Flowers and compliments.

She gave him a quick smile, her cheeks turning a bit
pink, and he hoped she was ready at last. That his sal-
vation was in sight. Her money would save him.

But she wouldn't meet his hopeful gaze and she
turned away to snap open her fan. 'I think it's almost
time for me to depart, Mr Hertford, but thank you so
much. I enjoyed our dance.'

Her hand slid off his arm and she started to turn
away, that ungrateful chit. James saw his last chance
slipping away from him and a red mist rose before his
eyes. How dare she turn away from him! From what
he could offer her!

Before he realised what he was doing, he grabbed her
hand hard and spun her around towards him.

She looked at him, her eyes wide and startled, and
he was glad he could ruffle her smug pride after all.

'Mr Hertford, what are you...?' she gasped.

'Miss Fortescue, I must beg you to listen to me,' he said, hating every begging word he gave her. Hating the dark hole he had fallen into. 'I need to tell you…'

'There you are, Miss Fortescue,' a voice said, light, full of laughter, yet insistent.

James turned to see Christopher Blakely standing there, watching them, a wry smile on his lips. James knew the man's reputation. Surely he was not after Miss Fortescue himself? Was he only trying to embarrass James?

'I believe you have promised me the next dance,' Blakely said. He smoothly took Emily's hand, drawing it into the crook of his arm.

Emily nodded and they hurried away to vanish into the crowd, not even glancing back at James. He had never felt such a burning anger before. How dared she, a tradesman's daughter, choose someone like Blakely over what James could offer her? He needed a new plan, one that would make her his—and then make her sorry.

Chapter Seven

When Chris arrived back at his lodgings the next day, after long meetings about the questionable German Herr Friedland and his possible errands in Paris, he found he was not alone. His brother William was waiting, sitting by the window with a book, a bottle of burgundy and a tray of sandwiches, as at home there as Will always was everywhere.

And Chris was secretly delighted to see him. Will had been at his post in Vienna for many months with Diana and the family had seldom seen them in that time. Not that Chris could blame him for protecting Di from the dark cloud of the Blakelys; Will had a career, a life to build. A wife he adored.

And Chris envied him that. Not that he would ever say so. He wouldn't give his brother the satisfaction of knowing he still felt sibling jealousy!

Chris grinned at his brother and tossed his coat and hat on to the table. 'I see you have not hesitated to make yourself at home.'

Will smiled back and poured another glass of wine as Chris sat down beside him. 'Your landlady is very obliging. She insisted on making me a repast while I waited and told me all about her rheumatism and the gossip about your neighbours.'

'Mrs Hodges. Yes, she does keep fine lodgings indeed, but she will also chatter on if she can corner a person. Especially an unwary stranger like yourself.' Chris reached for one of the sandwiches.

'It sounds as if she can rarely corner *you*, Christopher. She says you are "gadding about at all hours", seldom home.'

'I would think she would appreciate that. Saves her on my board.'

Will was quiet for long moment, the two of them drinking their wine in companionable silence, as if it had been only a day they were apart and not weeks. 'Is Ellersmere keeping you hard at work, then?'

'At times, yes,' Chris answered. 'I've been asked to go to Paris again, to look into the doings of a man called Friedland.'

Will frowned. 'Paris. Interesting. I am headed there myself.'

'Are you? I did wonder what brought you to London.'

'We're just here for a few days before we leave for France, doing our duty by subjecting Di to dinner with the parents. She has a commission from *Ladies' Weekly* to write a series about the new Parisian hats.'

'Of course she does. All the magazines want articles from Diana now, she's an amazing writer. And what will you do while she peruses the Champs-Élysées?'

Will shrugged, his smooth, angular face hiding his thoughts as always. 'Oh, make the diplomatic rounds of the embassies, as usual. The Exposition may have closed, but plenty of important people still linger there. They say the Prince of Wales may make a return visit soon—*without* the Princess. The races are starting.'

'I have heard talk of it at the office. Bertie's visits are a constant nuisance.' Chris took another bite of his sandwich, thinking as he slowly chewed. 'What have you heard of this Herr Friedland?'

'Not a great deal. He seems to be one of those radical sorts who seem to keep popping up everywhere lately. They don't like that sort of thing in Vienna. Stuck in the sixteenth century there.'

'I would imagine they don't.' Chris knew how etiquette-bound and strict places like Vienna could be. And yet he wouldn't mind trying such a job himself, not now.

'But he does seem to be acquainted with Empress Elisabeth, which is something of a worry. She is very— unpredictable in her opinions, unlike her very predictable husband. I am sure the Foreign Office in Vienna would be interested to learn all about Friedland.'

'As they would be here.' Chris toyed with the stem of his glass, thinking of Emily at the party, the enthusiasm on her face as she talked of her League. Her concern about being followed. He worried about her. 'It's been hinted that if my work is satisfactory in Paris, there may be a—change in my career direction.'

Will slowly nodded. He didn't seem very surprised. 'And what do you think of that?'

Chris shrugged. 'If a diplomat's post makes a man

look as happy as you, Will, I should consider it.' And his brother was indeed looking well, content and calm, a hint of laughter in his dark blue eyes that had never been there before.

Will smiled. 'I suppose marriage suits me. Maybe you should try it soon.'

'Me? Never.' Chris remembered Emily again, her face in the moonlight, the touch of her hand on his arm. 'No lady would have me.'

'If you were to become established in a respectable career, set up a real home...'

Chris shook his head. 'It's true I'm becoming too old for the work I've been doing. A young rogue is winked at, indulged. An old one just becomes pitiable. And I am rather bored at times.'

'Well, diplomacy is seldom boring in Vienna, I promise you. It's like constantly learning new, silent languages. I could never do it all without Diana's help.' Will poured himself more wine. 'Is the Friedland business the only thing taking you to Paris?'

'Well, there *is* the races. Like our good Prince Bertie, I am something of an aficionado of the turf. Have to take the perks of the job where we find them.'

Will studied him for a long moment. Chris could tell that his brother did not quite believe him—Will's career was built on reading people's secret thoughts, just as Chris's was. But Will said nothing, just nodded and finished his wine.

'Be careful with these people like Friedland, radical sorts,' Will said. 'Anarchists, suffragettes. They care only about their cause and will never hesitate to be rid of anyone who gets in their way. Now—will we see you at dinner at the family manse tomorrow? I know Di is eager to find out all about your doings of late.'

'Of course I will be there. Even dinner with the parents would be worthwhile to see my lovely sister-in-law again.'

After Will left, Chris sat staring out the window for a long time, not really seeing the crowds hurrying past. He thought about Will's words—*Never hesitate to be rid of anyone who gets in their way.* And he also thought of Emily and her father's worries about her. Had she got in someone's way? Was that why she was being followed?

He scowled as he remembered Emily's expression as she told him about being grabbed in the street. Emily never showed fear; she always tried to treat such things as jokes. But he had seen that look in her eyes, the slight tremble of her hand. He worried she was involved in something she couldn't understand, that her intelligence and idealism would lead her into more trouble. She had even seemed grateful when he took her away from James Hertford at the party, though she was very quiet as they danced afterwards.

He pushed himself up from his chair and crossed the sparsely furnished sitting room to his small bookshelf. One of the volumes was a hollowed-out copy of Aristotle, tucked amongst the other dusty volumes. Inside were hidden a few papers, a diary—and a fading pink-silk ribbon.

He took it out and turned it over in his fingers. It still smelled faintly of Emily's spring jasmine perfume and he remembered the day she gave it to him. The Parisian sunlight, the green, heated smell of the hedge maze, the laughter of the party. The way her lips tasted under his, making him hungry for more.

He wasn't really sure why he kept the ribbon. It should remind him of feelings he couldn't have, dreams he had to let go. But now he saw it as a sort of pledge. The chivalrous knight protecting the lady whose favour he bore—even if she never knew he did. Even if she would turn him away.

He closed his hand over the scrap of silk. He would go to Paris—and he would accept Mr Fortescue's task. He had to make sure Emily was safe.

There was a quick knock at the door and then a note slid underneath. He crept over to pick it up, listening as Mrs Hodges's heavy footsteps retreated. At least she was just delivering his mail at the moment, not being nosy. He slit the letter open and saw it was a note from Albert Fortescue.

The man wanted him to come to the Fortescue house and talk more about protecting Emily in Paris. The timing could not have been more perfect.

Emily saw the glow of firelight from beneath her father's library door when she returned home from an appointment with the silk importers' warehouses. She unpinned her hat, and called, 'Father, I'm just going to change for dinner now. Sorry I'm late!'

'Oh, don't worry about that now, Emily,' he called back. 'Could you just come in for a moment?'

Puzzled by his quiet, thoughtful tone, she hurried into the library. Her father sat next to the fire, wrapped in a loose, burgundy-velvet jacket rather than his dinner suit. There were no other lights in the room except the crackling fire, and a bottle of brandy sat on the table next to him. It was not his usual evening routine at all.

'Are you quite well?' she cried, rushing over to kneel beside him. She took his hands in hers and they were alarmingly cold. His face looked rather pale, too.

'The doctor did come to see me this afternoon,' he said. 'Just a touch of dropsy again. I just need a few quiet evenings and all will be well again.'

Emily felt terribly frightened. 'Father! I knew you were looking tired of late. Why didn't you tell me? We should go to Switzerland…'

'Emily, my dearest.' He gave her a gentle smile and laid his hand against her cheek. 'There is no time to talk about such things now. A caller is arriving soon.'

She was baffled, confused, alarmed. What was her father doing? 'A caller? At this hour, and in your condition? Surely they can be put off.'

Albert firmly shook his head. 'It is too important. We both have to see him. I have something to ask you both.'

'Ask *us*? I'm afraid I don't understand. Who is this caller? And no matter what, you should be in bed, getting some rest.'

'Soon, my dear, very soon. Just have some patience. I know that is not the easiest thing for you!' A knock sounded at the front door and she could hear the butler hurrying to answer it. 'Ah, there he is now. Most prompt. Always a good sign.'

Emily sat back on the chair beside her father, wondering if this illness was more serious than he claimed, if in fact it was making him lose his mind. Whoever this caller was, she would make sure he left quickly and her father rested.

To her shock, it was Chris who appeared in the library, his golden hair damp from the evening fog gathering outside. He looked almost as confused as she felt and Emily shivered with a cold sense of foreboding. What on earth was her father about?

'Mr Fortescue,' he said. 'Emily. I received your note. Is anything amiss? How can I help?'

'This is the first I have heard of you being expected here at all,' she answered.

Albert chuckled and poured out three snifters of the brandy. 'Not at all, Mr Blakely. I simply have a great favour to ask of you, of both of you. An indulgence to an old man, if you will. Please, do sit down. Have a brandy, it's becoming a wretched night out there.'

Chris sat down in the armchair across from them, backlit with the firelight, but Emily could see the lines of wariness around his eyes. 'I am happy to help friends, if I can.'

'Of course you are. You are a very good sort of chap, even if my daughter might not always agree,' Albert said with a laugh.

'Father!' Emily protested, mortified. 'Christopher is perfectly—entertaining.'

'Entertaining?' Chris snorted. 'Is that all?'

'Well, you know what I mean,' she said, feeling her cheeks turn too warm. She gulped down her brandy, wishing this strange evening was over. Or maybe she was dreaming it all?

'Which is just one of the reasons you are the only one I could call on for help,' said Albert. 'As you know, Emily is going to Paris soon to see to some of our business concerns. My doctor has told me I should not travel right now, but I can't see her alone so far away.'

Chris watched Albert very carefully, his eyes narrowed, his glass turning slowly in his hand. Emily wondered what that look could mean. He did not seem very surprised. 'I can understand that. And I am happy to look in on Miss Fortescue whenever possible, since I will be in France myself.'

'Chris!' Emily cried. 'You are not my nanny. I don't need looking in on.'

Albert waved his hand. 'Absolutely right, my dear. You need no nanny. But though I understand that you, Mr Blakely, are a good friend to my daughter, as well as brother-in-law to her best friend, I also understand that there is the danger of gossip when a man and woman are seen to be—friendly. What I would ask now, and this may seem rather outlandish, but do hear me out, is that you pretend to be my daughter's suitor. A serious contender for her hand. Maybe even her new fiancé.'

Emily was beyond appalled. She slammed her glass down on the table and glanced between the two men as if she could almost see the madness in the air. 'Father, what do you mean by this? I told you, I do not want a suitor right now. And Chris would be...' Chris would be—what? Too much fun? Too dangerous? Too painful once the charade ended?

'You needn't actually marry him, my dear. Merely give the impression that you are considering it. Then you can go about your business with everyone knowing you have a protector and I will know you aren't alone in a different city.'

Emily scowled. She looked at Chris, but somehow he did not seem nearly as surprised and appalled as she was by the suggestion. 'How exactly is he supposed to court me, then?'

Albert laughed. 'Oh, it's been too many years since I've had to do such a thing, but I'm sure it hasn't changed that much. Dancing, walking in the park, going for drives? The theatre, maybe. The Louvre. I used to hide letters in gifts of sheet music to your mother. That sort of thing.'

'It would not be so difficult,' Chris said carefully, shocking Emily deeply. Surely courting one lady would be injurious to his reputation?

'Chris, surely you can't be considering this?' she said.

He gave her a crooked little smile, the one that always seemed to make all her practicality melt away. 'It's never a hardship to spend time with you, Em. And we'll be in Paris. It might be fun. If we could spare ourselves a little unwanted attention from others…'

'Unwanted attention?' she said, puzzled. She imagined Chris might be something of a deterrent if someone wanted to keep sending her letters and following her home from League meetings, but how could she help him? 'What about Will and Di? Our other friends?'

'They know we're friends. I'm sure there wouldn't be a fuss later when they see you've thrown me over.'

Emily closed her eyes against the headache forming there as she tried to decide what was happening.

'It would be the only way I would feel right about letting you go to Paris, Emily,' her father said gently. 'Knowing that you have a friend to make sure no one bothers you again. And no one at all would think it strange you have a suitor.'

Emily glanced at her father in the firelight. He *did* look rather tired and worried. Suddenly she felt terribly guilty, worrying him in any way at all. And if men like James Hertford could be persuaded to leave her alone, would that be a terrible thing? She was so worried about her father, about their business, how she would carry it all forward, worried about the League and its important missions. It might be nice indeed to have a friend, to not be all alone in Paris. She knew all too well how it felt to be alone.

She looked back at Chris, who smiled at her. 'Then what would be in it for *you*, Chris?'

He shrugged. 'Well, it could be fun. We could discover Paris together, Emily! Art, restaurants, music. Also, I admit I have had a, shall we say, misunderstanding lately with a lady. She's become rather too serious, so a little distance wouldn't come amiss. If she heard I was being seen with you…' His cheeks turned red and he shrugged again.

Emily slumped back in her seat. Of course it would be about some unfortunate romantic entanglement with Chris. She had heard the gossip; she knew what his life was like, very well. She would never be so foolish to think that a couple of kisses, no matter how sweet and life-changing they had been for her, would mean the same to a man like him. She wondered if it was with Lady Smythe-Tomas. They had been seen together in a few places, though she didn't seem like the clinging type. It could be any one of a number of ladies.

And yet, she still felt a secret, painful little pang deep inside to think of him and his—entanglements.

She crossed her arms and looked away to the darkened windows. Spending more time with Chris was probably the very last thing a sensible lady would do. Every time she was with him, trouble seemed to come in his wake. But she did want to help her father. She wanted to see to their business in Paris and she did not want him to worry.

And Chris was right. It might even be a little bit fun.

She turned back to them and nodded. 'Fine.' She sighed. 'But only a few walks and a dinner or two! I have work to do while I am there.'

Chris smiled, a brilliant grin that lit up his face and made him too handsome to be real. Emily almost took back her words, realising the danger she could be in.

'I will not disappoint you, Emily,' he declared.

Her father clapped his hands, like he was at the satisfactory ending of a romantic comedy at the Savoy. 'Excellent! Then I won't worry about you at all while you are gone, my dear.'

'But you must promise to rest while I am gone, Father,' Emily demanded. 'And not do any work. You must leave it all to me.'

Albert gave her a satisfied little smile. 'Certainly I will. I'll be completely well by the time you get home. Now, Mr Blakely, will you stay for dinner? It is only a small meal tonight, very informal, but you're most welcome.'

'The doctor told you to rest...' Emily began.

'That is most kind of you, Mr Fortescue, but I have another engagement. I will call again before we leave for Paris, though,' Chris said.

Emily wondered if it was an engagement with the clinging lady. 'I'll show you out,' she said, abruptly standing up.

Once they were alone in the hall, hopefully out of earshot of her father, she leaned close to Chris and whispered, 'You don't really have to do this, Chris.'

He squeezed her hand and smiled, taking his hat from the butler. 'Of course I do, Em. I want to help if I can. And really, you would be helping me out of the most alarming pickle. See you at the Eiffel Tower!'

'Yes,' she murmured as she watched him stroll out into the night. She wondered just what she had let herself in for now. 'See you there.'

Chapter Eight

Paris was overwhelmingly beautiful. Every time she was there, Emily realised, she was bowled over by that realisation, by the awe over the elegance people could create when they were so inclined. The loveliness that could be in the world—and she got to be a part of it.

She tipped her head back to peer up at Monsieur Eiffel's tower from beneath her wide-brimmed hat. The first day of her Paris adventure. She had seen it before, of course, had even ascended to the very tippy-top during the Exposition, to see the city spread out far below. But she always fell in love with it anew. It seemed like the city itself, in its new Haussmann-designed guise of pale stone, grey-slate roofs, lacings of iron balconies and streets reaching out towards the silver ribbon of the river. It was modern, sleek, spare but luxurious, every detail perfect. Against the pale blue sky of early summer, it was intoxicating.

Emily wished she had paid more attention in art class, so she could sketch the scene before her and freeze it for ever. But all she could do was study it carefully, memorise it, lock it away to bring out on some faraway grey day. That was what she did with all her best memories. The smell of her mother's perfume, a game of tennis at Miss Grantley's, Alexandra's and Diana's weddings. Kissing Chris Blakely, here in this very city.

She suddenly longed for Chris to be there beside her, to share the beauty with her, to laugh with her at the people walking past. But she pushed that longing away. She had to concentrate only on the scene before her. The work she had to do. The promises she had made to her father.

The Champs de Mars was busy on such a lovely day, the gravel pathways lined with strollers against the shimmering dome of the École Militaire. She studied the ladies' gowns, the width of their hats, the trim on their sleeves.

She glanced behind her as a group of gentlemen approached, dark as crows in their suits and bowler hats, their footsteps heavy. They passed by with only polite nods, but she realised she had grown tense. It had been that way ever since she was followed in London; the dream of being chased along alleyways plagued her nearly every night. She had hoped in Paris she could forget about it, leave it behind, but she was still nervous.

She made her way to one of the green wrought-iron benches to sit down out of the way for a moment. She opened her parasol and tilted it against the sun to watch the city swirl around her. Two children dashed by with a hoop, followed by their watchful nanny; a tour group hurried past, noses in their *Baedeker*s.

A young couple drifted by, their arms entwined, smiling up at each other as if they were oblivious to the rest of the world. Their happiness made Emily feel terribly wistful. Terribly alone. Paris wasn't a city for melancholy.

'Imagine running into *you* here in Paris, Miss Fortescue,' a voice suddenly said, shattering her dreamy thoughts. Startled, she peeked around the lacy edge of her parasol and saw it was Chris.

For an instant, she was sure she imagined him, that he was only another daydream. But then he smiled at her, that wide, white, flashing smile, and she knew it was truly him. He swept off his hat and the sun sparkled on his golden hair.

'What on earth are you doing here?' she blurted. Then she remembered. Their 'courtship'. It was beginning. She wished he wouldn't startle her so. Maybe they should have made a more formal agreement as to when and where they would meet?

'Oh, much the same as you are doing, I suppose. Enjoying the *joie de vivre* of it all.' He sat down next to her on the bench and carelessly crossed his legs.

Emily felt much too pleased to see him. She had to resist the urge to lean on his arm, to breathe him in. 'So I suspect we are *not* in Paris for the same things, as I am here to work.'

'You do wound me,' he said, his smile widening. 'I do know how to be serious when I need to be.'

Emily gave a rather unladylike snort. 'Such as when?'

'Such as right now? What could be more serious in life than being with a beautiful woman in Paris? It requires a great deal of careful thought.'

'Thought about what?'

'About the perfect thing to do, of course. Shall we have a picnic, ride a *bateau mouche*, go shopping? Maybe stroll through the Tuileries? There are so very many choices, it's important to choose the correct one. We are meant to be courting, remember?'

She remembered her promise to her father all too well. But here, on this beautiful day, it didn't seem like such a terrible thing at all. 'Hmm,' Emily said, tapping her chin in pretended deep thought. 'It is true. So many choices, so little time.'

'I know what *I* would choose to do.'

Maybe kiss her again? Emily wondered whimsically. She studied his handsome face, glowing in the Parisian light, and thought that might be rather nice. No matter what happened afterwards. 'What is that?'

'I would sit here with you all day.'

She laughed, delighted by his silly words. 'You would be bored of it in an hour.'

'Not at all. From a park bench in Paris, a person could watch the whole world go by. And with you to talk about it all with—surely this is all I need.' He gestured at the crowds swirling past, the glittering life all around them, and for an instant he looked serious, solemn even.

Emily curled her fingers tighter around her parasol to keep from reaching out to him. 'Well, I can think of something I would like to do.'

'What is that, then?'

'Luncheon! My stomach is horribly a-rumble. I'm dreaming of a lovely steak tartare.'

Chris laughed, the sound rich and alluring, like

music or a cup of the darkest chocolate. 'Your wish is my command. I am your loyal suitor, remember?'

Emily remembered the maze, the ribbon. It hadn't felt so false then at all. 'Like a chivalrous knight?'

'Of course. Slaying dragons; finding the perfect café. Onwards, fair lady!'

He took her arm and led her out of the park, laughingly telling her about his mother's latest attempt at heiress-hunting.

'The poor girl was pretty enough, true, but she laughed like a peacock and could only talk about American baseball, which I cannot follow at all. What's wrong with a good game of cricket, I ask you?' he scoffed. 'Now, Em, what kind of life would that be over the breakfast table every day?'

Emily laughed at the image of Chris trying to play baseball. 'A most tedious one, I am sure. Though I admit, I can't even follow your beloved cricket, let alone learn some American game involving bats, so I would be a poor match for such a person, as well. We must never marry Americans.'

Chris pressed his hand over his heart as if wounded. 'Ah, but cricket, my dear Miss Fortescue, is the game of the gods! Anything else is just—uncivilised.' He pointed out a café across the lane from the park and led her to one of the inviting little marble tables under the shade of the dark red awning.

'What about you, then, Em?' he asked, as he perused the chalkboard menu. 'Any rich, handsome, non-American suitors since we last met?'

'Oh, dozens,' she said with an airy wave of her hand.

'We are running out of space for all the bouquets and chocolates.' She thought of days at home, when bouquets arrived after balls from various suitors, some of them quite persistent. Like Mr Hertford.

Chris leaned his chin on her hand, studying her with an unreadable glint in his blue eyes. 'I wouldn't be at all surprised.'

Emily shook her head. 'No one new, of course. Where would a girl find the time these days? Between the business and the League...'

'And which of those two brings you to Paris?'

Emily studied him carefully, wondering at the rather sharp note in his voice. But he just looked like Chris, impossibly handsome, impossibly—impossible. 'Work, mainly, as you know. Well, maybe a bit of both. And maybe just a soupçon of fun.'

'*Fun?* Fun for you, Em? Are you sure?'

'Of course!' He looked rather doubtful and she found herself wounded he didn't think her at all fun. 'I *am* fun, Christopher.'

'Certainly you are,' he murmured.

'I am.' She studied the café pavement around them, the ladies in their fur stoles with their little dogs, gentlemen in suits muttering about business in low voices, a pair of young lovers in the shadows, their heads bent together as they whispered. She glimpsed a band just inside the smudged plate glass of the windows, tuning their instruments. They launched into a rendition of one of the new, popular *musette* songs, all swirling accordions, and she had a sudden idea. 'Come along!' she cried, jumping up from the table.

'Come along where?' Chris said with a protesting laugh. But he let her take his hand and followed her willingly, as he always did when an adventure promised. That was one of the things she liked best about him: his appetite to try things in life.

As the tune grew louder, Emily made Chris slide his hand around her waist and nudged him into the first steps of a waltz. The musicians laughed and played even louder. 'How can anyone hear this and not dance?'

'People are watching,' he muttered, shooting a glance around them.

'Of course they are and when has attention ever stopped *you*?' Emily scoffed. 'I just want to have some fun, you see. And you are supposed to be courting me.'

He threw back his head and gave a wonderful, full-throated laugh. His arms tightened around her and he twirled her in a wide circle, her blue-striped skirts swirling. She heard answering laughter around them, blending with the music and applause. Another couple joined them as the singer went into the tune, a high, sweet voice that added to the atmosphere of light merriment, of a sudden festival on an ordinary day.

'What do you think the song is about?' she whispered as she and Chris spun and dipped, the café blurry around them. Two other couples joined in, the ladies' perfume a flowery, musky tangle in the air.

'I'm afraid my French is shockingly schoolboy,' he answered. 'I can only follow when they speak slowly and carefully, as to a four-year-old. Not sing-speak. But I think it's about seizing life when it's upon you. About love.'

Emily laughed. 'Of course it's about love. It's a French song.'

'Oh, but not just any love. The girl it seems is in love with a—bird?'

'A bird?' Emily scoffed.

'Indeed. I hear the word *oiseau* and I know that means bird. She watches it soar high above her little farmhouse, its feathers glittering like jewels in the sun, its song alluringly sweet. She wishes it would lead her far away from her normal life, beyond the clouds to something magical. Something where life has the—the…'

'The what?' she whispered, fascinated by the strange tale. Fascinated by Chris, by how he looked. As if he was indeed a golden Arthurian knight from another world.

He looked down at her with a crooked smile. 'The true intensity of feeling, the living of life. I think it must be a firebird.'

'A firebird.' Emily sighed. She leaned her cheek for a brief, sweet moment against Chris's shoulder, feeling the movement of his strong body against hers, breathing deeply of the scent of his citrus soap. 'When I was a little girl, my father went on a buying trip to St Petersburg once and he brought me back a painting of the firebird. I couldn't read the Cyrillic letters of the story, of course, but I was mesmerised by the image. The brilliant colours, the way the bird soared high into the night sky, all red and gold above the sleeping, cool blue city. The gold domes and river.'

'Would you like to see that city, Em?' he asked quietly.

She raised her head to look into his eyes, the endless blue of them. The beauty that hid so much. 'Of course. It must be like a fairy tale. But only if I could take all of my furs with me! I could never bear the cold.' She glanced out over the street, the glitter of sunlight on the windows of the pale buildings, the tip of the Eiffel Tower soaring behind the grey roofs. 'Can it be as beautiful as this?'

The song swirled to an end and Chris dipped her with a flourish, making the other dancers applaud in delight. Emily laughed as she tried to hold on to her hat.

'I don't think anything could be as beautiful as this,' he said quietly, his hand tight on hers, warm and safe.

He looked very un-Chris-like in that moment, almost sad. As if he, like her, didn't want this moment to slide away. Startled, she drew away and hurried back to their table. A plate of oysters and chilled glasses of champagne waited, and she gratefully gulped down the cool, bubbly liquid.

'Come with me to Longchamp on Friday,' Chris said as he sat down beside her.

'The races? Why?' she answered, deeply tempted by the thought of day away, with him. Just themselves and the horses, nothing to distract. Nothing to worry about. And yet it would surely be *everything* to worry about, alone with him.

'For the fun, of course. You said you are here in Paris to have fun. To be a courting couple. What could be more so than an afternoon at the races? Who knows, we might even glimpse Prince Bertie there.'

'I do have work…' she murmured, tempted. She *had*

promised her father to spend time with Chris after all. And a day at the races sounded alluring.

'I'm sure it could help with the work. You can see what all the most fashionable ladies are wearing and order in enough hats to make a fortune before anyone else knows the styles.'

'That is true.'

'Just don't hesitate too long,' he warned.

Emily laughed. 'Or you will find another lady to invite?'

'Or Friday will pass us by.' He held out an oyster and she opened her lips to let it slide past. The salty sweetness of it, the tinge of lemon, reminded her of his summer-day kisses. The lazy, wonderful feeling that it would always be a warm Friday with him.

But she had learned those moments always flew by much too fast, like the firebird.

'I'll think about it,' she said with a smile. 'In the meantime, do pass another glass of champagne before you drink it all up...'

Later that night, when the sun was fading like a swathe of lavender-silk scarves over the grey chimneys of Paris, Emily hurried towards her hotel after a meeting with the wine suppliers. It was only a short distance from their office to the hotel and she had thought it would be a quick, easy stroll, but now she wasn't sure. She had a sudden chill and rubbed her gloved hands over the sleeves of her jacket.

She hadn't realised the streets around her hotel became so quiet in the evening. In the afternoon, there were always business meetings in the lobby, at night, people rushing off for dinner and the theatre. But at that in-between hour, they all seemed to be tucked away inside, behind drawn curtains, getting dressed, sipping new-fangled cocktails. Perhaps getting ready for a rather naughty *cinq à sept*.

She imagined herself preparing for a lover, maybe Chris with a roguish glint in his beautiful eyes, and she giggled.

Her laughter was interrupted by a sound behind her. A rustle, a footfall.

She glanced over her shoulder, but saw nothing. Yet that unease lingered and she couldn't help but remember that hard hand that grabbed her on the street before, the cold rush of fear. She spun back around and half-ran towards her hotel.

Once inside the small, golden-lit foyer, hearing the murmur of the receptionist behind the desk, she sucked in a deep breath. Her heart still pounded.

'Mademoiselle Fortescue,' the doorman said. 'And how was your day?'

'Quite lovely, Pierre, *merci*,' she said, still afraid she sounded too breathless.

'This came for you while you were out.' He handed her a small nosegay of white roses and a letter attached to the stems with a green-velvet ribbon. Best of all was a striped red and white hatbox.

Surely it was from Chris, asking her to the races again! Emily felt absurdly delighted as she reached for the paper.

She tore open the note, trying to tell herself she

wasn't at all excited, that the whole faux-courtship scheme was an utter nuisance. But she couldn't quite hide her *whole* smile. She had to admit that Paris with Chris was indeed amusing, and she was much too curious to see what might happen next.

From your parfit knight.
See you at the races!

Emily opened the box, and found nestled in tissue paper the most chic, elaborate, silly hat she had ever seen, a garden confection of peach tulle and roses, pale green bows and streamers. She plopped it on her head and couldn't help but laugh and laugh. Life with Chris was always unpredictable indeed. And she had to admit that sometimes, just sometimes, she rather liked it.

Chapter Nine

'Welcome to Gordston's, Mademoiselle Fortescue,' the uniformed doorman said with a tip of his hat, as he opened the store's frosted glass doors for her.

'*Merci,*' Emily answered happily, glad to be back in the perfumed sanctuary of Gordston's, the air cool and delicious after the bright day outside. Surely no harm could come to her there. It was too elegant, too serene, too perfect.

Alexandra's husband had indeed created a luxurious oasis in the middle of the busy city. The main floor was an endless expanse of black and white marble floors, glittering glass cases, feathered hats and floating silk scarves offered by pretty girls in crisp black dresses. Above soared a gallery, lined with granite pillars in a touch of pink, where the curious peered down at the newcomers below. Emily could just glimpse the fashion displays up there. The air smelled of powders and perfumes, all flowers and spice.

There was so much to catch her attention, to lure her

in for a closer look, but she just waved at the attendants and made her way to the lifts at the back of the store.

She was whisked to the private top floor, where the store's offices lay behind discreet closed doors. Secretaries and managers hurried past on their errands, the Aubusson carpets underfoot muffling their quick footsteps, and Emily heard only the pinging bells of the lifts, the click of typewriters, the swish of fabric. She straightened her hat, a brown-velvet toque with topaz-coloured ribbons she had bought in that very store to go with her caramel walking suit, and knocked on the door at the end of the hall.

'*Entrez-vous,*' a soft voice called.

Emily pushed the door open to find Alex sitting behind a gilded antique French desk, a pile of order ledgers in front of her. Despite the fact that she was a duke's daughter and the wife of a wealthy businessman, her pale blonde hair was piled simply atop her head, and she wore a loose, flowered Liberty cotton morning dress with no jewels at all.

'Hard at work, Alex darling?' Emily asked with a fond smile.

Alex looked up, her pretty, heart-shaped face breaking into a radiant laugh. 'Em! Of course I am, I learned it from you. Who would have ever thought store-ordering figures could be so fascinating?'

She jumped up and ran around the desk to throw her arms around Emily. She was so petite, she had to stand on tiptoe in her kid boots.

Only when Emily hugged her back did she notice that her friend was not *quite* as tiny and fragile as usual.

'Alex!' she cried, stepping back to study Alexandra in astonishment. Beneath her loosely tied sash, there was a distinct bump. 'Are you…?'

Alex laughed, and gave a happy twirl. 'Yes, but not very much yet. We aren't telling anyone until next month, just in case—well…'

Emily nodded, remembering that Diana had had two miscarriages since she was married and they all worried for her. But Alex looked in the full, pink bloom of health. 'I am sure all will go very well with you. You look utterly luscious, like a pink-iced cake!'

'I do feel very well. I've been eating so many candied figs from the food hall, though, that I'm sure I will turn into one at any moment.' She twirled over and sat down on a brocade sofa near the window, with a glorious view of the bustling Champs-Élysées below, drawing Emily with her. 'Do sit down and tell me all about *you*, Em. I'm so excited you're back in Paris! Have you come to work?'

Emily decided not to tell her quite yet about the League and definitely not about the mission to have fun. And definitely not about the false courtship with Chris. Better to keep things simple. 'Of course. What else could it be? And I want to examine our lovely café here at Gordston's.'

'It's all going perfectly, as you know, the most profitable area in the whole store. Everyone wants to rest for a cup of tea with their friends before they shop some more!' Alex tucked a shining strand of hair behind her ear and she looked so very happy and relaxed, so unlike her old shy self. Emily thought Paris, and marriage, must be like magic for her. 'And you've come at just the right time. Di and Will are visiting from Vienna and even Chris is here. It will be quite like home.'

Emily thought of her dance with Chris at the café and she looked down to carefully smooth her skirt. 'Oh, yes, I did see Christopher. At the Champ de Mars.'

Alex looked surprised. 'Did you? How did he look? My aunt has been rather worried about him, as always. She thinks he will never settle down.'

Emily laughed when she remembered the baseball-playing heiress. 'Oh, he looked just like Chris. Handsome, full of himself. I think your aunt might be right.'

Alex sighed. 'I hope she is proved wrong soon. Chris is such a darling, he deserves to be happy, to have all his potential fulfilled. Maybe he is in Paris for a reason?'

A reason, such as a lady? Emily hadn't thought of that. Her hand tightened on her skirt. 'He said something about the races.'

Alex laughed. 'That's not exactly the sort of fulfilment I was thinking of! I must find out where he is staying and send him an invitation for dinner. I'm quite aching to show off my new house to all of you.' The small enamelled clock on her desk chimed. 'Oh, dear, is that the time? Come along, Di will be meeting us for lunch in the café.'

'Diana is at the store?' Emily cried, overjoyed to think about seeing both her best friends at the same time.

'It's meant to be a surprise, so don't tell her I told you.' Alex reached for a lace jacket she draped over her

shoulders and patted her hair into place. 'I am so happy
we three are together again! It's just as life should be.'

'I'm so glad the café is doing so well,' Emily said,
taking off her gloves. A large, domed skylight set with
stained glass bathed all the ladies and their stylish hats
in blue and green light, and their laughter blended in a
soft music with the clink of silver on fine china. It was
all most elegant, but also relaxing and fun.

'It's all thanks to you, so Malcolm says,' Alex answered. They saw Diana already at a corner table and
she waved at them exuberantly. Emily ran over to kiss
her cheek and exclaim over her chic new Paris suit.

Alex lowered herself slowly into her velvet-cushioned
chair, as though even at that early stage she wasn't yet
comfortable with her changing figure, and gestured to
one of the black-suited waiters for coffee. 'You have
done wonders with the decor; all the shoppers love to
linger here. And the menu suggestions for afternoon tea
have gone over wonderfully.'

'Well, everyone needs a project,' Emily said with a
laugh. 'I must keep myself busy somehow.'

'You've always done far more than that, Em,' Diana
said, adjusting the tilt of her hat on her upswept red curls.
'Extending your father's business, doing volunteer work,
dancing at every ball…'

Alex sighed as she poured out the coffee into elegant
eggshell-blue-and-gold china. 'So much energy! It's all
quite unfair. I can barely get out of bed in the morning,
I've become such a sloth.'

'You *do* have a good excuse,' Diana said with a

glance at Alex's waist. She looked strangely wistful for a moment, likely thinking of her own sadness, before she smiled again.

Alex laughed, and wrapped her lace jacket closer around her. 'I suppose I *am* very lucky. I haven't felt sick at all, just tired. So…well…*wallowy*. I haven't been to any good parties lately, so you two must tell me all about the glorious fun you've been having.'

Diana took a nibble of one of the iced cakes. 'I fear embassy life isn't terribly glamorous. I serve tea to the other wives and talk to old men at dinner, and dash around town leaving calling cards everywhere. But I *am* having fun writing those new articles for *Ladies' Weekly*, all the Paris fashions for summer!'

'You have to tell me more about what we should order for the Season,' Emily said. 'We sold so many of those feather-trimmed shawls last year, before anyone else knew they would be the fashion, thanks to you.'

'Have you been terribly busy lately with the business?' Alex asked. 'No time for fun at all?'

Emily flashed them a quick, mischievous smile, remembering the 'fun' they always got up to at school. Sneaking out of their rooms after lights-out for midnight picnics, swimming in the pond, organising lessons to learn the 'shocking' modern dances. 'Oh, there is always time for a bit of fun, just as there was at Miss Grantley's between studying. There have been some amusing parties in London this year. And I've been doing some work with the Women's Franchise League and have met some fascinating people there.'

Diana's eyes gleamed. 'Oh, do tell, Em! I have been reading about them. They have such wonderful ideas.'

'I would like to help them, too, if I can,' Alex said. 'If this child is a girl, imagine how the world could be different for her!'

Emily had known they would be interested. She told them about Mrs Hurst and the Pankhursts' salons at their Russell Square house, the wonderful ideas they were circulating, as well as a little about her errand in Paris to expand the League's reach. 'In fact, I have a meeting with them this afternoon, so I must be going soon.'

'Oh, no! We have so much to talk about still,' Alex cried.

'You must both come to dinner next week,' Diana said. 'I am planning a little party. Nothing grand at all, no business, just family. Which is you two, of course, and Malcolm. And Chris is in Paris, too. It would be such fun.'

Emily remembered dancing with Chris at the café and she felt her cheeks turn warm. She took a quick sip of coffee. 'Yes, certainly. I can't wait!'

Diana and Alex exchanged a glance. 'You should bring an escort, too, Em, if you like,' Diana said, in a much-too-casual tone. 'We always want to meet friends of yours.'

Emily looked at them suspiciously. 'What sort of escort?'

'Oh, you've always had so many admirers,' Alex said.

'And someone told us that James Hertford has been

most attentive at parties in London lately,' said Diana. 'He is so handsome!'

'And so sweet,' Alex added. 'He's always buying gifts for his sister and aunts at Gordston's.'

Emily had not been expecting to hear a specific 'suitor' named and felt rather flustered. Of course James Hertford was handsome, and had been kind, but surely that was just because he was ashamed of his erstwhile friend's bad behaviour towards her. 'Oh, no! That is, he *is* very nice, but you two know me. I am far too busy for serious romance.'

'Oh, but surely not always,' Alex protested.

'Even if I was not so busy, I don't think I would see Mr Hertford that way.' She had another flashing memory of Chris, laughing as he chased her through the maze, and she glanced away.

'If you say so,' Diana murmured.

Alex daintily dabbed her napkin at her lips and gave a sly little smile. 'But perhaps our darling Em doesn't need our help at all when it comes to finding an escort. Maybe there is a very good reason why Mr Hertford is not her type.'

Emily froze, wondering what Alex was implying. 'What do you mean?'

Di's eyes widened. She was always eager to spot a good story. 'Alex! Do you know a bit of gossip here that I do not?'

Emily tried to laugh, to keep from blushing. 'Oh, yes. Do tell me what I haven't learned yet about my life.'

Alex grinned and reached for the plate of dainty

iced cakes. 'Aren't these scrumptious? I just can't get enough of them lately.'

'Alexandra!' Diana cried. 'You are always so rotten at keeping secrets.'

Emily just wanted to sink under the table. No one could tease like her friends.

'I have heard that Emily has been seen around the city with none other than our own Christopher. He was even seen at her father's house in London one evening!' Alex said happily.

'No!' Diana cried. She sat back in her chair, staring wide-eyed at Emily. Emily tried to will herself not to blush even more, not to give away her thoughts at all. She and Chris were *meant* to be courting after all. She just hadn't counted on how hard it would be to fool Di and Alex. They knew her all too well.

'Em,' Diana said, 'are you and Chris really courting? Oh, how wonderful! We would be truly sisters then.'

'It's not like that, really,' Emily quickly protested. 'Chris is doing some business with my father and we just happened to see each other now and then. He's always been friendly. He likes all the ladies.'

Alex suddenly went from looking smugly happy to rather concerned. Emily wasn't sure which way was worse. 'Oh, but surely there has always been a—a rather wonderful little frisson between you.'

'Not at all,' Emily said briskly. She tried to butter a bit of toast, but ended up crumpling it. 'He is my friend. *Our* friend. He is doing me a favour of sorts. That's all.'

'A favour?' Diana gasped. 'Do tell us.'

Emily was saved at that moment by a commotion at the café doorway. Lady Smythe-Tomas appeared, surrounded by at least five handsome admirers. She held on to the arms of two of them, the tall emerald-green feathers on her hat waving as she laughed.

Alex glanced over at her. 'Ah, Lady Smythe-Tomas. I wondered when we might see her. She comes nearly every day to the store when she is in Paris.'

Diana frowned. 'Was there not some dispute last year about her bill?'

'Oh, that's all done now,' Alex answered. 'Her accounts are paid most promptly.'

Emily thought of Lady Smythe-Tomas, her dashing reputation, her high style. 'She seems much more the sort of lady for Chris than me. Glamorous, fashionable, confident…'

'And busy,' Diana murmured, examining the lady's coterie of suitors.

Alex giggled. 'She is the sort of lady for the man Chris once was, maybe, but surely we are all growing older. Our lives are changing. Even Chris's. He couldn't go on behaving like that for ever.'

'And I am growing older, too? A grey spinster?' Emily teased, even though she did feel a pang at the thought. She saw how happy Alex and Di were in their married lives and she had to admit she rather envied that.

'Oh, not you, Em!' Alex declared. 'You will never age a bit, drat you. All that boundless energy, that glorious hair. You are a wonder and you deserve to be happy with someone who deserves you.'

'If one could be found.' Alex sighed. 'I know no one good enough.'

'Oh, but Chris is wonderful, you all know that,' Diana said. 'And then I wouldn't be all alone in that family any more.'

Luckily, the waiter brought more coffee, and they dropped the 'romance' questions and chatted about other things until Emily had to leave for her meeting. She tried to ignore all the tempting displays on her way to the door, all the hats with their luscious satin ribbons, the wafts of sweet perfume, but it was not an easy task.

As she waited by the grand staircase for the doorman to call her hansom, Emily drew on her gloves and tried not to buy another hat. She studied the streams of shoppers flowing in and out of the doors, eavesdropping on their words as she tried to imagine what supplies she should suggest her father purchase next.

Suddenly she glimpsed a familiar face among them. James Hertford, sweeping off his silk hat to reveal his glossy dark hair. Had she somehow conjured him by listening to Alex and Di's gossip? There was no avoiding him, for he had seen her, too. She couldn't help but remember the ball in London, when Chris had to sweep in to carry her away from Hertford when he was insistent about talking to her. But then again, many men were like that when they decided to court a lady, so awkward. She was certainly overreacting. She made herself smile at him.

'Miss Fortescue,' he said, bowing over her hand. When he looked up at her, his smile was wide, his eyes glowing. He really was very handsome. Why could she not feel that strange little flutter when he looked at her, the one Chris could always conjure? Surely it could make her life easier.

'Mr Hertford. How extraordinary to see you in Paris. And at Gordston's!'

'My mother sent me on an errand here. It's her favourite shop.'

'I can certainly see why,' Emily said with a smile.

'Maybe you could help me? I need to find the fans. I am tasked with procuring one with an...er... Versailles design, painted on silk. I'm quite hopeless with it, I must say.'

Emily laughed. 'Now that I can help you with. It's on the way to the door—shall I walk with you?'

They made their way through the grand, galleried foyer, thronged with shoppers and gawkers, and the uniformed doorman bowed and opened the glass portal to let in the heat and light of the real world outside. She took him to the fan counter, its glistening glass spread with feathers, silk, bamboo.

'It is so lovely to see you again, James,' Emily said. 'Are you in Paris long?'

'Long enough to see you again, I hope,' he answered. 'Would you join me for supper at Véfour one night soon?'

Emily thought of her friends' teasing about 'romance', and Le Grand Véfour was nothing if not a romantic place. Even a modern lady like herself couldn't be seen courting two men at once. She turned away, busying herself with adjusting her gloves. 'I am going to be so busy while I'm here. Business is so prosperous these days.'

He smiled down at her, his brown eyes wide with eagerness. He had always been such an insistent suitor and it seemed any rumours about her and Chris had not put him off yet. 'Surely a lady as lovely as you must make some time for fun! Life cannot be all work.'

He sounded just like Alex and Diana. And maybe he was right. Maybe she *should* have more fun. Maybe if she made room for suitors in her life, Chris would lose some of his strange attractiveness. But Mr Hertford was not that man. 'No, indeed. I *have* been wanting to try the lobster bisque at Véfour, everyone says it's heavenly. I'll send you a message if my schedule lightens.'

'I'm at the Perrier Hotel.' James took her hand and pressed a lingering kiss to it. 'I look forward so much to seeing you again.'

Emily smiled at him and stepped out into the crowded street. She automatically scanned the pavements for any threat, as she always did lately when she was outside. She still grew tense and cold to remember how it felt to be chased, grabbed, to feel so helpless. But there was only the usual noise and motion of Paris, the crush of carriages, the sea of feathered hats, the tangle of laughter. At the end of the Champs-Élysées, she glimpsed the Arc de Triomphe rising out of the sunny mist, solid and reassuring, the French flag fluttering above it.

Even if someone there *did* mean her harm, she never could have found them in such a press. She tugged her gloves tighter and looked about for a cab.

* * *

The Paris offices of the League were in a much quieter neighbourhood than Gordston's, a narrow lane ending at the river that was lined with tall houses, their windows shuttered. Respectable, but not grand. Emily checked the address she had been given and found her way through a courtyard gate and up a winding staircase to a flat on the top floor. She could hear the murmur of voices behind some of the doors, smell the scent of luncheons cooking, garlic and wine, but the corridors were empty.

To her surprise, a familiar face from London society opened the door. Laura, Lady Smythe-Tomas. As usual, she was dressed in the height of fashion, a walking dress of bright green-and-gold-striped silk, a velvet hat on her whirls of auburn hair, emeralds winking in her ears. Just like when she was at Gordston's earlier. But her eyes were narrowed, almost cautious.

'Miss Fortescue, you are here at last!' Lady Smythe-Tomas exclaimed happily, belying that flash of an expression. She took Emily's arm and tugged her into the flat, quite as if they were at a society drawing-room soirée and were the best of friends. 'Would you like something to drink? I have the most charming Parisian elderflower liqueur.'

Emily was rather flustered. She had been expecting someone rather more—stern and businesslike. 'I—well, I was looking for the offices of the Women's Franchise League.'

'Yes, of course. That's me! Well, me in Paris, for now. We are searching for new offices, more officers, as we speak.' Lady Smythe-Tomas made her way to a glass and gilt cart, laden with crystal decanters and pyramids of glasses. Besides the cart, the rest of the furniture was dark, old-fashioned, solid, matching the green-velvet curtains at the windows, the dark carpet underfoot. Lady Smythe-Tomas looked like a peacock dropped into a haunted, dark forest. 'I am so glad you're here. Mrs Hurst does so sing your praises. Ladies with your business acumen are just what we need.'

Emily took off her hat and gloves and cautiously perched on the edge of a velvet sofa. 'I do find the work to be of such importance.'

'And so it is, vital. Both for ourselves and our descendants, if we are to reach our full potential in life. Exercise our intelligence and talents.'

'Of course.'

'Herr Friedland will be here very soon.' Lady Smythe-Tomas handed Emily a glass and took a sip from her own. 'Delicious, isn't it? So refreshing in the warm weather.'

Emily took a tentative taste and almost choked on the strong mixture of herbs, lemon and, shockingly, gin. She feared she could get too used to it. 'Delicious.'

'Now, tell me, Miss Fortescue, how much do you know about our work here in Paris?'

'Not very much, I fear. There wasn't time to learn much about it before I left London.' Emily quickly repeated what she had learned before she came to France, about the former Queen of Prussia, Crown Princess of Prussia and Herr Friedland. Talking seemed a good excuse not to gulp down the elderflower drink. She didn't quite trust Lady Smythe-Tomas, yet she couldn't really explain why. Maybe it was the sharpness hidden behind fluffy laughter. The lady rather reminded Emily of Chris in some strange way. Maybe they *would* make a suitable couple.

'It is so important that we make good contacts in Germany,' Lady Smythe-Tomas said. 'But, as I am sure you know so well, we must be careful who we trust, at all times.'

Her words echoed Emily's thoughts precisely. 'I do tend to be cautious. It's the only way not to be taken advantage of in business.'

'Exactly. And we ladies are always underestimated. That is one of our strengths. We can strike from the shadows and no one expects us.' A knock sounded at the door and Lady Smythe-Tomas smiled as she drank the last of her glass. 'Ah, there is our guest now.'

Emily watched cautiously as Lady Smythe-Tomas opened the door, admitting a corpulent figure in an astonishing bright blue-checked suit. He looked rather walrus-like, with a sweeping brown moustache, pink cheeks and a fringe of grey and brown hair escaping from beneath his bowler hat. But his eyes, small and bright green, were sharp. Behind him was a tiny, bird-like lady in brown velvet, her dark eyes sharp as she took everything in.

'My dear *fräuleins*, how lovely to meet you at last,' he boomed, bowing low several times. 'You know my friend, Madame Renard? She is the French counterpart to your Mrs Hurst.'

Lady Smythe-Tomas smiled at the sparrow-like lady.

'We have not met, but I have heard of the *madame*, of course. This is my friend Mademoiselle Fortescue, also from the League. She can be trusted with any of our business. Do join us for a drink.'

As they settled themselves around the table, Lady Smythe-Tomas poured drinks and chatted about the League's work, its aims, with Madame Renard murmuring agreement. 'Of course, we are always hoping to expand the reach of our message,' Lady Smythe-Tomas said.

'As do we, *fräulein*,' Herr Friedland agreed, gulping down his drink. 'And certainly our dear Princess. She wishes to aid you in any way she can, but she must be very discreet.'

'We could expect nothing less,' Lady Smythe-Tomas said with a smile. She watched the *herr* closely, as Madame Renard watched her.

Emily frowned, wondering what was really happening. What was not being said.

'Perhaps your own Mrs Hurst could be the answer,' Friedland said. 'She has many contacts, including some in the naval office, who I am sure will always have their Queen's daughter's interests at heart. If we could meet with some of them…'

'I am quite certain that could be arranged,' Lady Smythe-Tomas answered.

'Then you can meet me in the countryside soon, somewhere more—quiet,' Madame Renard suddenly said. 'We can discuss our mutual contacts there and come to an arrangement that would suit us all.'

Lady Smythe-Tomas narrowed her eyes as she studied the strange couple, then she nodded. 'Of course. You must give me a few days to make a few enquiries. Mademoiselle Fortescue here can join me. She is our League's officer here in the city.'

Her—go with them to the country? Emily had no idea how she might help there, or what was going on, but she found herself intensely curious to know. It was a dangerous trait in her life. 'I would be happy to join you,' she said with a smile. 'At any time.'

Chapter Ten

'Chris, my most darling brother!' Diana cried as she opened the door to their hotel suite to let Chris in for their little family dinner party. She went up on tiptoe to kiss his cheek, leaving a trace of her rose perfume behind, as sweet as her smile. 'I can't tell you how excited I was to hear we were all going to be together again. You are looking utterly lovely.'

Chris kissed her cheek in return. 'And so are you.' Di *did* look lovely, just as Will did lately, glowing with quiet happiness. Chris remembered how his brother used to look, always so solemn and watchful, so careful. Now he had laughter and light in his life.

Chris thought of Emily, making him dance in the café, laughing up at him as Paris swirled around them. What would it be like to feel that way all the time?

He pushed away the memories, the feelings that shouldn't even exist in his heart, and gave Diana another hug.

'I went to Gordston's today,' she said, leading him into the sitting room as a footman brought in sherry. 'It was so wonderful to see Emily and Alex again! We are having them to dinner very soon and you must come back then. We will have such fun, just like our Miss Grantley's days.'

'Maybe Chris won't have time for much fun, darling,' Will said, coming in from the small office he used. 'I hear he will be hard at work here in Paris.'

Diana threw Chris a wry glance, as if she doubted he could be 'hard at work' at anything. Not that he blamed her. It was a role he carefully cultivated. 'You sound just like Emily, business all the time. But I'm sure everyone has time for fun, Will. Especially Chris. And I have heard he has plenty of time for our Em lately.'

Chris did not trust the sly smile she shot his way. 'I'll try to come, Di. It would be nice to see all the old crowd together again.'

'Yes, indeed.' Diana glanced down into her wineglass, a wistful look coming over her usually merry face. 'Did I tell you, Alex is in the family way! She looked positively glowing. So it won't be *quite* like Grantley's days.'

Will gently touched her hand and she smiled up at him. For a moment, it was as if the two of them were alone in their own small world.

There was a knock at the suite door and the butler came and spoke in Will's ear. Will nodded and turned to Chris.

'I need to take care of a bit of business from the office before dinner, Di,' Will said with an apologetic smile. 'It won't take long.'

Diana waved him off, obviously used to such things.

'No matter, the hotel kitchen is always running late. I'll just work on my new article.'

Will kissed her again and gestured for Chris to follow him to the small library. Chris couldn't imagine what emergency work had been sent so late at night and hoped it wasn't a true emergency. To his surprise, it was Lady Smythe-Tomas who waited for them, her violet-silk evening gown glowing in the windowless office.

'Sir William, Mr Blakely,' she said with a smile. 'So sorry to interrupt your dinner! I was just on my way to meet a lovely old *comte* for the opera, but I thought you might like to hear about the Friedland meeting this afternoon.'

'Of course,' Will said, shutting the door behind them. 'Lady Smythe-Tomas is our contact here in Paris, Chris, connected to the Women's Franchise League.'

'Yes, and you're terribly lucky to have me here,' Lady Smythe-Tomas said merrily. 'Mrs Hurst and her ladies can be rather suspicious of men like you, no matter how handsome. But I did think the meeting went rather well. Miss Fortescue does seem wary, of course, but Friedland has certainly learned his lines. I was almost convinced he *did* know the Princess. I do think you might consider recruiting Miss Fortescue, she is so very clever.'

Chris felt a flash of concern, a protective instinct towards Emily. 'Surely she has her own work to worry about. She shouldn't be dragged into our messes, as well.'

Lady Smythe-Tomas and Will exchanged a glance. 'Quite,' she said. 'But Miss Fortescue did agree to go with me to the country in a few days, to meet Herr Friedland again and the mysterious Madame Renard. I shall certainly like hearing her perspective on them.'

Lady Smythe-Tomas went on to tell them about the rest of the meeting, though Chris still worried about Emily. He would have to keep his word to her father and watch her closely until the whole German matter was resolved.

'Now, my dears, I must be off,' Lady Smythe-Tomas said, wrapping her velvet evening shawl around her shoulders. 'I will send you details of our next meeting soon.'

Will went to show her out and Chris stared out the window at the Parisian night. He wondered what Emily was doing that night, if she was watching after herself, if she was safe. It was almost all he thought of lately, which wasn't good for his job. Nor his emotions. Was he failing in his promise to her father, to himself?

Will came back into the room and poured them out another brandy. He seemed to know what Chris was thinking, in that uncanny Will way of his. 'She will be fine,' Will said. 'She's a Grantley girl and they're the strongest ones of us all. I should know.'

Chris smiled. 'Yes, they are certainly that.'

'And they're also insane-making. Beware.'

Chapter Eleven

Emily put on one of her new hats and peered at herself in the mirror, turning her head to all angles to study it. It was a Gordston's purchase, a confection of pale straw, feathers and silk roses in shades of pink, from lightest shell to bright fuchsia, frivolous and pretty, and very French. Was it perfect for a day at the races? She didn't want to look too—English. It would be bad for business. And somehow she didn't want to share the hat from Chris yet. It felt like something just for her, not for business at all.

But Emily suspected it wasn't business she worried about. It was Chris. Would *he* think she looked pretty in the hat?

She sighed and tore off the chapeau to toss it on to the bed. A few curls of hair fell from their pins and she impatiently pushed them back. It was ridiculous to think about Chris that way. He was never serious; she couldn't be, either, not about him. They were much too different that way.

And yet—yet she could never quite forget the way it

felt when he kissed her, so sweet and light and marvellous, as though she was floating free up into the sky, heavy earth falling away. She closed her eyes, blotting out the bright morning sun from the window, and in that darkness she saw again the summer day by Miss Grantley's lake. The maze. Chris's face, all golden like a young Greek god, his smile as he leaned towards her, the feel of his lips on hers…

Emily shook her head. Once, she had thought herself infatuated with that pig of a man Hamilton, after only one mediocre kiss. Yet Chris's touch made her feel so very much more than that, made her forget herself entirely. Sometimes it didn't feel like he was just *pretending* to court her.

And that made Chris so much more dangerous than anyone else ever could be. He made her long for things she had never dared think about, things like fun and romance and true understanding, when all she had ever really had, ever needed, was work. And now she had the League, the chance to help other women make better lives for themselves.

She knew Chris was not like most men. He had a sunny, boyish carelessness about him that seemed to make him see the world differently from most people. He saw people as just people, not men and women, and was interested in them as they were. But all men, all marriages, expected a woman to retreat, to become less, to take care of home and hearth and give up her essence. Di and Alex had found another way to be in love, but it was all so complicated and difficult.

Emily sighed. A day at the races didn't seem to warrant such worries, she reminded herself. It was just a bit of fun. And no one was better at fun than Chris. Surely she deserved a day away from work, from the League? She just had to be careful.

Mary hurried into the room, Emily's pink-and-white-striped dress over her arm, freshly pressed. 'I'm so sorry it took so long, Miss Emily, but these new pleated seams are a bear to smooth out. Whatever happened to your hat?'

The day was indeed a beautiful one at Longchamp, the sun golden and warm in a pale turquoise sky. The stands, and the rolling green lawns around the course, were a sea of lacy parasols, feathered hats, elegant black tailcoats. Laughter, chatter and happy cries rose like a cloud above the carriages packed so close together. The breeze smelled of the spice of expensive perfumes, the sweetness of sugared almonds sold from handcarts, the peaty loam of the earth and the animals. The Ladies' Box across the way, where all the French ladies in highest society gathered, was a rainbow of colours, satins, feathers, diamonds.

Emily raised her own silk parasol, studying the scene with a rising sense of excitement—and, yes, even of fun.

She rather enjoyed the races at home, Ascot and Goodwood, but this had something quite different about it all. Something elegant and light-hearted that was so French. She was glad she had worn the new hat.

'What do you think of it all, then?' Chris asked, returning to her side with the racing papers in hand.

Emily smiled up at him from under the feathered

brim. He *had* liked it after all, looking rather thunderstruck when she first appeared in her hotel lobby to
meet him, and it gave her a lovely little glow of satisfaction. Though she knew she should *not* care what he
thought of her looks, not after promising herself to be
so careful around him.

And he looked rather nice himself. He was dressed
like the other men in his dark suit and pale grey waistcoat, his face shadowed by the brim of his tall hat, yet
he carried it off as none of them did, with a graceful
carelessness.

'It's all quite festive,' she said. 'Tell me, what do
those flags over there mean?'

'That's where the famous hill begins, a true chal-
lenge for any thoroughbred. And that's the starting post
for today's first run.' He took her arm and led her closer
to the railings along the track, pointing out the perils
of the hill, the sharp corners where jockeys had to beware. All around them in the stands were bright, laughing crowds, a cloud of merriment.

'Monsieur Blakely!' a voice cried and Emily turned
to see a man weaving his way towards them through the
colourful crowd, followed by a gaggle of ladies in vivid
satin gowns and beribboned hats, young men in daring
striped jackets. All of them held champagne glasses and
were obviously enjoying themselves very much indeed.

'Monsieur Jouet,' Chris answered boisterously.
They shook hands, laughing merrily as if they were
old friends long parted. 'Good to see you again! I was
hoping to see you here in Paris.'

'Ah, yes, it has been too long,' Monsieur Jouet, a

man with most impressive mustachios, Emily could see up close, and a bright blue jacket quite different from the requisite black. 'We had such fun the last time you were here, did we not, ladies? The boats on the river you stole...*ooh-la-la*.' The ladies all giggled and Emily couldn't help but wonder what happened in those stolen boats. Which ladies Chris had taken out there before. She was a fool if she forgot what life with him would *really* be like on an ordinary day. But an extraordinary one like this—that was different.

'I do hope you gave them back to the boatmen,' she murmured.

'Of course,' Chris protested. 'With ample compensation. Em, may I present an old friend, Monsieur Jouet? Jean-Paul, this is Mademoiselle Fortescue, a friend from London.'

'Ah, and the most lovely friend!' Monsieur Jouet proclaimed, bowing over her hand. 'Anyone who knows Monsieur Blakely is most welcome. Have some champagne?'

Chris took Emily's arm and led her to where Jouet's crowd waited with bottles of bubbly.

'You do know so very many people,' Emily said. And it was true. Everywhere Chris went, he seemed to find friends. To know the secrets of everyone. She wondered what he knew that he did not tell. What really lay in his past.

Chris looked after Jouet and his party with a strangely serious look on his face. 'Of course. People are endlessly fascinating. You never know what you might discover about them.'

Emily remembered what she had once thought about Chris, that he seemed to have so many masks. Bright, shining, lovely masks, full of laughter, but concealing none the less. She did so long to know what was behind them.

'Now, who do you fancy for the Grand Galop?' Chris asked. He tilted back his hat on his tousled, gleaming gold hair, which gave him a rakish appearance, and studied the racing sheets.

Glad of the distraction, of something else to think about besides the mysteries buried deep behind Chris's vivid blue eyes, Emily leaned closer to study the smudged ink. But that, too, was a mistake, for that close she could feel the warmth of him against her arm. His scent, that spicy citrus soap of his, wrapped all around her, a stealthy, steel-strong bond that she couldn't seem to break from. Or even want to break. She just wanted to be closer and closer.

And that showed she was entirely right to be wary of him.

She held herself very still and forced herself to focus on the words of the page. 'Oh, Jeune Fleur, I think.'

Chris gave her a startled glance. 'Really? But he's the longshot. Has a reputation for unreliability, though he can be wondrously fast at times. Cinnamon Trade is favoured to win.'

'But I like the name. Young Flower, so sweet. And it's so dull to go for the obvious,' Emily said with a laugh. 'Low risk, low reward, where's the fun in that? So much more fascinating to go with the rebellious outsider and watch him astonish everyone with victory.'

Chris frowned as he studied her. 'And you think Young Flower is a—rebellious outsider?'

'Certainly he is, or why would he have such a fabulous name? Can't you just picture it? He kicks against his traces—he runs in the wrong direction, goes places he shouldn't. But he's fast, magically fast, and all he needs is someone who understands *why* he needs to run to give him his wings. To let him achieve his destiny by winning here at Longchamp. And bringing the faithful few, such as us, rich takings.'

Chris laughed, an astonished, bright sound. 'Why, Em—who would ever think you're hiding such fanciful dreams? You *do* know how to have fun.'

'Of course I have fun,' Emily said indignantly. 'Sometimes, when it's appropriate. What did you think? That I was just made up of dusty ledger books?'

'Hardly that.' He reached out and gently touched one fingertip to a loose curl coiling from beneath her hat. She leaned her cheek into his touch, unable to stop herself. 'No one could ever think you were made of dried-up dust at all.'

'But you do think I'm too serious,' she whispered, entranced by his touch.

'You are responsible about your work, like my brother is. And you're both all the more admirable for it. Yet I'm beginning to suspect you do know how to have fun, too. That you have hidden aspects.'

Emily was beginning to think that about him, too. Could they ever understand each other?

The crowd swirling around them jostled against her and she caught Chris's arm to keep from falling.

His muscles flexed under her touch, hard and lean, the power of him hidden under finely tailored wool. 'Shall we place that bet?' she said, her voice hoarse.

He looked down at her for a long moment and she was sure he was going to say something. She felt terribly breathless, on edge. But he just shook his head and that brilliant, sunny smile, the smile she was beginning to suspect was something of another mask, was back in radiant force.

'Of course,' he said. 'You wait here, I'll be right back. I'll try to find some strawberries, too.'

Emily watched him disappear into the crowd, his tall figure standing out among all the others, and she sighed. She took a deep breath of the warm, earthy air and tried to compose herself. It was most unlike her to get so flustered and over nothing.

She tilted down the wide brim of her hat to shade her eyes from the sun, which was climbing higher overhead, and studied the crowd pressed against the railings as they waited for the next race to start. She could hear brassy music from some unseen band nearby, could see the swish of lace fans from the expensive boxes that rose at the end of the track, could hear laughter growing louder as parties became more raucous, as champagne and bright yellow elderflower liquor was consumed.

A man in a box just across the track from where she stood turned towards her and, with a start, she realised she recognised him. James Hertford, with his glossy dark hair and fine, pale features. He seemed to appear everywhere lately, even here at Gordston's in Paris. Yet now, as he, too, caught sight of her, his lean, handsome face lit up and he gave her an enthusiastic wave.

Emily waved back, wondering what had brought him to Paris. Business? What exactly did he do, besides being a gentleman?

As she studied James Hertford, she heard again her father's voice saying he wished she was settled and happy, respectably married. She saw Di and Alex and their contentment. Maybe she *should* consider it. She was no spring deb—what if one day work and the League were not enough? One day when her father was gone and she was alone. A man like James Hertford could be a most suitable choice. He had a fine name, a place in society and seemed nice. Conventional, steady—a girl could predict exactly what sort of life she would have with him. Running a house, having children, doing charity work, the Season in the spring, shooting in the fall. One day like another. Not at all like...

Not at all like a meteor such as Chris.

Emily frowned. If she *was* in the marriage market, Chris would be a poor investment. Quicksilver, full of laughter, uncertain. What would life be like with him?

Never boring, she knew that much.

Emily knew that most men claimed a strange chivalry to protect women from life's challenges, wrap them in cotton wool and put them on a shelf. Keep them from bothering themselves with pesky things like intelligent thoughts or genuine worries. Even James Hertford had said she should not concern herself with business, that her father was not right to force that on her. Chris never did such things. He was different from most men. He was free and he saw no reason why other people should not be so. It made him so attractive—and so dangerous.

She turned away from the box and made her way a little deeper into the crowd. They pressed closer around her, chattering, laughing shrilly, chattering like a flock of jungle birds, the swirl of so many perfumes making her lightheaded. She started to feel too warm, almost struck with an arrow of panic, and she remembered too well that sudden attack in the street. Someone grabbing on to her arm in the darkness.

Just as she was sure she would start screaming, she felt a lighter, more careful touch on her silk sleeve, and she whirled around to find herself facing Chris. His brow was creased with concern as he looked down at her.

'Are you ill, Em?' he asked.

'Oh, Chris,' she choked. 'I've never been so glad to see anyone!'

Unable to stop herself, she threw her arms around his neck and held on tightly. He felt so strong, so steady, so warm, his scent comforting now.

'Emily?' he whispered, now sounding slightly panicky himself. He patted her gently on the shoulder, as if she might break. 'It's quite all right, I'm here now. By Jove, it *is* getting hot here today, no wonder you're out of sorts. Come on, let's find a place to sit and wait for your Jeune Fleur to run and rake in our winnings.'

Emily smiled weakly and took his arm to let him lead her out of the thick of the crowd. She felt rather silly—she never had such moments of weakness! She didn't have time for them. Surely it was just the heat, maybe working too many hours lately, the memory of that attack in the street. The unthinkable possibility of getting married one day. It was enough to drive any girl a little batty.

Strangely, it was Chris now, of all people, who made her feel steady again. He was calm and careful, speaking to her gently, holding her arm close. Another facet to him.

'I shouldn't have left you alone there in the sun,' he said. 'Most thoughtless of me. Are you sure you're feeling better? Should I find a physician? There is sure to be one about.'

'I am quite well now,' she said. 'This French light is so much brighter than at home! Quite disorientating. No wonder the English get a little crazy here.'

'Should I fetch you something to drink? Some chilled champagne?'

Emily was sure champagne was the last thing she needed. It was sure to go straight to her head, make her feel even less like herself. 'Just a bit of shade and I will be perfectly all right, I promise.'

'Miss Fortescue! Mr Blakely. How perfectly extraordinary to see you here,' a woman's light, flute-like voice called out.

Emily glanced up and saw Lady Smythe-Tomas making her way towards them. It was hard to miss her; everyone else seemed to part before her, staring after her as she sailed past in her gown of purple-striped satin, her tall green hat, the sparkle of her emerald jewellery. She swooped in to press a quick kiss to their cheeks, leaving the trail of her expensive jasmine perfume behind.

Emily wondered if they were going to see everyone they knew that day. Mr Hertford, Lady Smythe-Tomas…

'I didn't know you were a devotee of the turf, Laura,' Chris said with a tight smile.

Emily was startled. How did he know her well enough to use her first name?

'Oh, I go wherever a party calls me, my dear, you know me,' Lady Smythe-Tomas said with a laugh and a wave of her purple-gloved hand. 'I am in a box today with some dear friends, including a darling little Bavarian strudel of a man called Friedland. James Hertford has come along, too, so handsome. You must join us! We've ordered the most lavish luncheon, there is no possibility we could eat it all.'

Friedland? Emily wondered what game Lady Smythe-Tomas was playing now. Was she sending some sort of message? Emily glanced up at Chris to see what he made of it all, but his laughter had faded and his face had gone unreadable again.

'I don't think we plan to stay so long,' he said.

'Oh, but surely you will stay through the Galop,' Lady Smythe-Tomas protested, gesturing to the marked-up racing papers in his hand. 'You've placed your bets.'

'Maybe we could join you for just one drink,' Emily said, curious to see what was really happening. 'It's rather warm today and I would enjoy the shade of a box.'

'You certainly must come and sit down, then, your

cheeks are rather pink,' Lady Smythe-Tomas said. She took Emily's arm without another argument and steered her towards the boxes rising like tiered cakes above the track. She left Chris to follow. 'The style of hats these days are charming, but so useless against the sun! I often think we could wear a nice, sturdy canvas pith helmet, as they do in India and Egypt. Then we should be quite ready for any adventure at any moment.'

'Have you been to India, then, Lady Smythe-Tomas?' Emily asked her curiously. She realised how very little she knew of the lady, beyond her flamboyant fashion, her devotion to women's suffrage.

Lady Smythe-Tomas gave another airy wave of her hand. 'My dear, I have been so many places, how can I possibly remember them all? Ah, here we are.'

A liveried attendant opened the door, and Lady Smythe-Tomas ushered them inside. It was indeed luxurious, with silk-papered walls, a needlepoint carpet underfoot, a buffet of delicacies laid out in the shadows. Along the wall of open windows, looking down at the track, sat a cluster of well-dressed people on rows of satin chairs, sipping champagne.

Lady Smythe-Tomas took Chris's arm and drew them forward. 'My dears, look who I found wandering about like lost sheep! I had to rescue them. It is Mr Blakely and the lovely Miss Fortescue! Of course, you both know the Duc d'Aimiens, and his friend, Mademoiselle Ferent. A ballet dancer, of course, the toast of the Opera, she veritably flies across the stage!' The elderly *duc* and his ballet dancer, an elegant young lady with Titian hair and a white tulle dress, nodded. 'And the

Pointons, from Bath, they just arrived in Paris. Mr Hertford, Mr Chester—he rented the box, so kind of him.'

'And I am sure you remember me,' a voice boomed. Herr Friedland stepped from the shadows, his yellow plaid suit a slant of light. 'I would be quite wounded if such a lovely lady had forgotten me.'

Emily studied him, wondering why he had appeared at the races. If she was missing something in his scheme with Lady Smythe-Tomas. 'Of course I had not forgotten you, *mein herr*. It is good to see you again so soon.'

'Madame Renard was meant to join us, but had a last-minute engagement,' Lady Smythe-Tomas whispered in Emily's ear. 'We shall see her in the country tomorrow.'

Emily gave a brief nod and sat down in one of the satin and gilt chairs by the windows. A footman brought her a glass and she sipped at it as she studied the track below, the swirling kaleidoscope of the crowd.

'Monsieur Blakely, I have heard of you,' the silvery, fairy-like ballerina said, giggling behind her painted ivory fan. 'Do come sit beside me. Are you a great admirer of the dance, by any chance?'

Chris gave her one of his most charming smiles, he was being the Chris that was more blinding than the sun. The *duc* did not seem pleased.

Emily watched him as he chatted with the lady, making her giggle even more, but Emily could see that he did even more than that. As he seemed to give her his whole attention, he also watched everything going on around him, so subtly it was almost imperceptible. She wondered what his game was, what was really going on with him.

A loud blast of trumpets signalled the start of the race. One of the footmen handed her a pair of opera glasses and she turned away to watch, grateful to have a distraction from Chris and his mysteries. His flirtations. She watched the horses burst from the starting box, trying to glimpse her Young Flower.

She spied a movement near the railing, a tall, lean man with distinctively bright hair. Hair much like Gregory Hamilton possessed. A knot clenched in her stomach. Could it really be Hamilton, here in Paris? She hadn't seen him in a long while, yet the old fear was still there, hidden so deep. Could he really have followed her, after he had been gone so long? Was that what happened that night in London?

She almost jumped out of her seat when someone suddenly touched her arm. She spun around to see it was just Chris, his brow creased with concern as he looked down at her. She pressed her hand to her pounding heart.

'Is something wrong, Em?' he asked quietly.

She shook her head and made herself smile. 'Of course not.'

'It's the last lap now, thought you might want to keep an eye on your Fleur.'

Her breathing a bit ragged, she turned back to the course. The man, whoever he was, had vanished. She was sure it must have been her imagination, too many late nights, too much work lately.

The horses swirled around the corner in a thundering blur and she watched them through her glass. At first, she could make out nothing, until at last a horse caparisoned in pink and chocolate silks, Jeune Fleur's colours, broke free of the pack and sailed over the finish line. She impulsively threw her arms around Chris in a burst of happiness.

Chris grabbed her hand and kissed it in excitement, whooping with laughter. 'Look, Em! You were right. You must be my magical charm.'

She smiled, but inside she suddenly felt so unsteady, unsure of everything, which wasn't like her at all. She felt like she understood nothing, not about Chris, about the world around them, or even about herself.

'I'm surprised to see you here, Christopher. Are you not tired after your day at the races?'

Chris glanced up from his desk to see Lady Smythe-Tomas standing in his office doorway. It was indeed rather late; the rest of the building was dark and quiet, everyone sensibly gone off to their lodgings to prepare for the next day's work. Chris, though, had found that sleep would not come. Once he was alone in his room, with only the silence and a brandy, he could only see Emily's face. Hear her laughter, feel her arms around him as her horse won, smell her perfume.

The pretend courtship was feeling too real indeed.

He tossed down his pencil and sat back in his chair. Even work was no distraction that night. He was actually glad someone else was there, even if it was Laura, who always seemed to know everything that everyone kept hidden.

'There's so much work to finish before we leave Paris,' he said.

Lady Smythe-Tomas sighed and sat down on the edge of his desk. She was dressed splendidly, in a theatre gown of ruby-red satin and spangled black tulle, black feathers in her dark red hair, but she looked rather tired. 'Indeed there is. And things like trips to the races just take up too much time.'

'Sometimes socialising is an important part of the task. You know that. Is that not a big part of why I was hired in the first place?'

Her lips quirked in a wry smile. 'Because we are so dramatic? So charming? I suppose so. Someone must know how to make wary people reveal themselves without even knowing that they do it.'

Chris thought of the hearty German in her box at Longchamp. 'Herr Friedland?'

'Of course. He thinks he is so clever. All those old Prussians do.' She took off her black-silk evening gloves and stuffed them carelessly into her handbag, almost as if they were another useless male she had no need for. 'But what of you, Chris? You have been spending a great deal of time with Miss Fortescue lately. She is a wonderful volunteer for the League, and a great help to me, but I doubt she is in cahoots with the Germans.'

Having people see him with Emily was exactly what Chris had wanted, for people to think they were courting. Yet something in Laura's tone made him feel cautious. He sat up straighter. 'Her father and I belong to the same club. He asked me to keep an eye on her in Paris.'

Laura's brow arched. 'Really? But she seems so capable, so intelligent.'

'She is, yet she doesn't work for us. She needs to be kept safe.'

'Perhaps we should think about recruiting her. I've been quite impressed with her work at the League and she is going with me to meet Friedland. She doesn't know what is really going on, of course, but I definitely think she could be trusted. She could be a real asset.'

Chris firmly shook his head. He would never, ever put Emily in any danger. 'I do not think that would be a good idea. Nor should she go to the country to meet Friedland without me. I am supposed to protect her, that's the deal.'

Laura studied him carefully, *too* carefully, for a long moment. She shrugged and slid off the desk. 'You know best, I'm sure. Just don't underestimate her.' She gave him a strange, sad little smile. 'But if you ever need to make her a wee bit jealous, I am always here to help.'

Chris was puzzled. 'Why would I do that?'

She laughed and gently patted his cheek. 'Oh, Chris. Sometimes a bit of jealousy is all a person needs to think clearly. I'll be going now. Don't work too hard.'

Chris waved at her and in the silence Emily was there with him again. And he found that she was all he wanted.

Chapter Twelve

Despite her worries about all that was happening with her work, all the details Lady Smythe-Tomas hadn't been able to discuss about the Friedland business, Chris felt rather strangely—buoyant as he made his way through the streets of the *arrondissement* in the soft light of morning. Paris always had that effect, of course. Unlike the heavy, grey gloom of London, Paris always seemed suffused with glimmering gold, the streets filled with beauty and laughter. Time moved more slowly there, filled with endless glasses of *pastis*, smelling of exotic flowers and fresh baguettes.

Yet he knew very well that it wasn't just Paris that made him want to break into ridiculous song that day, to dance along the pavement. It was Emily. She was the one who made him want to do a fancy waltz step right there on the cobblestones, if it wouldn't have shocked the black-clad gaggle of matrons hurrying past.

He remembered their day at the races yesterday. How serious she looked as she perused the runners, her expression as intent as a farmer reading the weather report, but with a soft pink light from her delightfully frivolous hat cast over her face. That was so perfectly Emily. As deliciously pretty as a bonbon, as hard as steel, her brain always whirling with thoughts he wished he could read. Wished he could kindle an approving light in those beautiful eyes.

He thought of what happened when her longshot horse won and she leaped up with a burst of laughter. The feel of her arms thrown around him, her hand under his lips as he kissed her. How he wished in that moment that *he* had created that burning flash of happiness for her! That he could make all her days just as light and free. That their false courtship could be real.

Chris paused on the street corner, staring up at the façade of an ancient church, St Gervais, pale pink in the morning light. It made him think of her pink hat and just how quickly that effervescent moment faded. How fast the shadows came over her face again. She had quickly turned to Lady Smythe-Tomas and the German, chatting with them for the rest of the afternoon, and then she was so quiet on the journey back to her hotel. So full of thoughts he couldn't read.

Chris frowned at the thought of the German. What was Emily's business with them, really? How much did she know of what was happening? He had warned Laura not to involve Emily, that his job was to protect her.

He knew she was not a soft, delicate lady to be protected, to be made to sit at home sewing as her men shielded her from the world. He had always known that about her. She was hard-working, always plunging ahead, not caring what the world thought. Chris had seen that in her the very first time they met and that answering determination inside of him yearned for her. Yearned to know everything about her: every thought, hope, dream, even the fears he knew she would never show, even to herself. That attraction never faded, but only seemed to grow stronger, more dangerous, every time he saw her.

But he couldn't let her in, as he sometimes longed to. He *would* keep her safe, even though she would never know it. And now she was in danger. Even her father knew that was so, but they also knew locking Emily away would do no good. Em would never back down to anyone.

He just had to figure out how to keep himself safe, as well, to guard his feelings very carefully. That would be the hardest part of all.

He crossed the street and made his way towards Emily's hotel. The pavements were more crowded now, Paris coming to life. Men in their black hats hurried to work, maids strolled past with their market baskets, shutters went up, doors opened, while the flower cart on the corner was bursting into bright colours. Chris paused to buy a red rose for his buttonhole and a small bouquet for Emily, before making the flower girls giggle and continuing on his way.

In the gilt and marble lobby, heavy with the scent of large arrangements of lilies in silver vases, people were also bustling past, arriving and checking out, mountains of trunks zipping past on carts, lapdogs yapping. Paris was always full of such life, everywhere he went. Chris glanced around for Emily, but couldn't glimpse her face, or her distinct chestnut hair under any of the elaborate hats. He took the lift up to her floor and knock on the door of Suite Cinq, as she had told him, careful that no one saw him in the quiet corridor.

At first, all was silent and he started to worry she had gone out and been followed again. But then a pink-cheeked maid opened the door and smiled up at him. 'Oh! Mr Blakely, isn't it?'

He wondered how she knew him. 'So I am. Here to call on Miss Fortescue. I thought she might like a *petit dejeuner*, maybe a look at the Louvre. It's not so busy there in the mornings.' In truth, he had just wanted to see her again. Make sure she was all right after their long day at the races.

'Oh, I'm sure she would, but she's gone out.'

Chris felt that jolt of worry again. 'So early?'

A door slammed down the corridor and the maid glanced past him a bit nervously. 'Would you like to come in, Mr Blakely? I can find some water for those flowers.'

'Of course,' Chris said, slipping inside. The sitting room looked like Emily, elegant, clean lines, sunny, pretty but not overdone. The only hint of untidiness was the tray the maid had been clearing from a break-fast table by the window.

'She was gone nearly before first light,' the maid said, smoothing a pale green-satin cushion on a *chaise*. 'That Lady Smythe-Tomas came to fetch her, they were going to have luncheon at some inn in the country and meet some other people. Miss Fortescue said she prob-ably wouldn't be back until later this evening.'

Chris frowned to hear that Emily had gone off with Lady Smythe-Tomas. He thought they had agreed last night not to involve Emily. 'Luncheon in the country?'

The maid shook her head. 'I think that what's they said, sir, though it seems a little odd. I mean, we're in Paris, restaurants on every corner! No need to find a train and all that fuss. But they did seem determined, very serious. Miss Fortescue is like that about her work.'

'So she is. Do you know where this inn could be?'

'A village called Chaton sur Mereille, maybe. Lady Smythe-Tomas said they are renowned for their trout *amandine* there.'

Chris nodded. He knew of the place, it was not terribly convenient to the city at all, though a train stopped at a station not too far away for his purposes. Why was Laura taking Emily there? 'Thank you very much. You have been very helpful. I'll look into it all.'

The maid suddenly reached out and shyly touched his sleeve. She looked very concerned. 'Oh, Mr Blakely— do you think she could be in some kind of trouble?'

'Why do you think that?' he asked gently. Servants so often knew everything that was going on in their households, better than their employers could ever realise.

'She has—well, there has been a bit of bother lately, not that it can slow her down at all. But I do wish she would have a care. I've been with her ever so long, you see, and she's a wonderful employer.'

'I'm sure it's just a meal with friends,' he said reassuringly. 'Not a thing to worry about. She is most capable.'

The girl nodded, but she didn't look especially reassured. 'It's just—I've been a bit concerned about her lately. That's all.'

'Why is that?'

She shrugged and turned away to stack the tea things on to her tray. 'I'm just a worry-wart, I suppose, sir. Never mind me.'

'I am sure it is all quite well,' he said with a smile, realising he would get nothing more out her that day. 'Here is my card, let me know if anything else worrisome comes up. I will call again later.'

He left the hotel, not seeing the chaos of the lobby as he stepped outside into the sunshine again. He had to find the next train to Chaton sur Mereille.

Emily was quite fascinated. She would never have thought a small, riverside village would attract foreign conspirators of any stripe. It was too far from Paris to be easy to find, via a train ride through beautiful, rolling farmland and then a short, jolting carriage jaunt on dusty lanes past a walled, crumbling chateau. There were no palaces or bridges or tall office buildings, only sleepy sunlight, dappled shadows, meandering goats.

But it *was* very pretty in the village, with its cobblestone square and red-tile-roofed houses, its ancient stone church tower, music drifting from the open windows of a café. A few tourists wandered about with their open guidebooks, peering up at the church, watching women in red aprons gather water at the fountain.

'They say Joan of Arc passed this way,' Lady Smythe-Tomas said as they stepped down from the carriage. She led Emily away from the central square with the tourists and the curious village children, and hurried down a narrow, shady alley. The windows in the whitewashed walls were mostly closed, despite the warm day, and even grated, but lines of laundry flapped overhead. It smelled of garlic and herbs, laundry soap, the sharp earthiness of the wandering goats.

Emily tried to picture the warrior-girl saint there, but the silence didn't let in any images of battle. 'Is that true?'

Lady Smythe-Tomas shrugged. Her coral and black hat gleamed in the shadows, incongruously modern and stylish against the old walls. 'I wouldn't think it would be on her battlefield path. But who knows? It's a nice story, isn't it? History soaking into the cobblestones.'

'Yes. It seems like Joan is rather a Mary of Scots figure. Put her name on a place, any place, and you have a romantic tale. But they can't have lived long enough to have seen *all* the places that claim them.'

Lady Smythe-Tomas laughed. For a moment, she looked less remote, less careless and full of brittle style than she usually did, and Emily was surprised to notice how young she actually was. She so often hid behind brisk efficiency, bits of sharp-edged gossip. But after their talk on the train, long and serious and full of the necessity of women's suffrage, what it might take to win it in the end, Emily found she rather liked her. They had a lot in common.

But what was Lady Smythe-Tomas to Chris? That kept nagging at Emily's mind, making her worry.

Lady Smythe-Tomas knocked on the door of a tall, narrow brick building at the end of the lane, quiet but

petty, laced with bright flower baskets outside the
gleaming windows. The handpainted sign declared it
to be an inn and café. A maid in a crisp white apron answered the door and nodded when Lady Smythe-Tomas
said they were meeting Madame Renard.

The maid led them through a common room, where
other servants were cleaning out the grate and laying
tables, and up a narrow flight of stairs. It was just like
the village itself, sleepy and pretty, not really the place
Emily would have said was ripe for secret meetings.

The door at the top of the landing opened, and Lady
Smythe-Tomas herself appeared, wearing what Emily
imagined a 'professional beauty' might think a country business meeting required, a heather-blue tweed
suit and tilted felt hat that should have looked silly but
instead looked just right. Emily thought she had to find
out where the lady shopped.

Behind her was a thin, tall woman with iron-grey
hair swept into a neat chignon, a tidy, dark grey dress,
her eyes bright and shrewd—much like a French ver-
sion of Mrs Hurst, Emily considered. 'Ah, Mademoiselle Fortescue,' Madame Renard boomed. 'Do come
in and have some *cassis*, they make it locally.'

'Thank you, *madame*,' Emily answered, feeling a
little bit overwhelmed. She sat down at a table laid by
the fire, following Lady Smythe-Tomas who gave her
a reassuring smile, and watched as Madame Renard
poured out the wine.

'As you know, Mademoiselle Fortescue,' Madame
Renard said, 'Germany is not at all like your England, or
indeed like our own France, where women have always

been very influential. They have none of that lovely open outspoken quality. They are all concerned only with order and obedience, with military matters. The Princess is so gentle, so caring, that it is a great pain to her. And, of course, many ladies there are just as concerned for their own advancement, their own freedom, as English ladies.'

'Of course,' Lady Smythe-Tomas said solemnly. There in that small room, far from glittering parties, she looked utterly different from her usual merry self. 'Discretion *is* the better part of valour sometimes. We are eager to help those of like minds wherever we can.'

'Perhaps we could begin with these letters,' Madame Renard said, taking a sheaf of papers from her case. 'Herr Friedland has been gathering them for us. They must be destroyed after, but perhaps they might be of assistance in seeing what is required.'

Lady Smythe-Tomas took out a lorgnette and studied the messages carefully as Emily read over her shoulders. They appeared to be from Princess Vicky's ladies-in-waiting, outlining what they would like to see happen from the English League, what they might do to assist. None of the names were familiar to Emily.

Lady Smythe-Tomas finally tucked away the notes and turned to give Emily a long glance. 'My dear Miss Fortescue, perhaps you would be so kind as to fetch some papers from my case? I left it in the corridor, I think,' she said.

Emily wondered what game she was playing, what she would tell Madame Renard about the notes. But she knew a speaking glance when she saw one. 'Of course. I will return quickly.'

She made her way back downstairs to the common room, wondering what was really in those letters. Was it a code of some sort? A way to reach real contacts? Still puzzled, she told the maidservant what was required and went into the public sitting room to wait for the drinks. She did know one thing for certain—she had no idea why she was there, what part she was meant to play. And she never liked being kept in the dark.

She froze at the sight of Chris lounging at a table by the window, his golden hair turned to sparkling gilt by the sunlight, looking lazy and leisured and perfectly at his ease. But surely it was no coincidence. No gentleman seeking a pleasurable day out would come to Chaton sur Mereille.

'Chris, what on earth are you doing here?' she demanded, marching over to his table. She glared down at him, hands planted on her hips. Yes, they were meant to be courting, but no one was there to see them in the country.

He grinned up at her, unrepentant. 'Just looking for a bit of fresh air in the countryside. Imagine seeing *you* here, Em!'

'Oh, don't be so silly, Chris. Did you follow me here? Why?'

He leaned across the table, looking suddenly serious. 'I called on you at your hotel and they said you had gone away with Lady Smythe-Tomas. I was a bit worried. Wherever she goes, trouble is sure to follow her.'

'Chris.' Emily shook her head, feeling a mix of happy

that he worried about her and irritation that he thought he had to. 'I am touched you care. I know it might not look that way sometimes, but I really can usually take care of myself. Lady Smythe-Tomas is a safe enough companion.'

'Compared to some, maybe.' Chris reached out and took her hand, holding it tightly. She was so surprised by the touch that she couldn't pull away. 'Em, there are so many things you haven't thought about. Shouldn't have to worry about. I just want you to be careful.'

Emily was confused, both by Chris's words and whatever was happening in the sitting room upstairs. She hated not knowing what was going on, hated feeling like she was deceived. 'If you know something, you should tell me what it is. How else can I be on my guard?'

He shrugged and sat back. 'You know me, Em. I am utterly clueless about everything. I just want you to be safe, that's all.'

'And you think I *don't* want that?' Emily sighed in deep frustration, sure he was hiding something from her—again. 'I cannot live my life always frightened, always hovered about. It's impossible. I am happy you care about me, but there is no need. If you can't be honest with me...'

'Emily...'

The maid appeared in the doorway with the tray of refreshments and Emily shook her head at Chris. 'I must get back now. I will see you in Paris.'

'Em, wait!'

She whirled around and hurried away. She felt like

her life was suddenly submerged in a murky river, she couldn't see two feet in front of her, couldn't see what was happening around her, and she was churning frantically to get away. To see clearly again. She hated not being in control.

Upstairs, she found Madame Renard and Lady Smythe-Tomas talking about the structure of League meetings, as if nothing else had ever happened. But still that feeling of disquiet lingered at the edges.

Once she was back in Paris, she was determined to confront Chris once and for all, and find out what was *really* happening.

'Blast it all!' Chris growled, and curled his hand in a tight fist to keep himself from pounding it on the table. He had made a right mess of that, as he so often seemed to do with Emily. He'd lost all his subtlety, all the arts of acting and subterfuge that served him so well in his work, and just plunged ahead like a clumsy old bull.

He would never be able to keep his promise to Mr Fortescue, or his promise to himself, to keep her safe. In fact, he should not have left her to return to Paris and would not have if he hadn't known Laura was there with her. If he was to succeed in his mission, and it was vital that he did, he would have to learn some artifice again. Quickly.

Emily was no fool. She could surely sense *something* was amiss. But she couldn't know about his true work. No one could.

He had to find some distance within himself, see Emily not as his friend, not as a beautiful woman, but as an assignment. That was the only way he could make sure he returned to England safely.

He had to forget everything else.

He made his way back through the crowded streets of Paris, not really seeing anything around him, the flower carts, the barking dogs, the café terraces. He only thought about Emily. In his quiet, cold room, a stack of correspondence waited for him as usual. Not official business; that went to the Foreign Office's central post. There was a letter from his mother, more news about a likely heiress she had met, a lecture passed on from his father, a note from an old friend inviting him into a new wine club. A *billet-doux* from an old dalliance who'd heard he was in Paris again.

All of those seemed to belong to someone else, to an old Chris who was gone now. He tossed it all in the wastepaper bin and only then did he notice a letter marked from the Poseidon Club at the bottom of the pile. Curious, he opened it and his eyes narrowed at the signature.

Albert Fortescue.

He swiftly read it, then had to read it again.

My dear Mr Blakely,
Thank you for your kind, if brief, note informing me of my daughter's safety in Paris. I am most content with the situation and most grateful. I only have to say if you ever called on me to ask for my daughter's hand in reality I would be only too happy to consent.
I know I ask a great deal, but I also know what

a prize my dear Emily is, and I do not make this offer lightly. I know of your old reputation, but I also know reputations can be misunderstood. I see deeper than some men, as I have had to do for my business. And I see that you are a man to be trusted.

It would not be an easy task. You know my daughter well enough to see her independent spirit, but I also believe you see her sensitive heart, her vulnerabilities, and understand my deep wishes and fears for her happiness. I think you are the man who could help her.

You would find me a generous father-in-law, of course, if you consider my request. And I need not say that Emily needn't know anything of this conversation.

I look forward to seeing you at the Poseidon Club as soon as you return to London and to a satisfactory conclusion to our business.
Your friend,
Albert Fortescue

Chris dropped on to the nearest chair, staring at the letter in astonishment. No respectable man had ever wanted him as a son-in-law before, especially not a man he admired as he did Albert Fortescue, a fine businessman and loving father. As for what the man suggested...

Chris had to admit he found it more than intriguing. And much too dangerous.

His feelings for Emily had been strong even from the first moment he saw her and now they grew whenever they were together. But he could never put her in any danger. Never hurt her. He was not worthy to be her husband.

Still, he could not quite bring himself to toss away the letter. Someone, someone as important as Emily's own father, actually thought he could be worthy of her. Maybe he could even think that about himself one day, though he would not be with Emily.

He put it in the desk drawer, where only he would know it was there. Only he would know the hidden words there he longed to hear, even as he knew they could not come true.

Chapter Thirteen

'This letter came for you this morning, Miss Emily,' Mary said as she deposited the breakfast tray on the bedside table. Teapot, toast rack, the post, just like always.

But not quite. Emily remembered too well her quarrel with Chris.

Mary threw back the curtains, letting in the pale morning light of the city. 'What do you have pianned for today, miss?'

'I'm not sure,' Emily murmured. 'Just work, I think.'

Mary made a tsking noise as she opened the wardrobe and sorted through the suits and day dresses arrayed there. 'You work too much, Miss Emily. Surely that can wait until we're back in London. Paris is—well, it's Paris! You should go up the Eiffel Tower. Stroll in the parks. Buy a hat.'

Emily laughed. 'I already have enough hats for the Season!' She gestured at the rows of chapeaux atop the wardrobe: feathers, fruit, lace, straw, felt. 'But you are right. Paris is indeed Paris. I should do something a little special.'

'That Mr Blakely called yesterday, wanting to take you to the Louvre. That might be nice.' Mary shook her head at a jacket whose hem needed mending. 'You are young, miss. I worry sometimes that you forget that.' She laid out a mulberry-silk skirt and smoothed the lace trim. 'You're always working, working.' But there had to be time for their courtship, as well. For people to see them.

'Someone has to do the work, Mary. There are hats to pay for. What else would I do with my time?'

'Just enjoy yourself a little, that's all I'm saying, Miss.' With one last sniff over a small spot on the skirt, Mary bustled away with the clothes over her arm.

Just enjoy herself. Emily sighed. If only it was that easy. She always seemed so preoccupied by so much— her father and his health, ledger figures, imports and exports, the household, the League. How could there be room for much fun?

Yet with Chris, there always seemed to be fun. Dancing, garden mazes, the races, even a dance became a merry game with him, despite when they quarrelled. He made her laugh as no one else could, made her forget the rest of the world. With him, everything looked different, brighter, lighter. He was like Paris itself. Always changing, always alluring.

But like Paris, there were shadows lurking behind. Secrets.

Emily shook her head. She didn't understand Chris, yet she longed to know what he was hiding from everyone. Probably she would never even have an idea. She knew what it was to hide behind a mask, how hard it was to lower it once it was fixed in place. How hard it became to even know where the mask ended and real life began.

If he was in some kind of trouble—how she wished she could help him. Yet she knew him well enough to be sure he never would let her. He had Blakely pride, and stubbornness, just like Will. Chris just hid it behind that bright laughter.

Emily sighed, and poured out another cup of tea. She saw that letter left on the tray. Eagerly, she broke the seal and scanned the short message.

Sweetest Em,
I am sorry we quarrelled. It was much too lovely a day for any cross words! Friends still?
Let me make it up to you. Come out with me to the Moulin de la Galette tonight. We can have some of that elderflower liquor and a dance or two.
Send me word, I hope you will come.
Your repentant Chris

Emily bit her lip to keep from smiling like a fool. She knew she should be mad at him still, following her out of the city like that. Yet it seemed like a sign. She had just been thinking she needed more fun, and here was Chris offering it up. She had heard so much about the Moulin de la Galette, the famous pleasure garden in Montmartre, haunt of scandalous artists and can-can dancers. She had secretly been longing to see it.

She knew she shouldn't go. It would not be sensible at all. But she very much feared—no, she *knew*—that she could not stay away.

* * *

'It's so astonishing,' Emily whispered, holding tightly on to Chris's arm as he led her through the gates of the Moulin de la Galette. The moon hung low over the wind-mill in the background, sparkling along with the fairy lights strung through the trees and around the crowded dance floor. Swarms of people gathered there, waltz-ing, lounging on the benches as they chatted together, waiting at the bar for their drinks, as music swirled and dipped all around them. The pleasure garden was like a painting come to vivid, noisy, crowded life.

Paris was very different at night, she realised as they dived into the sea of people. Mysterious even as it was noisily merry, shadows and light twined together. The people were different, too, free and full of laughter. It was amazing.

She had left behind her Worth gowns and dressed as she knew the Parisian shop girls did on their free eve-nings, in a slate-blue skirt and jacket piped in red, with a red scarf tied at her neck and a small, straw boater pinned to her upswept hair. She felt so light, so free— like a different person. Like a real Parisian, even.

She smiled up at Chris in a burst of excitement. He, too, looked very different than he had before. Casual, tousled, yet still so maddeningly elegant in his effort-less charm. Of all the many aspects of Chris, she rather liked this one the best. It made something flutter with nervousness inside her just to look at him, so golden and laughing and free in the lantern-light.

'Do you like it?' he asked.

'I love it. What a grand idea to visit! I've never been here before.'

'Never?'

Emily studied the couples swirling around the dance floor, much closer than they would ever be in a ballroom, leaning against each other in laughter. 'It's not the sort of place a lady can just wander into, is it?'

'Especially if that lady is always busy working,' he teased.

Emily laughed. 'You sound just like Mary.'

'Mary?'

'My maid. She's been with me since I was tiny, so she is very outspoken. She thinks I am wasting Paris by never having any fun.'

'Mary sounds like a very wise person. You can assure her that I am here to help correct the matter.' He tossed a coin to one of the barmaids and took two glasses of bright yellow liquid. 'Here, try this for a start.'

Emily took a tentative sip and shivered with delight at the sweet-sharp taste of it on her tongue. 'It's like— like liquid sunshine!' She remembered when Lady Smythe-Tomas gave her something very similar and she thought if that was what Parisians drank all the time, she would never want to leave.

Chris threw back his head and laughed, and he, too, seemed like sunshine in that morning. Warm, alluring, full of life. Life Emily craved. 'Why, Em, that's quite poetic. I knew you would like St-Germain.'

She drained the small glass. 'May I have another?'

He shook his head doubtfully. 'Maybe in a minute.

They're surprisingly strong, as I learned from hard experience.'

Emily could feel what he meant. She suddenly seemed so warm, so tingling, so longing to laugh. 'Then let's dance!'

'Now *that* I can definitely do.' Chris swept her into his arms and swung her out among the press of the other dancers. The music, with accordions and violins, seemed to reach deep down into her with its swaying rhythm.

Emily laughed. It was like flying through the air yet held safely in his arms. He felt so strong, twirling her amid the lights and the stars.

The music grew and grew, winding ever higher as everyone danced faster and faster, and Emily couldn't stop giggling with delight. At last it all crashed down and the music ended with a great crescendo. Laughing, the dancers moved towards the tables and bars, and Chris offered his arm to lead Emily towards a seat.

'Is that what you do so secretly with your time, Chris?' she teased. 'Dance under the stars?'

'Of course. All the time. Drink, and dance, and eat lobster *bisque*!' He gestured for another glass of St-Germain.

Emily rested her chin on her palm, feeling very giddy herself, as if for once she was part of the merriment around her. As if Chris's light-heartedness became hers, just for a little while. 'No, I don't think I actually believe that. You would be all fat and dissipated, with a red nose just like Lord Troxell's.'

Chris laughed, but before he glanced away Emily

glimpsed a serious expression in his eyes. 'I look very dissipated on the inside, I'm sure. One day it will all come out and lovely ladies like you will never want to be seen with me. I'll be reduced to sitting around the club, bragging about all the conquests I once had. Remembering brighter days.'

Emily sighed. 'At least you will have wonderful memories of all the fun you had when you made legions of conquests, right?'

He gave her a puzzled frown. 'It was hardly as merry as all that.'

'At least you *live*,' she said wistfully.

'Don't you, Em?' he said, squeezing her hand.

'I just work, really. Everyone is right about that.'

'I thought you enjoyed your work.'

'Oh, I do! I love making a difference. Thinking through problems, finding solutions. I'm fortunate to have that in my life, I would go mad sitting at home sewing a fine seam. But maybe, just sometimes, there *is* more to life. Like music! And dancing. And St-Germain in pretty glasses. And moonlight!' She gestured to the moon, silver and shimmering, rising above the trees that ringed the dance floor.

'Maybe we should take advantage of all that, then. Music and moonlight. Just so you have some memories of Paris. Shall we dance again?' He stood and held out his hand to her.

Emily studied his face, the sharp, elegant angles of it, in the lantern-light, and she suddenly felt such a deep, sad spasm of longing. 'Yes. I think we should.'

She took his hand and held on to him tightly as he

swept her into the dreamlike flow of a waltz. The other dancers carried them along like waves and all she had to do was let them buffet her about, cresting and falling. She rested her cheek against Chris's chest, feeling the rough wool of his coat on her skin, hearing the beat of his heart and the swell of the music blending inside of her. It was all she knew; Chris was all she could hold on to as the world shifted under the bright moon.

Usually her life moved so quickly, so full of noise and colour and busy tasks, that she had no time to stop and just *feel*. Now the sensation of time pausing was almost overwhelming. She had time to smell the warm air, filled with the flowery scent of the drinks, Chris's clean, citrus cologne, to hear the music and the laughter of people who were forgetting the outside world just as she was. She almost sobbed with the raw rush of longing.

Chris seemed to sense how she felt, even with no words. His arms tightened around her and he kissed her hair. They were just together in that moment, bound by so much. By Paris and music, and the sense that so much lay just beyond their grasp.

The music ended and suddenly time rushed forward again. Emily blinked hard and made herself smile brightly before she dared to step back and look into his eyes. She knew she couldn't allow herself to be so very vulnerable.

'That was lovely,' she said. 'Thank you, Chris.'

He just nodded, and for an instant he didn't look like Chris at all. He looked like someone so much older, sadder. 'Shall we sit down for a moment?' he said hoarsely. 'Maybe have another sip of St-Germain?'

Emily laughed. 'Sitting down sounds good, though I think I should just have a plain lemonade. I feel rather dizzy.'

He smiled and the old Chris was back again. She wondered if she had imagined anything different. 'Quite right.' He took her arm and led her back to one of the tables set up under the light-strewn trees. Another group was nearby, laughing loudly, bringing the world back into close focus.

Emily watched Chris disappear through the crowd back towards one of the bars, his hair shimmering in the lights like rare, ancient gold, and only then did she let out her breath in a great whoosh. Only then could she start to be her non-fanciful, sensible self. When he was near, she felt like a different person entirely. One who could not trust herself.

'Emily Fortescue? Whatever are you doing here?'

Startled, she turned to see James Hertford standing behind her. She wondered how he managed to appear seemingly everywhere in Paris. But he was a reminder of real life.

'Much the same as you, I would think, Mr Hertford,' she answered. 'Dancing! You seem to be enjoying Paris.'

'Are you here alone, Miss Fortescue?'

'I am not quite so daring as all that,' Emily said. 'I…'

'She is here with me,' Chris said, emerging from the crowd with glasses of frothy lemonade in hand. He watched Hertford with a suspicious narrowing of his bright blue eyes.

James looked startled. 'Blakely. I wasn't aware you and Miss Fortescue were so acquainted.'

'His brother is my best friend's husband, of course,' Emily said, feeling suddenly a bit bewildered. She wished she knew what was going on with James Hertford and with Chris.

James glanced between her and Chris, as if trying to read something himself. 'If you require an escort here in Paris…'

'I have that quite in hand, Hertford, thank you,' Chris said brusquely. He took Emily's hand and drew her close, as if to show off their courtship to everyone.

'Certainly,' James answered. He gave Emily a bow, a quick smile. 'Perhaps I may call on you, while we are both in Paris?'

'Thank you,' Emily said. 'I am the Hotel d'Or.'

James bowed once more and hurried away. Two ladies approached him, laughing up at him, and they vanished into the throng.

Chris handed Emily one of the glasses and sat down beside her, quiet. His expression was remote, unreadable. Different from the usual Chris.

'How do you know Mr Hertford?' she asked.

'From our club,' Chris answered shortly.

He didn't seem as if he would say more. He stared at the dancers, his thoughts seemingly far away, and Emily sighed and watched them, too. The kaleidoscope twirl of colours and noise, which she had felt a part of only moments before, now seemed terribly distant. She sipped at her tart drink and watched the swirl of ruffled skirts. The night suddenly seemed dimmed, tired.

'Shall I take you home, Em?' Chris asked. 'I hadn't realised how late it was.'

Neither had she. For just a little while, she hadn't noticed anything at all but how she felt. She couldn't let herself be so distracted. 'I am rather tired, thank you.'

When she finished her drink, he offered her his arm and she took it to let him lead her past the gates of the pleasure garden and into the silent night beyond. They made their way down the steep streets of Montmartre, the city spread out below them like a sparkling carpet. They walked in silence, as if they were each wrapped tightly in their own thoughts, making their way into the quiet neighbourhoods beyond.

'There's my lodgings,' he said, gesturing to a building on a street corner. Tall and narrow, grey stone, the windows dark, it looked quiet and respectable. 'Not as grand as your hotel, I'm sure.'

'It looks quite nice and peaceful,' she answered honestly. She was rather surprised he didn't stay in a loud, bright, crowded hotel, somewhere more sparkling, more—temporary. But she had learned Chris was always changing, always surprising. 'I do sometimes wonder what it would be like to have one's *own* room in Paris, not a hotel where one dare not move anything and the staff is always following people about asking to fetch things. Not that everyone at the Hotel d'Or isn't quite lovely, of course. It just doesn't feel—homely.'

'The concierge here is not lovely at all, I'm afraid,' Chris said with a laugh and just like that his serious, silent self was gone, vanished behind the brightly painted mask. 'She is always lurking in the shadows, waiting to see if she can catch me with a lady and then yell at me about the rules of the house.'

'I am sure you are much too wily for her, as you are for everyone else.' Emily laughed, trying to picture a concierge leaping out to shout at her tenants. She ignored the pang that the image of Chris with various ladies tiptoeing past the office gave her. Had he even been there with the glamorous Lady Smythe-Tomas? 'Let's try it, shall we?'

Chris looked startled. 'What do you mean?'

Emily felt suddenly terribly daring again, as if the fun of the Moulin de la Galette was still there inside of her. 'Let's see if we can sneak past her. I am quite sure I could. I was very good at bringing in contraband chocolates at Miss Grantley's, I was never caught.'

'Em...' he said cautiously, and she rather liked being the daring one for once. She grabbed his hand and drew him across the street. Laughing, he gave in, following her, and she loved the feeling of being partners in mischief.

There was no light in the concierge's room just past the front doors and it was dim on the winding iron staircase just beyond. Chris led her to the second floor, past silent apartments, and opened the door on the landing. Hardly daring to breathe, she tiptoed past him into the apartment beyond, wondering if she stepped into the secrets of Aladdin's cave.

She had never been in a gentleman's bachelor home before and she was a bit disappointed at the lack of decoration, though she wasn't really sure what they might be. Chris's apartment was small, a corridor leading to a sitting room, the alluring peek of a bedroom beyond. The furnishings were simple, sturdy, plain, a desk, a sofa, a table and chairs, a blue rug, a window shaded by blue curtains.

Emily went many places ladies usually did not— offices, boardrooms, warehouses, but not men's chambers. She had never wanted to go to such places before. She knew she really should be nervous, ashamed, but with Chris it was impossible to feel that way at all. Chris was always different from other men, from anyone else.

She peeked out the small window, expecting to see only night-dark rooftops, and gasped at the view. The lights of the city sparkled and she saw the Eiffel Tower silhouetted against the sky. 'How ever did you find this place?'

Chris shrugged and tried to surreptitiously shove a pile of laundry under a chair. Emily pretended not to see. 'Through a friend. I like the location, near the river, easy to get places.'

'Near cafés and bars, too, I'm sure.'

He laughed and went to a small cabinet where there were glasses and bottles. She wondered if he entertained there often. 'Of course.'

'It must be the perfect place to look at this city view, and just—well, think. Be quiet for a while.'

'I don't do much of that.'

Emily studied him carefully as he mixed two drinks. His hair fell over his brow and he looked thoughtful, far away. Masked again. 'You should try it some time. It can be most interesting, if you do it right.'

'I am sure your thoughts are most interesting, Em.

Mine are dull indeed.' His voice was growing faint behind her.

'I'm certain that is not true.' She glimpsed a small desk against the wall in the next room, piled with papers. It looked much used, as if to point out the fact that Chris did use this room for real work. Curious, she drifted closer, glancing over some of the documents. They seemed to be letters to the government office where he worked, requests for favours, appointments.

But one letter, half-tucked in a pigeonhole, caught her eye. The handwriting was rather familiar, bold and black, and she suddenly felt a cold touch of unease. She slowly reached for it and saw that it was indeed from her own father. And it was about her.

Her father urged Chris to make their courtship real—and to not tell her about it. That he would be a 'generous father-in-law'. Were they really plotting to marry her off without her knowledge? Had she really been so foolish?

Emily read it over more slowly and couldn't believe what she was seeing. Chris had been guarding her, watching where she went! At the behest of her father.

Shocked, a burning flare of anger rushing over her, she spun around to face Chris. He watched her warily, as if he knew.

'You have been working for my father? Marrying me off for real?' she choked out.

'Of course not,' he answered, but he wouldn't quite look at her. 'That is—Mr Fortescue did ask me to make sure you were all right. You know that. He was worried after what happened in London. I am worried, too. But I am not working for him.'

'So you would be paying me so much attention even if there was no bargain? Even if no one had been following me?' She wasn't so very sure. Chris had his own life after all. A life apart from here, even if she had forgotten that.

'Em, these things cannot just be dismissed! You must be kept safe. And really, his request was only an excuse for me to ask you to the races,' he protested. 'How else could I get you to go with me?'

But Emily could hardly hear him. Her feelings were in a whirl and she hardly knew what to think. She was hurt, angry, confused. She dropped the letter and strode towards the door, unable to look at him any longer. 'It's late. I need to return to the hotel.'

Chris put down the bottle with a *thunk*. 'I'm coming with you.'

She gave a bark of laughter. 'Because following me is your job?'

He took a sudden step back, as if she had pushed him. Wounded him. 'Because I am your friend and want to make sure you're safe.' He held up his hands. 'I won't say a word. You won't even know I'm there.'

Emily wanted nothing more than to be alone, to forget how foolish she had been, letting herself have fun with him. Enjoying being with him. She felt so terribly, terribly silly. But she also knew he was right. She certainly had no wish to be caught alone on the street again and assaulted by some strange villain.

She nodded and they made their way down the stairs and back out into the night. The edge of the sky was turning a pale grey, dawn was close, and the magical night was ending. She felt as if she would never have such a time again, could never again so forget herself. Chris was as good as his word. He said nothing, walking beside her in silence as they passed shops whose windows were opening, doors letting out the smell of fresh-baked bread. But she could sense him watching her, casting her quick, concerned glances. But she could not look back at him. Not yet. Not in the same way she had earlier and maybe never again.

He left her outside the hotel and she gave him a brusque nod. In her own suite, she gratefully locked the door behind her, kicked off her shoes and sank down on to one of the satin *chaises* with an exasperated sigh. She knew her frivolous evenings were over. No more dancing, no more races, just work. She had no more time for Chris Blakely, or the wild, laughing way he made her feel. She had been a fool, but no more. She had been right not to trust.

Chapter Fourteen

Chris watched the sun rise fully over the Parisian rooftops from his window, dry-eyed from lack of sleep. He hadn't been able to close his eyes at all after leaving Emily at her hotel and his thoughts were still whirling.

'Fool,' he muttered.

He had been an idiotic fool, leaving her father's letter on the desk and then letting her come to his room. But when she'd grabbed his hand and laughed up at him, her face full of light and fun, he hadn't been able to do anything else. He had been able only to follow her, as if under a spell.

He had to explain to her, to make her understand, even if he didn't fully understand himself. He had to make it up to her. The thought of his life without her in it was shockingly dry and dusty, empty even. He needed her friendship.

He pushed himself up from his chair and caught a glimpse of himself in the small mirror on the opposite wall. After the long night, he looked quite disreputable.

His jaw shadowed with whiskers, his hair rumpled, his shirt wrinkled, his eyes reddened. Emily would never accept an apology from someone who looked like that. He had a huge mountain of work ahead of him, making up to his sharp-edged Emily.

A few hours later, bathed, shaved, dressed in his best suit and brocade waistcoat, he set out for her hotel. The city was buzzing around him, a very different place from the silent streets he had walked down with her, and the sun seemed to make everything look a bit more hopeful. Surely she could not push him away again, not in such a glorious place. He stopped to buy a bouquet at one of the bright flower stands, the biggest bunch of roses and lilies he could find, and he dared to think all might be well.

'I am sorry, *monsieur*,' the hotel manager said. 'Mademoiselle Fortescue left a half-hour ago, she said she had an errand in Chaton sur Mereille and needed to catch an early train from the Gare Saint-Lazare.'

'Chaton sur Mereille?' Chris asked sharply. Why was she going back there again? Was she in danger there by herself?

'*Oui.* For her business, I believe.'

Chris could just imagine what sort of 'business'. The League and Herr Friedland. He left the flowers for her and made his way towards the train station, determined to keep protecting her—no matter what.

Emily stared out the window as her train gathered speed leaving the city, watching but not really seeing the blur of rooftops and back gardens giving way to fields. She couldn't stop thinking about last night and her own silly behaviour. The things that happened when she let go of her control.

She sighed and turned over the file of papers in her lap. She had her life to return to now. No one could make her behave so foolishly as Chris could! With him, she had felt too free, too reckless. She could not account for what had happened last night, getting as giddy as a schoolgirl over dancing in the moonlight. Forgetting the world that existed outside.

And then to find out that her father was scheming to marry her off for real! It was beyond embarrassing. Emily felt her cheeks burn hot just thinking about it.

She snapped the folder on her lap open and stared down at the papers Lady Smythe-Tomas had sent her. Work was the answer. Work never failed her, never made her feel like a fool.

The door between the train carriages opened and then closed, and footsteps sounded on the carpeted corridor. Emily glanced through the little window of her compartment and froze at the sight of the man in the pale grey suit who was making his way past the windows, peering carefully inside. It couldn't be Chris! Surely she was just imagining things because she had been thinking about him far too much that day.

She looked again. No, it really was him. He was looking at the next compartment down from hers and she heard a girl giggle as he raised his hat, smiled and moved on.

'There you are at last, Em,' he said. 'I thought I would have to search this train from one end to the other!'

'What on earth are you doing here, Christopher?' she demanded. 'How did you know I was here?'

'They told me at your hotel, when I called there earlier.'

Emily folded her arms. 'Did my father ask you to follow me? To compromise me so I would have to marry you?'

He glanced down the corridor, looking rather abashed. She wasn't sure she had ever seen that side of him before. 'Please, Em. Can I sit down with you? Explain everything? I've come all this way to apologise and if I stand here much longer they are sure to toss me off this train.'

She gave a grudging nod and he slipped into the compartment to sit down on the narrow seat across from her. Emily realised her mistake at once. The compartment was rather small and he was too close to her, so close she could smell his cologne. Feel his warmth, see his smile. But she could hardly toss him out now and cause a scene on the train.

'I *am* sorry, Em, truly,' he said softly. 'I shouldn't have concealed it from you, shouldn't have concealed anything from you at all. I was just—well, dash it all, I was worried about you. I could see how concerned your father was and it made me concerned, too. I couldn't stand it if you were hurt.'

Emily felt herself start to soften at his gentle words, the look in his eyes, and she tried to steel herself. 'You, and my father, as well, could have been fully honest with me. I am not a child.'

'Of course not. You are one of the most sensible people I know. I just didn't want to worry *you*.'

'You didn't have to waste your time nannying me at the races or the Moulin de la Galette, either.'

Chris gave a crooked grin. 'I'm afraid it was all rather an excuse to get away from work and have some fun with you. We *did* have fun, yes? Even your life can't be serious all the time, can it?'

Emily bit her lip to keep from grinning back. His charm was much too dangerous. 'That is of no account. You still didn't have to follow me today.'

'I did. I told you—I had to apologise for hiding things from you. I won't do it again.'

But Emily wondered if that was true. If he could not help but hide things from the people who cared about him. She glanced at the window to see the red-tiled roof of a farmhouse slide by, the golden ripples of fields of grain. Everything felt so far away again, as if she and Chris were the only people in the world.

'What are you working on?' he asked, gesturing to the papers on her lap. 'What takes you all the way to a country village?'

'Oh, just some tasks for the League,' she answered, wondering how much he really would want to know. Even her father was rather dismissive of the League, which made her even more determined to press on for them. Women had to fight for themselves, for their place in life.

'Isn't the League for British women's suffrage?'

Chris said. He looked genuinely curious. 'Why French meetings?'

'Women everywhere are realising they must fight to realise their true potential in the world,' Emily answered. 'We might actually have a German benefactor soon, there have been meetings here in Paris to gauge their interest.'

'German?' he said with a frown.

Emily nodded. 'The man you met at the races. Herr Friedland. I can't really talk about it yet. Honestly, I don't know much about it myself at present. It's all quite new. I do wonder if…'

The train gave a sudden lurching jolt and Emily glanced out the window, startled. The train was definitely slowing down.

'What could be happening?' she asked, watching as everything seemed to slide a bit sideways, then came to a stop.

Chris looked outside. 'Sheep on the track, maybe? Such things happen when you leave civilisation and go to the back of beyond countryside.'

'We're only a few miles outside Paris! It's hardly the Ardennes Forest.' Yet something was happening. The train gave another hard jolt, nearly knocking her to the floor, and then ground to a halt with a metallic squeal. She heard a wave of cries in the corridor.

Emily put down the window and peered outside, craning her neck to try to see what was going on there. A puff of greasy smoke blew in her face and she sat back, coughing.

'I can't see a thing,' she said. 'At least we don't seem to have crashed.'

'I'll go see,' Chris said. 'You stay here.'

Emily nodded as he left and sat back down, trying not get impatient with the moments ticking by. The nervous chatter in the corridor grew louder, but no one seemed to have any more idea than she did. She tapped her foot, packed and re-packed her case, until at last Chris returned, his lovely suit streaked with smoke.

'Something to do with the engine, they say,' he said. 'They're not sure when we'll be on the move again. We're going to be pushed off to a siding.'

'Oh, no!' Emily cried. 'I'm supposed to meet Madame Renard soon.'

Chris frowned as he looked out the window. 'I don't think we're very far from Chaton. Shall we leg it?'

'Walk?'

'I could carry your case for you.' He smiled teasingly. 'Or carry *you*, if you're not up to it.'

Emily pictured being swept up in his arms and felt her cheeks turn hot. She turned away to stuff her papers in her bag. 'That would be taking your apology a little too far. But I think we could walk. Better than sitting here twiddling our thumbs for hours.'

Chris hoisted their cases up and they made their way out of the station and down the lane towards the village. As they crested a hill, she could see the red-tile roofs of the farmhouses amid their green fields, the old tower of the church in the distance. It all looked peaceful, timeless.

'You didn't have to travel all this way to find me

today,' she said, clambering over a fallen log in the lane. 'A note saying "sorry" would have sufficed.'

'Of course it wouldn't. You would have just crumpled up my letter and tossed it in the fire. This way you had to look directly at my contrite face and who could resist my sad eyes?'

He gave her an exaggerated, wide-eyed, tragic look and she laughed. He was probably right. What lady *could* resist those eyes?

'Besides,' he continued, 'a day in the countryside seemed most alluring. Wouldn't you agree it was worth the journey?'

They had reached the top of a hill and Chris gestured to the picture spread before them. The red-tiled roofs of the houses, their old, mellow gold stone walls, an ancient church tower, the vineyards snaking across the hills just beyond in green glory.

'It is certainly lovely, like a painting,' Emily agreed. The day was turning out to be much more fun than she had planned, thanks to him.

'Paris is beautiful, but who could resist such rustic Gallic charm? Fresh air, little cafés, sunshine…' A clap of thunder rolled out over the hills and Chris glanced up ruefully at the suddenly darkening sky. 'Maybe not so much sunshine at the moment. But still, a place to renew the soul.'

Emily studied his face, as serious as those gathering clouds. 'You do surprise me, Chris. I would have thought you a man of the city through and through.'

He gave her a crooked smile. 'That's because you don't know everything about me.'

Emily was beginning to think that was very true. He changed like the weather, sudden and surprising. But she didn't have long to contemplate the mystery of Christopher Blakely. A fat raindrop landed on her nose, making her gasp.

'We'd best make a run for it,' Chris said, tugging his hat lower on his brow. 'Where are you meant to be?'

Emily took the letter with instructions from her handbag. 'The inn, again. Where we met before. It's just by the church, I think.'

'Come on!' He grabbed her hand and they ran for the village just as the skies cracked open above them. Emily laughed helplessly, trying to hold on to her hat.

At last they found the half-timbered old inn, its red window awnings sagging under the sudden downpour, and tumbled through the door, gasping with giggles. The elderly lady behind the desk gave them a stern glance and a loud 'tsk'.

'*Puis-je vous aider?*' she asked, narrowing her eyes on the puddle they brought with them on to the tile floor.

'I am sorry to be so late, we weren't expecting the storm,' Emily answered. 'I am meant to be meeting Madame Renard?'

'The *madame* is not here, my son tells me the trains are delayed today.'

'Yes, it is why we had to walk,' Emily said. She wondered if that meant she and Chris were stuck there at the inn for the foreseeable future and if that annoyed her—or made her feel glad for the weather. 'I'm afraid I didn't bring much with me for a longer stay.'

The landlady seemed to have some pity on them

then, in their drowned-kitten state, or perhaps she re-membered them from the last time they were there. 'You must have some *dejeuner*, a warm *digestif, non*? I'll have the maid send you to a room, *monsieur* and *madame*, and find some dry clothes for you to borrow.'

Before Emily could protest that they were not ac-tually '*monsieur and madame*', the formidable lady marched off, calling for the maidservant.

Chapter Fifteen

'Well, I must say that was the finest *dejeuner* I can remember,' Chris said, sitting back from the table that was littered with the plates and bottles that were all that remained of their meal. 'We must contrive to get caught in the rain more often.'

Emily smiled and realised that she had to agree. Her whole life seemed to be 'hurry, hurry, do more'—there was seldom time to enjoy a bottle of wine, a good joke. It was—quite nice. Better than nice. She would never have thought a thwarted appointment, fruitless waiting, could be the finest pleasure. And it was all thanks to Chris.

The landlady had ordered a fine meal of roast chicken and raspberry tarts, local cheeses and wine, and had it laid next to the fire in a private sitting room. The rain pattering at the old, wavy glass of the window, muffled by the heavy velvet curtains, made the space cosy and warm and small, a place outside the cares of the world.

And Emily's sides ached from laughing at Chris's

merry tales. He could mimic society matrons and clerks at his office with perfect pitch, making her giggle helplessly.

'It's been worth the journey out here,' she said. 'I feel terribly fat and lazy now. I don't even care about missing any meetings!'

Chris leaned back in his chair and gave her a crooked smile, a penetrating glance, as if he searched for something from her. 'The meeting was for your suffrage work with Lady Smythe-Tomas?'

Emily couldn't help but remember that he had called her 'Laura' before, as if they knew each other well. 'Yes, in a way. Important fundraising, things like that. It's rather dull, but without such help the work can never increase. I'll do what I can to bring whomever I can to the cause.'

'It's very important to you.'

'Yes, of course.' She turned her half-empty wineglass in the firelight, watching the deep ruby-red gleam in its depths. 'Women are so helpless when they're thrown on to the mercy of the world. They can't raise themselves by their own intellect, their own labour, they are helpless to any who would take advantage of them. Victimise them. I never want another woman to feel as I did when I was followed in the street. When I read those notes. I never want that feeling of fear to prevent women from enjoying the world. Life is too full, too wondrous, to miss.'

'I never want that, either.' He reached out and gently touched her hand, a warm, comforting brush of his fingers. 'I want to help, Em, truly I do. I knew I went about it all in the most wrong way, that I was blasted clumsy, but I do want to help you. I want you to be safe.'

Emily swallowed hard, trying not to burst into tears in front of him. Trying not to let him see how very much his words meant to her. 'Yes. I do believe you, Chris. I could never think you were—well, anything like the man who attacked me.'

Chris gave her a crooked, rueful smile. 'You just think I am a careless ne'er-do-well.'

Emily remembered her doubts about him lately, those flashes of something solemn, serious, hidden behind his eyes. Could she trust him? Were there more secrets in his life? 'Not entirely.'

He turned her hand lightly on his palm, studying her fingers against his skin. 'Do you have any idea at all if someone you know might have been the one who followed you in the street? If it could have been someone besides an opportunistic vagrant?'

She thought back, remembering all the sleepless nights she had spent trying to decide that very thing. Trying to remember everything, everyone she had ever met. She studied Chris carefully, and realised she could truly confide in him. That he could be trusted. 'I— something did once happen, in my first Season. I felt so foolish about it all and I never told anyone. Not Father, or even Alex and Diana. But the memory has rather nagged at me.'

His brow creased in a concerned frown. 'You can tell me. I promise your secret is safe.'

She thought of the masks Chris wore, layers and layers of them, just as she wore her masks. Masks of strength and work, but they weren't all the story of her. Just as his were not all of him. Yes, he probably could keep a secret. Lock it up safe.

'Well, for a time, a very short time, I rather fancied myself in love with someone. We had always read some rather silly novels at Miss Grantley's and I think they turned my head, even though I always laughed at them. This man seemed quite charming. But then…' Emily forced herself to go back to that night, to the girl she had once been, even as she wanted to run away from it all for ever. 'Then he tried to take advantage of me at a party. I had gone out on to the terrace with him, thinking he might be about to propose, but instead he kissed me, tried to reach under my skirts. He laughed when I was outraged, said I was just a girl in trade and should appreciate his attentions. I slapped him and ran away. I tried to forget it all. But I thought I saw him at the races.'

Chris looked outraged. His fingers closed tightly over hers. 'And you think it could be this person following you, sending the notes?'

'Not really. Maybe? No. He seems to move from lady to lady as easily as changing his stockings, I'm sure he didn't think of me at all after that night. As far as I know he's gone to India And I haven't heard he is in Paris, though I did wonder if I saw him that day at Longchamp.'

'I'm sure you have many admirers, some with just such mistaken ideas. Has anyone else dared to behave so outrageously?' he asked tightly.

Emily wondered if he was angry with her suitors—or with her. She felt a hurtful pang that he might think that.

Surely they knew each other better than that? 'I don't encourage anyone, Chris! I have no time for romance now. I would never be less than honest with anyone.'

'Of course you would not. You are Emily. You're never less than honest. Even when it could wound a fragile male heart.' He laughed and kissed her hand quickly.

'Oh, you're teasing!'

'Not at all. Have any of your suitors become—more insistent lately? Have you received any more strange letters here in Paris?'

Emily thought of James Hertford, how he always seemed to appear where she was. But he seemed harmless enough. 'No one that I can tell. But every time I travel somewhere new, I'm always looking over my shoulder now.'

'Yes.' Chris squeezed her hand, his silence heavy, his face serious and thoughtful. He stood up, drawing her with him. 'Come, let me show you something.'

'Is this another tease?' she asked suspiciously.

'Certainly not. I'm just going to show you a few things I've learned in my disreputable life. Going to prize fights and such, you know.'

'Oh, really!' Emily clapped her hands in delight. 'Will you show me how to break someone's nose in one blow?'

'Two, maybe. Just come here, I'll show you. It should help give you an element of surprise, at least, some time to get away.'

Emily leaped eagerly to her feet, only to realise that her borrowed skirt was much too long to engage in fisticuffs. She tied it up like bloomers and hurried to follow Chris to an open patch of carpet by the fire.

'Now, if someone comes after you, you need to move fast, aim for their most vulnerable points. Their, er, trouser area.'

Emily giggled. 'Yes, I see.'

'Kick, or punch. Or drive your nails into their eyes, with a twist up into the socket…' He took her hand and showed her the correct gouging motion. 'Or if they come from behind you, drive back your elbow into their midsection, as hard as you can, and stomp back with your heel on their instep. This is especially good if you're wearing those heeled shoes.'

Chris went around behind her and, before she knew what he was doing, grabbed her around the waist. Her instincts took over and she did just as he had instructed, driving back her elbow and stamping down with her foot. It felt surprisingly empowering and, when he gasped, she whirled around and landed a blow to his cheek.

'Ouch!' he shouted as her fist made contact with his jaw. 'Very enthusiastic.'

'I'm rather good at it, aren't I?' she said, half-gleeful and half-sorry she had hit him harder than she intended.

'Rather *too* good. There is also the method of distraction.'

'Distraction? Like shouting, "Look over there!" and then running? Is that how you get away from all the ladies pursuing you at parties?'

'You underestimate the power of pointing out an eligible duke across the room and then ducking into the crowd. Works a charm.'

Emily laughed in delight at the image of Chris bobbing and weaving through a ballroom, a pack of misses in white tulle in pursuit. But when she spun around to face him, she found he wasn't laughing at all. He watched *her*, his expression thunderstruck, almost as if he had never seen her before.

'What is it?' she whispered.

Chris shook his head. 'It's just—you're so very beautiful when you laugh, Em. It's like the sun coming out and lighting up the whole world.'

Emily couldn't breathe. 'Oh, Chris.' She took a tentative step closer and reached up to touch his cheek with her fingertips. His skin felt like roughened silk under her touch, warm and alive. 'You are so much like the sun all the time. Too dazzling for us mortals to look at. You are a distraction just in being yourself.'

'Perhaps I should distract you like—this.' Before Emily could tell what he was about, before she could think at all, he reached out to clasp her by the waist and pull her close, so close there was nothing between them at all. His lips descended on hers in a quick, crushing kiss, full of hunger and need.

Emily arched back at first, startled. But her own desire and confusion, all the fun and excitement and strangeness of the last few Parisian days with him, sparked into a roaring flame. It burned away all rational thought, all the complications of their past, and left only pure, hot emotion. Pure need.

She threw her arms around him, her fingers driving into the rough silk of his hair, holding him against her as her lips parted for his kiss. He groaned, a deep, primitive sound of need to equal her own, his tongue touching hers, tasting, their mouths and bodies and even spirits enmeshed. He seemed as caught as surely she was, bound by something they could never be free of.

What did it all mean? Emily didn't know and in that moment she didn't care. She only knew, only wanted, his kiss, his touch. How could he make her forget, with only a certain look, how wrong they were for each other? How different their lives were?

Pulling him with her, Emily stumbled backwards until she fell on to the *chaise*, sinking down into its cushions. She drew him down on top of her, their kiss frantic. She wrapped her legs tightly around his hips, kicking the knot of her borrowed skirts free. She felt the roughness of his woollen trousers on her skin, the heavy proof of his fierce desire pressing against it. But it wasn't enough for her now, not nearly enough.

She let her head arch back against the cushions, revelling in the shivery sensations of his lips against her jaw, the arc of her throat. The hot rush of his breath, his heartbeat, all around her, part of her. How alive he was, how real and vital! She had lived too much in her mind, keeping her distance from everything else, and now she wanted his impulsive heat. His passion. No matter how maddening he was, how frightened she was, she knew now they had been coming to this moment ever since they met.

When she was with him, she knew real emotion, the primitive urgency of craving and passion and life. When she was with him, she felt alive herself. She didn't want to let that go, not yet.

Her eyes still closed, absorbing every feeling, she slid her hands over his strong shoulders, down the lean line of his chest, until she found the buttons of his waistcoat. She made quick, hungry work of them, pushing the heavy cloth back so she could unfasten his shirt and could at last feel the heat of his skin against her palm. The beat of his heart.

Chris groaned, his face buried in the curve of her neck as he let her explore him.

She had never seen a real naked man before, only cold marble statues, flat oil paintings. She had never imagined the male body could look this way, feel this way. She traced her fingertips over hot, smooth flesh, roughened by a sprinkling of coarse, pale golden hair. His breath caught under her caress, but he didn't move away, didn't try to snatch control from her in the moment. He lay wrapped in her arms, his lips against her shoulder where her gown drooped away, and let her explore.

Emily tightened her clasp on his shoulders, rolling him to the *chaise* as she rose above him on her knees. She could hardly breathe, dared not think! All she could know was him, that unbearable need that had been building inside her for so long. She'd tried so hard to deny it, push it away, fight against it.

She couldn't do it any longer. It was like a dam breaking open.

She shrugged off her dress, letting it fall to her hips, and Chris moved at last, sliding off her chemise so that she knelt above him wearing absolutely nothing. She suddenly longed to hide behind her hair, but she knew she had to be brave now. She shrugged the loosened, damp strands back over her shoulder and held her breath, staring down at him in a tense, silent moment that seemed to last for ever.

Chris's bare chest, golden as a gilt god, rose and fell with the force of his own breath and he couldn't look away from her. As she looked into his eyes, as dark blue as a storm, she knew that he did want her, just as she wanted him. She had half-feared that once she offered herself to him, he would not want her. Would change his mind. Then she felt the slide of his touch on her bare waist, easing her away so he could sit up. So they were eye to eye, in that moment together, nothing else outside them.

'Will you—kiss me?' Emily whispered.

Chris groaned and their mouths met again in a desperate, hungry clash that held nothing of artful romance or cool seduction. She couldn't deny it any longer. Love him, hate him, he was a part of her and always would be, no matter what happened after that moment.

She broke off their kiss only to pull off his shirt, then wrapped her arms around him again, leaning into the sharp edges of his lean body to feel the press of naked skin to naked skin. Heartbeat to heartbeat. They fell down to the *chaise*, limbs entangled.

'Emily,' he gasped. 'You're a lady, and I—we shouldn't do this.'

'I don't think we have a choice, do you?' she cried, suddenly desperate at the thought he might leave her now. That she might lose that moment. 'I might be young, and, yes, a virgin, but you know I'm not such a

squeamish miss as all that. And I—well, I know some things. From women in the League. Things I can do after so we don't have to worry about—consequences.'
She felt her face flame bright red at the words and let her hair fall over her cheeks.

He gave a startled laugh and she dragged him back on top of her, silencing his words with a kiss. Soon there could be no words at all, no rational thought, just emotion, sensations, the joy of being together and alive.

He quickly shed his trousers, sliding into the welcome of her parted legs as if he was always meant to be just there. Their bodies *fitted*, their movements perfectly co-ordinated like the most beautiful dance. Emily closed her eyes, revelling in the feel of his mouth at her breast, the delicious friction of their hot, damp skin, the frantic need that built and built inside of her.

Then he joined with her and she didn't know anything else at all.

The rain was heavier against the window and roof now, a loud, soothing song that seemed to move in time with Chris's heartbeat against her cheek. Emily closed her eyes and let the moment wrap around her like a soft eiderdown.

What had happened between her and Chris was so very momentous, she could hardly take it in. She certainly couldn't think about it coldly, clinically, with distance, to decide how to deal with any possible consequences at all. She knew that would come later. That real life would crowd in on this hazy dream.

But not yet. Not until the storm outside passed and they had to step out into the world again. Had to be their separate selves with their separate lives. She could see no way they could join them, could reveal all their secrets and live like other people in their conventional houses and lives.

Emily closed her eyes and curled up closer to him, letting his heat and strength hold her up. It was very strange, she thought, how a man so known for being so careless, so unreliable, made her feel safer and more at peace than anyone else ever had.

Chris's arm tightened around her. 'Are you cold, Em? Should I build up the fire?'

'Not at all. It's very cosy here. Don't move just yet.'

'I don't think I could, anyway.'

She glanced up to see that his eyes were still closed, but a small smile curved his lips, and he looked so young and carefree in that moment. She ached with how beautiful he was.

'I do love the sound of the rain,' she said. 'It reminds me of when I was a little girl and rainy afternoons were the only time I wasn't strictly marched around the park by my nanny. I would hide in the attics when she wasn't looking and listen to the fall of it on the roof.'

'How shocking of you. I would imagine you were always diligently reciting your lessons in the schoolroom, no slacking at all.'

Emily felt a tiny pang of hurt that he would think her so lacking in fun. 'I usually did. Except on rainy days.'

He smiled lazily and his fingers trailed lightly over

her arm, tickling and making her giggle. 'And what did you do there? Sneak cream cakes up from the kitchens? Read novels?'

'Sometimes there were cakes. But mostly I looked through my secret box.'

'Your secret box? That sounds intriguing.'

Emily remembered her box, an enamelled case her father brought her once from Switzerland, with its own little lock and tiny velvet compartments inside where things could be hidden. 'Mostly it held things that were my mother's. Some pressed roses from her wedding bouquet, her photograph, a baby bonnet she was embroidering for me but never finished. My father will talk about her a little bit now, but back then it would make him too sad. I never wanted to see him sad. I just wanted to know her in some way. Up there, with just the rain, I felt like I was with her.'

'Oh, Em,' he said softly. She felt him press a gentle kiss to her hair and she tried not to cry. Her throat felt tight with the tears she had always held back. 'I am sorry you went through that.'

She just nodded, trying not to cry. Not to let even an instant of sadness into that moment. She felt safe there, with Chris. 'What were *your* childhood secrets?'

'Hiding sweets, mostly, or refusing to do my lessons. My parents were both there, of course, but sometimes I wished they were not. I liked going off to school, after Will was gone. Our house was such a quiet, cold place.'

Emily could well imagine that the Blakelys did not make 'home' a fun, welcoming place. Every time she saw them, they were disapproving of something. Yet they had not managed to crush Chris's irrepressible spirit. 'I do sometimes wish I had a house like this one.'

'This one?'

'Yes. Old and cosy, full of character and stories. Even better if it's in the French countryside, of course, with lovely vineyards all around. Maybe a goat in the yard.'

Chris laughed, a golden, merry sound that made her very toes warm. 'And will you be a milkmaid? Gather eggs, crush grapes to make your own wine?'

'Why not? It would be so—simple. Useful.' She remembered what waited outside those old walls, real life with all its work and responsibilities, and she wished she could hold it back a little longer. But it still waited there, patient. Ready to swallow her up.

'Simple and useful. I think you might be right about something like that. I can barely imagine what life could be like then.'

Emily closed her eyes and tried to picture it. A lovely old house, curtains fluttering in the open windows, chickens scurrying in the garden. Chris sitting in the shade of a tree, waiting for her. It was an image to take into her dreams, as she drifted on amid the soothing patter of the falling rain and let sleep and dreams take her while she lay safe in his arms.

Chapter Sixteen

Laura, Lady Smythe-Tomas, sighed as she looked over the letters in front of her. All seemed to be going ahead just as planned. Her real contacts in Berlin reported that Friedland thought she was on his side, deeply rooted in his schemes to discredit the Crown Princess, while Princess Vicky had no idea what was really happening around her. Her mother, the English Queen, who railed against female suffrage, would never know what other, independent women went through to keep her safe.

Laura had once been rather like the Queen, herself. Married much too young to the older Lord Smythe-Tomas, sheltered and spoiled, knowing only the silk-covered walls around her. It had taken her a while to realise that those walls, as luxurious as they were, could only be a prison. Everything, everyone, around her conspired to keep her from thinking, doing, even feeling for herself. She was just a toy for others, an ornament for their world.

But she knew how to read, how to listen, how to use that disregard to her own advantage. Lord Smythe-Tomas never realised how she took back her own power, one hard-won inch at a time.

And then he died and she found out that all the money was gone. Lost by him in foolish investments. Everyone expected her to marry again right away, because a beautiful, pampered woman like her could surely do nothing else. One daring friend had even suggested she try being a courtesan; her style and looks would surely be worth a great deal in such a market.

She had even considered it. Surely it would be better than being married and in her widowhood she had discovered that men could even be rather fun in their place. But she had also realised she could never again give up even a fraction of her freedom. And then Lord Ellersmere had come along to offer her new work. A new purpose.

The clock on the mantel chimed the hour, and she suddenly realised she would be late for her appointment across the *arrondissement*. She put down her pen and reached for her hat, a confection of blue taffeta bows and peacock feathers from Gordston's. Looking her stylish best, she had found, was just as important for her work than if she had indeed become a courtesan.

She smoothed the skirt of her blue-silk gown, reached for her gloves and reticule, and made her way downstairs to the cobbled street. At that hour the lanes were quiet, filled with flower carts and the scent of fresh-baked baguettes, lovely and peaceful. She was quite sure she could happily stay in Paris for ever.

'Lady Smythe-Tomas,' she heard someone call and

looked up to see James Hertford across the pavement. He looked the very image of handsome English aristocratic manhood, with his fine grey suit, his glossy dark hair, but she had learned long ago not trust appearances. He was always a bit too eager.

'Mr Hertford, how delightful,' she said, with one of her brightest smiles. 'Where are you off to this evening?'

'The theatre, though not until later. Are you on your way to an engagement yourself?'

'Supper at Le Grand Véfour. Would you care to walk with me for a while? It's a wonderfully cool evening, is it not?'

'That is kind of you. I would—well, I would rather like your advice on a matter.' He looked intriguingly abashed.

'Of course. I am always more than happy to share my wisdom of the world.'

He offered her his arm and they set off down the lane towards the busier squares of the city. 'I saw that you were with Miss Emily Fortescue at the races.'

Laura realised it was romantic matters he wanted advice about, and on her possible protégée. Interesting. 'Yes. She is quite a lovely lady, I think.'

He nodded eagerly. 'And so do I. I would like to pursue her, seriously of course, but I cannot think she sees me in the same way. She never seems to give me any consideration at all, and it makes me feel quite maddened. Perhaps she considers me to have some— uncomfortable friendships and she associates me too much with matters I have no control over.'

Laura thought it might be his too-desperate grasping that put the lady off. 'Unfortunate friendships?'

'Yes. People she does not like. I would do anything to make her see me in a new way. It is driving me quite mad.'

She felt a touch of disquiet and wondered if this was a moment to trust her intuition. Mr Hertford had always seemed to her a rather nice sort of man, if a bit too insistent on that 'niceness'. 'What do you like so very much about her?'

'She is quite beautiful and, as you said, has a great deal of conversation. Maybe a bit too much independence for a lady, but what can one expect with a father like Fortescue? I am sure she is just waiting for a proper marriage, a proper home. She is so gentle underneath, she would make a fine hostess for any man's house.'

Laura realised he did not care so much for the 'real' Emily, a woman of rare independence and fortitude, but instead saw her as an angel in waiting, a lady just longing for the kiss of a man to bring her to her true purpose, her true worth. She'd seen such things many times before. 'Perhaps she wants to be appreciated for who she is, her real accomplishments. Her brains, her talent for business.'

He looked astonished. 'But she is a lady. Surely she wants a home to run, a family? And I can give her that. If she saw what I can really do for her, how I can see her true desires! If she could see what I have already done…'

Her doubts grew stronger. 'What you have done?'

He shook his head, a quick, jerky movement of frustration. 'But she will not see. She sees only rogues like that Blakely, who can never give her the life she deserves. Like so many women, she can't see a nice man like myself. I must *make* her see. But how?'

Laura was suddenly worried, about both Emily and Chris. When someone started decrying the fact that women were perfidious creatures who only wanted men who treated them badly, not *nice* men like themselves, it never boded well. Self-proclaimed nice men were never nice at all.

'Mr Hertford, if you truly do care about her, you must be honest with her. Tell her your feelings, let her make up her own mind. I have found Miss Fortescue to be a lady of sense and intelligence, she will listen to you fairly.'

He shook his head again. 'I have tried and she will not. I must do something more.'

They had reached the door of Véfour and Laura saw her group waiting for her in the foyer. She felt relieved to be soon free of Mr Hertford's suddenly oppressive company. 'I must say, that is my best advice, Mr Hertford. There can be no way forward in romance without being honest with a lady—and accepting what she has to say in return. Romance is no easy task, no matter what poetry tells us. I am sorry I could not be of more help.'

His mouth was drawn tight, but he gave her a polite bow. 'No, indeed, Lady Smythe-Tomas, you have been of tremendous help. I see now what I must do to save her. I must show her what I have done.' He tipped his hat to her. 'Good evening, do enjoy your party.'

Laura watched him disappear into the evening crowd gathering on the stree, and she shivered a bit with the sudden cold touch of doubt. She had made a career of reading people—and she had met men who sounded like Mr Hertford before. Men who thought themselves entitled to a woman's attention just because they wanted it.

She should talk to Emily, warn her. And soon.

Chapter Seventeen

Chris stared at himself in the mirror as he tied his cravat, smoothed his hair. He was due for dinner at Diana and Will's in an hour and he was most uncharacteristically nervous about attending a family dinner. His hands were even shaking a bit.

Maybe, he thought, it was the tiny velvet box in his pocket than weighed so heavily on him.

After he left Chaton, left Emily at her hotel with a kiss on her hand, he didn't know what he thought or felt at all. His romantic encounters were almost always of the light variety, ladies who wanted a bit of fun as much as he did, and who laughingly tossed him out of their boudoirs after. Women who didn't want anything emotional, dangerous. That was what had suited his life of secrets and shadows perfectly.

Emily was entirely different. She was something he had never encountered before. She haunted his thoughts and he couldn't think of anything but her. Of anything but what had happened to them in that rain-wrapped chamber, hidden in the countryside.

When they parted, after a silent train ride, she had tried to laugh it off, too, kissing his cheek and sending him away outside her hotel. Yet he knew Em. She was strong, yes, and fiercely independent, but also a lady. She had a name to protect, a business. She was his friend. He had to do the right thing by her. Yet how was he to know what the 'right thing' was, when Emily was not like any other person? What had happened had cracked his world open, made him see everything differently. His next step could make everything far worse, if it was the wrong one.

When he saw the ring, a modern, fashionable ruby surrounded by diamonds, in the jeweller's window on the Rue Faubourg, the next step suddenly seemed clear to him. He had to ask Em to marry him. What was more, what really shocked him to his core, was that he *wanted* to ask her to marry him. He wanted her in his life.

But marrying her would mean lying to her, possibly for the rest of their lives. He couldn't involve her in his work. He had to keep on protecting her. He was good at acting, yes, but could he carry it off for so long? And with Emily, whose hazel eyes seemed to see everything?

He only knew he had to try. He felt the fierce, primitive urge to keep her safe, from everything in the world that could hurt her—even himself.

He put on his coat and felt the weight of that ring box in the pocket. Whatever happened tonight would surely change everything.

'The amber combs, Miss Emily, or the diamond aigret?' Mary asked.

Emily, startled out of her faraway thoughts, glanced

in the mirror to find her hair was already curled and pinned in place without her even noticing. Mary held up the two ornaments.

Emily just couldn't decide. Maybe it was knowing that Chris would be there that had her worried about her appearance. Usually she just chose a fashionable gown, put it on and left. Now she wondered what looked best. What looked attractive but respectable, distant but kind? 'The combs, I think. They should go well with the gown.' She had chosen one of her more subdued new gowns, black lace over dark green satin, drapes of black beads over the narrow sleeves. She didn't want to look as if she was trying too hard, but she did want to look pretty.

'You've been terribly distracted since you got back from your errand in the country, miss,' Mary said, pinning the combs to the back of Emily's hair. 'I hope that rainstorm hasn't brought on an ague.'

'Hmm?' Emily knew she had been distracted. How could she help it? Her world had changed utterly. She couldn't even focus on her work, which had been her life for so long. Instead she remembered what it felt like when he kissed her, the way everything else just disappeared. She wondered what he thought of her now. What would happen when they saw each other next.

She had managed to stay busy, to avoid him for a few days. But he was there none the less, in the bouquet of white roses on her desk that he had sent just that morning. She was sure he would be at Diana's tonight.

Emily took a deep breath. She had to stop being a coward, to face Chris and what had happened! To face her own feelings, once she could decipher what they were. Emotions were so much more difficult than ledger books.

She reached for her emerald earrings and fastened them on, hoping her jewels, the new gown, would be like armour tonight. She needed them.

'Oh, my dear!' Diana cried as Emily stepped into the Blakelys' hotel sitting room. She saw to her relief that Chris wasn't there yet, that the room was dimly lit, cosy and intimate in its green-silk walls. 'I am so glad you could come tonight. It's all been dull embassy events for weeks and weeks, it seems, they are never-ending. But tonight we can have some fun. Chris should be here at any moment and Alex and Malcolm. It will be just like old times.'

'It *is* lovely to see you again, Em,' Will said, handing her a glass of champagne. 'Though Di does rather exaggerate. I haven't exactly been chaining her to the embassy yoke. She's managed a visit or two to Gordston's, and one ruinous fitting at Worth.'

'I only bought one Worth gown! Every embassy wife must have one. But I found this one in Gordston's own new fashion line,' Diana said, twirling in her aqua silk and ecru lace dinner gown. 'Isn't it divine? I do think Malcolm has hired the most clever designers. It's the least Will owes me for all the work I have done for him lately. Trying to chat with Frau Wiesbach, wife of the German consul, over tea this morning. She barely speaks English and never reads a book or sees a play. Conversation is most trying, it's all about her ten children and shooting parties in the Black Forest. Germany sounds dreadfully dull.'

Emily thought of the slippery Herr Friedland and had to agree. 'They say Herr Wiesbach believes ties with England must be loosened if Germany is to reach her full potential.'

'Do they say that indeed?' Will said with a frown. 'You are well informed on our German friends, Em.'

'I do try to keep up with the news. We do a great deal of business with German wine merchants these days. Surely the Queen must find the treatment of her daughter in Berlin distressing?'

'I was thinking of writing an article for the *Ladies' Weekly* on Princess Vicky's charitable work, all the good she tries to do that is suppressed in her own court,' Diana said. 'But Will and Chris say I should wait, as things are quite delicate at the moment.'

'Chris thinks that?' Emily said, wondering why he thought about politics at all if he merely pushed pencils around his desk, as he claimed.

Will's eyes narrowed. 'His work does concern foreign matters, as well, whether he likes it or not.'

Emily took a quick sip of her champagne, trying to conceal her interest. 'I thought he counted pencils at a desk all day.'

'He is moving upwards,' Will said. 'My brother is far cleverer than people like to credit him. Or that he will credit himself.'

Emily knew that very well. Chris was a slippery one when he wanted to be, concealing so many things. 'I have often thought he gives himself far too little credit.'

'He is quite fond of you, too,' Diana said, with a secret little smile, and Emily remembered them teasing her about her 'courtship' at Gordston's. Was it all becoming real now?

The sitting room doors opened and Alex and Malcolm appeared. Alex wore a very stylish, Grecian-draped blue-silk gown and embroidered shawl that barely concealed her growing waistline and she glowed all golden and cream. Malcolm kept a protective touch on her shoulder. Behind them was Chris, unusually subdued in plain black and white evening dress, watching them all carefully, quietly.

Emily gulped down the last of her wine and gave them a bright smile, determined to pretend nothing was amiss. That nothing at all had changed in their little world.

At first, all went well and she even began to relax a bit among her old friends. Chris did not come near her and she was able to chat with Malcolm Gordston about their plans for more cafés in his stores. Alex's husband looked like a medieval warrior, tall and powerful, with long, dark gold hair, complete with a lovely Scottish brogue, but he was a kind and intelligent man, and a very shrewd businessman. It was just the sort of conversation to put her at ease.

But then Di was called away to see to some dinner difficulty and Alex went to play a tune at the piano to distract everyone. Emily went to follow Malcolm, when Chris gently took her hand.

She looked at him, startled, and he gave her a small, wary smile.

'Will you walk with me on the terrace for a moment, Emily?' he asked quietly.

Emily glanced across the room, but no one was paying attention to them. They were too busy drinking champagne and singing along to the piano. 'I don't…'

'Just for a quick word, please, Em,' he said and she reluctantly nodded. Otherwise, she would spend the rest of the evening not being able to look at him.

Chris offered his arm and they slipped through the glass doors on to the dimly lit terrace. Paris was spread about beyond the hotel garden, a sparkling blanket of bright windows beyond which she imagined every sort of party happening. But their terrace was silent and the marble balustrade was chilly when she leaned against it.

She steeled herself to face him. He looked very solemn in the shadows. 'Chris, we really don't need to speak of—of anything at all, really. Not here. Not anywhere, I think, and—'

'Emily,' he interrupted. She had never heard him sound quite like that before, almost stern, and it made her fall silent. He seemed to be steeling himself, too.

She swallowed hard. 'Yes?'

He reached inside his evening coat and took out a tiny velvet box.

Emily suddenly couldn't breathe. 'Is that—what I think it is?'

He opened it and she saw that it was indeed what she thought it was. A gorgeous ruby ring gleamed in the Parisian night.

'Oh, no,' she whispered.

'Just listen to me, Em,' Chris said. 'We have been

friends for a long time. We know each other well enough. Perhaps I am not exactly what you may have pictured as a husband...'

'Indeed,' she muttered.

'But I—like you. I think you like me. I would give you as much freedom as you would like, anything you want. I just—want to do the honourable thing.'

Emily stared at him in growing horror. He *liked* her? He had to do the honourable thing? This was certainly *not* the way she had ever imagined getting engaged. Especially not with Chris. Not after all they had been through.

'You like me?' she gasped. 'You want to—to be honourable?'

He frowned. 'I know everyone thinks I am a useless fribble, but I *do* have honour. I want to do the right thing for you.'

'The right thing for me is not to be married to a man who feels obligated to be with me!' She grabbed the box and snapped it closed, then shoved it back into his hand. 'I have to leave. Now.'

She ran into the drawing room before he could stop her and saw Diana coming back into the room. She ran up to her and grabbed her hand. 'I have to go, I'm sorry, Di,' Emily said quickly, gesturing to the footman to bring her cloak. She didn't dare look at her friend, Diana would see right away what was amiss.

'Emily, my dear, are you ill?' Diana asked, frowning in concern, her hand on Emily's arm. 'Let me send for Will to take you home...'

'No, I'm quite well. I just—just remembered some

business I must attend to at once,' Emily said. She took her cloak, kissed Diana's cheek and hurried out of the now oppressively cosy suite. She could only think of getting away, of trying to breathe again. She had been so caught by surprise—and she hated being surprised, hating losing control.

'What's wrong?' she heard Chris ask Diana and the sound of his voice hurried her steps to the lift. She had to get away from there.

'Em, wait!' she heard Chris call and she couldn't look back at him. She tried to outrun him, to reach the stairs, but he easily caught up with her. He caught her hand before she could duck into the stairwell.

'Please, Em, I never meant to insult you,' he said.

Emily peeked up at him. His golden hair tumbled over his brow, giving him that earnest, boyish look that always seemed to drag people into his orbit. It dragged her in, too, made her want to hold on to him and never let go. But she couldn't do that to him, to the rest of his life. Couldn't bear to see that glow in his blue eyes fade when he looked at her. 'No, of course you didn't. You said it yourself—you wanted to do the *honourable* thing.'

'Why should I not want to do the right thing by you? I care about you.'

His words were like a sharp-pointed dart to her heart. He cared about her; he was sorry for what had happened. 'And I care about you. That's why I won't ruin your life because we had one reckless moment. You always say you can't marry. We care about each other now, but we will be miserable if we come to resent each other. If we are trapped together.'

'How could we ever come to resent each other?'

'Because you will be sorry you married me! That you closed off all other possibilities in your life. And I must do my work. I don't have it in me to be happy just being a wife.'

'Please, Emily, give me a chance to try to make you happy. There are things I haven't told you about myself, things I can't talk about with anyone. But I would never stand in your way of you living your life however you wish.'

Emily was utterly confused. What did he hide from her? 'Then how could we really be happy if we can't share our full selves with each other? You think you love me as I am now, but it would soon be like other marriages, I'm sure. A woman must give up her passions for work when she has to take care of a house and family, no matter what intentions she has at the start. Surely we should just remember our time in the countryside for what it was—a happy moment?'

'But it can be more than that! Please, Em, just listen to me...'

But she couldn't, not at that moment. She was completely overwhelmed by emotions she couldn't yet understand. She shook her head and spun away to hurry around the corner and down the stairs. She heard him behind her and rushed on faster, determined he would not see her cry. Outside the hotel at last, she turned on to a quiet, narrow lane that led towards her own hotel and hoped she had left him behind, that he would give up on her now.

She was too determined to get away that she didn't

see the figure in the shadow of a deserted doorway until it was too late.

'Just listen to me,' a man's gravelly voice growled, and a hand reached out for her. Emily felt a rush of freezing cold panic—how could this be happening again? She opened her mouth to scream, tried to twist away, to kick out as Chris had taught her. A gloved hand clapped down hard over her mouth and she was dragged off the street towards the dark doorway. She jabbed back with her elbow and heard a grunt as she knocked out her attacker's breath. His hand tightened, cutting off her breath, and the world started to swim hazily around her.

'Let her go!' she heard someone shout, muffled as if down a long tunnel. She managed to twist around and saw Chris running towards her, his face full of fury.

His fist shot out and landed square in her attacker's face, right above her. He was caught by surprise at Chris's speed and stumbled back, giving her an instant to wrench free. She lurched into the street and in the chaos she saw Chris grab the man by his black coat lapels and slam him into the wall.

'Run, Em!' Chris shouted, but Emily knew she couldn't leave him. She glanced frantically down the street, searching for a *gendarme*, anyone to help. The lane was empty.

She whirled back around just in time to see the flash of light on something metallic in a gloved hand. Burning fear rushed over her.

'Chris, a knife!' she cried, but it was too late. The blade sliced down and landed in Chris's shoulder. His grasp loosened, and the attacker broke free and ran, disappearing into the night like a phantom.

But the pain he left behind was all too real. Chris fell to his knees, pressing his hand against his shoulder. He looked calm, disbelieving, as he stared down at the red seeping through his fingers.

Horrified, terrified, Emily ran to his side and knelt down next to him. She gently slid aside his hand and studied the wound. She could see little in the dim light, against his black coat, but she could see the stain spreading slowly, inexorably.

She tore off a ruffle from her gown and bound it tightly over his shoulder, but the satin and lace seemed terribly inadequate to the task. 'We need to get you to a doctor.'

Chris shook his head. He looked worryingly pale. 'I don't need a doctor. Just a bandage and a glass of brandy.'

'I think you need a great deal more than that. Here, lean on me, we'll get you back to your lodgings and then I am sending for a doctor. No arguments.' Emily slid her arm around his waist, taking some of his weight as he lurched to his feet. She tried to stay calm, not to panic, not to rush. 'This is all my fault. If I hadn't run away like a fool, if I hadn't forgotten...'

'No, Em,' Chris protested, his voice fading. They made their slow, halting way to the end of the street. 'It's only the fault of the villain chasing you. When I think it could have been *you* who got that knife...' He shook his head and even that motion seemed to weaken him. He turned even whiter.

'My father should never have asked you to protect me!'

'It was never because your father asked me, Em, you know that,' he said. 'I would do anything to keep you safe.'

He suddenly swayed against her and Emily bit back a flare of panic. They reached his lodgings, and in the hall the concierge peered out her office window.

'Here, now, we can't have blood on the floors,' she shouted.

'Send for a doctor—now!' Emily shouted back. She helped Chris slowly up the stairs and, once in his room, made him lie down on the sofa. She pulled back the makeshift bandage and his evening coat, and carefully examined the wound. It was not wide, but looked fairly deep and was still bleeding.

'Where are your cravats?' she asked. 'I need to make a better bandage and clean this up a bit. The doctor will surely need to stitch it.'

'In the second drawer over there,' he answered, sounding very far away. 'More important, the brandy bottle is on top of that table.'

Emily poured him a generous measure of the amber liquid and pressed it into his hand before she went to sort through the drawer. Beneath the piles of cravats and clean handkerchiefs, she glimpsed a tiny hint of pink. Curious, she pulled it out—and almost burst into tears at what she saw.

It was the pink ribbon from her hat that he had taken when they chased through the maze. Carefully pressed and tucked away, like it was a treasure.

Emily dashed away her tears. There was no time

for them at that moment, no time to decipher what had shifted inside her at the sight of her ribbon. She could have no fears now, no uncertainties. She just had to make sure Chris was all right, that he would recover.

Chapter Eighteen

Just as she had suspected, Chris's lodgings were not exactly as equipped as Miss Nightingale would have liked. There were no proper bandages except his own cravats and few medicines, aside from some headache powders for overindulgence, and only a lemon-scented Italian soap that reminded her of the wonderful way he always smelled when he held her.

As she inhaled its clean, citrus sharpness, she felt a wave of sadness and fear wash over her. She closed her eyes and there in the darkness she saw again the whole terrible scene. The flash of the blade, Chris falling.

What if she had lost him in that second? Until that one flashing instant, she had never realised what that could be, an earthquake chasm splitting her world in two. With Chris, the world was bright, exciting, full of possibilities. Without him, it was shadowy. A cold blank.

And it was her fault! If they hadn't quarrelled; if she hadn't been foolish. None of this would have happened.

She would never be so selfish again. She would leave

Chris to his own life, far from the chaos of her own. It was the only way. When they were together, it only meant trouble. *Delicious* trouble, sometimes, just like that perfect afternoon at the country inn. She would never forget that. But she would never let him be put in danger because of her again, either. She couldn't bear it.

Resolved, knowing she had to stay strong to get Chris safely through this crisis and then leave him, she reached for the soap and a pile of towels, plus a clean sheet she found in a cupboard, and discovered a bottle of brandy and pitcher and basin of water on the sideboard. She went back to the small sitting room to find Chris trying to sit up by himself. His face was as white as the linen, his jaw set in a hard line.

'Here, let me help you! You're going to start the bleeding again,' she cried. She ran over to take the hem of the shirt from his stained fingers. She eased it away and carefully examined the cloth she had bound around the wound earlier. It was already soaked through.

Trying to hide her panic, she tsked and said, 'See, it's bleeding again. I think you need stitches. Let me get you a bit tidied, then I'll fetch a doctor. It seems the concierge isn't going to do it.'

Chris scowled. 'Can't you do it?'

'Me? Surely you can guess my level of embroidery skill. You need a proper physician. Now, sit down before you fall over.'

Emily spread the clean sheet over the sofa and plumped a few pillows behind his back to help make him a bit more comfortable before she took a closer look. He took a deep swallow of the brandy.

She dabbed at the wound with the dampened cloth, clearing away some of the dried blood so she could see it clearly. Luckily, it did not look too deep, but it was still oozing blood, and she feared it could become infected. 'Oh, Chris,' she whispered. 'I can never tell you how sorry I am. If I wasn't so impetuous…'

'Em. Em, no.' He reached out and caught her face between his hands. When she looked up at him, everything blurring through her tears, his golden hair like a halo, his expression was so worried. His touch was so tender, light as a feather on her skin, as he brushed away her tears with his thumbs. 'Don't you know I would do anything to make sure *you* are safe? You deserve to walk free, *run* free in the world. I would do anything to make that for you. Go through any danger.'

'But you shouldn't have to! You have your own lovely life to lead. The Moulin de la Galette, the races—you should never have to worry about me.'

'But without you, my life is no fun at all. I never danced like I do with you before, never saw Paris the way we do together. I see things I never could before and I—I have to tell you…'

He suddenly swayed, his face turning grey, and Emily felt a rush of fear. 'No more talking, Chris. Lie down, let me clean this up and then I am going to get a doctor, no arguments.'

'Will you stay with me until I sleep?' he murmured, reaching for her hand. 'I am sure I won't bleed to death any time soon.'

Emily smiled at him gently. 'I will sit with you for a while, if you promise not to worry, or exert yourself.'

She washed the wound as carefully and gently as she could, trying not to cry out when she saw the fresh blood. She tore a strip from the towel and wrapped the makeshift bandage over his shoulder, tying it tightly before she mixed up a dose of the headache powder for him.

'Hopefully this will take some of the edge off the pain before help can get here,' she said. Morning light was beginning to appear at the window. 'Just lie still, try to sleep. I won't be gone long at all.'

'Em...' His eyes were already a bit blurry, but his hand was strong when it grasped hers. 'You cannot go out alone.'

'I have to! It's light outside now. I will stay on the busy streets and watch very carefully. I won't be so foolish again, I promise.' She pressed a kiss to his forehead, worryingly warm now. 'Just sleep, my darling.'

'There's an umbrella with a sharp tip by the door,' he murmured, his eyes closing. 'Take it with you.'

'I will.' While she still had the strength to leave his side, she tucked the blankets tightly around him, snatched up the umbrella and hurried down the stairs. True to her word, she studied the crowds carefully as she went, but all she could see were bleary-eyed gentlemen heading home. No one who looked suspicious at all, but surely he was long gone now.

Once she found the physician's office, which was just opening for the day, and sent him back to Chris, she found herself suddenly shaking, as if all the strength that sent her dashing through the streets drained out of her. She made her way to a bench in the shade of a beech tree, near where a noisy group of children on their way to school chased the birds, and sat down with a long sigh. She let the sadness and worry wash over her.

She remembered again that split-second moment of the attack. The tall, shadowy figure appearing out of nowhere. Chris—who fought most skilfully for a man who liked to play the dilettante.

She frowned as she thought back over it all. Surely something was strange in that scene. Surely Chris, as she had long suspected, was so much more than he wanted anyone to believe.

But how had it all led them *here*, to this moment? Why were they surrounded by so much danger? Who was after them?

She glanced around at the passers-by, suspicious, tense, about all the world around her. It was only nannies and their charges, a few businessmen, ladies going on their calls, but she felt cold, unsteady, most unlike herself.

She stood up, clutching tightly at the umbrella handle, and turned towards Chris's street. A group of men in their sombre, dark professional suits and bowler hats pulled low waited to cross at the corner. Among them, she glimpsed one familiar face. James Hertford. Just like at the races, the Moulin de la Galette.

And on his cheek was a long, red scratch.

'No,' she whispered.

His eyes widened as he glimpsed her and Emily spun around to run away before he could cross the street. The scratch could be coincidence, of course, yet some icy feeling deep inside told her it wasn't. He had been so attentive to her in the last few months, had appeared at so many places. Could he really be her insistent suitor? Chris's attacker?

She found herself at the corner of a quiet, wide, prosperous lane, lined with fine shops and apartments. It was quite a long walk back to Chris's lodgings, but she knew what *was* nearby. The Foreign Office post where Will worked, and Chris, too, as he claimed. Surely she would be safe there and maybe even find some answers.

She ignored the clerk who called out, *'Mademoiselle, non!'*

'I am looking for Monsieur Blakely,' she answered, running up the gilded stairs. 'Or Lord Ellersmere. Anyone!'

'Perhaps I could help?' a gentle voice said from one of the office doorways.

Emily looked up from the landing and to her surprise saw Lady Smythe-Tomas standing there. She was as stylish as ever, in a purple-velvet walking suit, amethysts glinting in her ears, but her face was very serious. Not even curious to see a dishevelled, blood-stained lady racing through the silent, elegant building.

'Chris has been hurt,' Emily blurted. 'And I think I know who did it. But I am not sure why.'

Lady Smythe-Tomas smiled. 'You had better come in, then, Miss Fortescue. Should I send our physician to Christopher?'

'No, I have sent one already. He was sleeping when I left him.' She went through the door Lady Smythe-Tomas held open, feeling rather dazed. 'Do you work here, too, Lady Smythe-Tomas?'

'Oh, Laura, please. We do know each other quite well now, don't we?' She sat down behind a carved Louis XV desk, piled with papers, and indicated a velvet armchair across from her. Emily dropped down on to it gratefully. 'And I only have an office here when I need it. A base, if you will. My real task is wherever it may find me.'

'You are not just a professional beauty.'

Laura laughed. 'Those photographs do make me a penny here and there, which a widow always needs, but, no, it is not my only job. It's a useful front. Like with your Christopher, as I am sure you have guessed.'

Emily had guessed, but the knowledge of it was still startling. She had always thought she knew Chris so well. 'I think you had best tell me what is really happening.'

'I think so, too.' Laura went to a small table near the window and poured them two cups of tea from the silver service laid out there. A 'base' it might be, but obviously a comfortable one. 'I have worked for this office for a few years now, travelling around, meeting people at house parties and embassy balls, things like that. Herr Friedland claims he represents Crown Princess Victoria in Germany, but of course we know that can't be true. We keep a close eye on the Princess and her court, as her mother does rather worry about her there. And of course, the *herr* and his contact, Madame Renard, needed watching. It turns out they were indeed trying to find information about the Princess on behalf of her son. Kaiser Wilhelm is a dreadful character, one who we fear will make trouble for England one day. Mrs Hurst has many contacts and they were hoping to use her to gain access to some of them, especially in the naval office. Kaiser Wilhelm seems especially interested in expanding Germany's sea power. I am sorry I could not tell you all this before, but I do assure you that the League in London is a legitimate, and very important, organisation.

'Now,' Laura said with a sigh, 'do tell me what happened last night and where Christopher is.'

Her head spinning, Emily told her about the attack in the street, though not the foolish way she had run away from Diana's hotel, and her suspicions of James Hertford. 'But I don't know if he has anything to do with this plot, or is just a disappointed suitor who has, shall we say, overreacted.'

Laura shook her head. 'Mr Hertford has been in our sights for a while. He is in terrible debt and such men can be dangerous when they are desperate and foreign agents approach them.'

'So he has probably been courting me so ardently for my money.' Emily thought back, trying to think of any signs of trouble she might have missed. She had probably overlooked them since he was once so kind about the embarrassing incident of Mr Hamilton. 'He seemed nice. He helped me once when I needed it.'

'And he probably thinks you owe him for ever now. Such men often do.' She tapped her fingers on the desk and gave a brisk smile. 'Well, he will soon be taken care of. I should find William, I think he is in the office now, and then I will take him see to our young Sir Lancelot. You need not worry any longer, Miss Fortescue. Let me call you a carriage to take you back to your hotel. You must be exhausted.'

Emily nodded, but she knew very well her worrying days were far from over.

'You are sure it's Hertford?' Chris demanded from Laura. His head was still fuzzy from the medicine the doctor had given him and his shoulder ached like burning devils, but it was nothing to his anger. He tried to push himself up, but the pain made him gasp.

'Oh, do be careful, Christopher, the doctor says you must rest,' she whispered, glancing at the door as if the torturing, bossy man with his needles and scissors was lurking. But he was talking with Will in the corridor and for the moment Chris was alone with Laura. She had just had time to tell him quickly about Emily's suspicions of Hertford and the fact that Em had gone safely back to her hotel in an Office carriage.

That bastard Hertford. It was always the quiet, meek ones who were such trouble. Chris would skewer him, roast him alive for hurting Emily.

'Of course we don't know for certain yet, but I am setting some of our best men on it this afternoon,' she said, plumping up his pillows and jostling his shoulder. She really was a terrible nurse. 'But we know he *has* been in contact with the Germans, thanks to our information on Herr Friedland. He has sizeable debts he's eager to keep secret. I'm sure he thought marriage to a rich heiress like Miss Fortescue would help. And men such as him don't like to take no for an answer.'

'Quite so,' Chris said grimly. 'I will take care of it.' He shoved back the blankets.

'Not right now, you won't,' Laura said, again batting him down with her bejewelled hand. 'You must recover your strength first, you're no good to any of us this way.' Her glance softened as she smiled at him. 'You really were very gallant. You must care about her a great deal.'

Chris thought of Emily, her laughter in the sunshine of their country idyll, the light on her chestnut hair. 'Very much.'

Laura sighed. 'Then she is lucky. She really is a most intelligent lady, you know. She could be very useful to the Office.'

'Certainly not,' Chris said fiercely. He wouldn't let her put herself in danger ever again.

Laura's eyes narrowed. 'If you think so, though I do wish you would consider asking her. She is smart, perceptive. Just think about it. And in the meantime, don't do anything reckless. So many people rely on you.' She laid her hand gently on his arm and leaned closer. 'I also think you need to tell her more about your own work. She cares about you and she can be trusted. It's a rare and enviable thing.'

'Is everything well?' Emily asked softly. 'I'm sorry, but I had to come look in on you. Will and the doctor say you will recover.'

Chris glanced up to find her standing in the doorway, freshly dressed in a blue-and-white-striped walking suit and veiled hat, her face pale and worried, but so, so beautiful. The loveliest thing he had ever seen.

Laura smiled brightly and stood up to pull on her

gloves. 'Quite well, my dear. I was just admonishing the patient to follow doctor's orders. No dancing yet.'

'I will make sure he does,' Emily said.

'Then Will and I shall call again later and have some provisions sent over from Gordston's food hall,' Laura said. 'Caviar does wonders to strengthen the blood! Goodbye, my dears.'

After Laura and Will left, Emily straightened the bedclothes around Chris and sat down beside him. She did look beautiful, but also tired, worried, and Chris hated that he was the one who had done that to her. His strong, wonderful Emily.

He also wasn't sure where to start in telling her the truth, how much to tell her. How much she would hate him after. 'I suppose you know now that my work is not just sitting behind a desk,' he blurted.

Emily gave him a weary smile. 'I gathered as much from Lady Smythe-Tomas. But I don't really understand.'

He gently took her hand in his. It didn't feel soft and delicate like other ladies' hands. Her fingers were long, elegant, strong, with ink-stained tips and a few light calluses along the edge of her palm, as if she was no stranger to moving a crate of wine or a bale of silk if needed. Just like Emily herself. Strong, independent, smart, serious. All the things he had always admired about her. She was always, unabashedly, herself.

She was like him in so many ways, wanting to use what talents they had to make the world a better place. But his job involved danger, too. When it was only himself, it didn't matter. Emily was an entirely different matter. He had to protect her at all costs. Chris knew that her father felt in a very similar way, as did their friends. Emily was special and the thought of the world without her was unbearable. He had thought he had to keep her away to keep her safe.

Chris saw so clearly now that he had been very wrong to think that. Emily could bear anything, understand anything, overcome anything. And that was why she was so wonderful.

'When I left university,' he said, not daring to look up into her eyes. If he did that, he would be lost. 'I had no idea what I wanted to do. Will was already well on his way at the Foreign Office, but I was young and foolish and had no patience for his sort of work.'

Emily gave a wry little smile, as if she understood his old impulsiveness, but she said nothing.

'I had no discipline for the military,' he went on. 'My father suggested the church, as he had an uncle who would assist me to a living, but I am no good at sermons, either.'

'I dare say all the ladies in the congregation would be in love with you, anyway,' Emily said. 'You would be quite distracting.'

Chris laughed. 'Perhaps that would have been the only perk of the job? I suppose there could always have been a tea plantation in India. But I went a bit wild for a time, was quite aimless.'

'So then what happened?'

'I had a visit from Lord Ellersmere, Will's superior at the Office. He had heard that I had a knack for making friends rather easily...'

'Which you certainly do.'

'It never seems like a career skill, though, does it? But I discovered that when people like someone, they tend to spill their secrets. And some secrets are very valuable indeed.'

Emily frowned at him. She looked adorable even then. 'Have you been discovering *my* secrets all this time, then?'

'I wish I could. I want to know *everything* about you. Though I doubt your secrets are quite the sort the Foreign Office is interested in.'

'What sorts are those?'

'Sorts of people who are not as devoted to Queen and country as they should be. It was useful to play the silly wastrel, the flirt, the one who pays no attention to anything but his cravats and the next pretty woman.'

Emily stared down at their joined hands for a long, silent moment. 'I have always known there was more to you than that. You just seemed so insistent that there was *not*.'

He squeezed her hand tightly. 'I know that. You always see too much. That was why I always had to be more careful with you than anyone else.' He remembered their first kiss, in the sunlight at the lake at Miss Grantley's, and how it had shaken his whole world. How nothing had really been the same since then. 'And right now, it's important that Friedland doesn't realise we know he is working with Kaiser Wilhelm rather than the Crown Princess. Germany poses many dangers to England. But I've been good at my job until now and have enjoyed it. But lately…'

'Lately?'

'A man can't do such work for ever. I see what Di and Will have, the security, the friendship, their partnership, and I—I don't know what to do next. I shall have to think very hard about my work once we leave Paris.'

Emily sighed. 'You and me both. I know my father worries about me and worries about how I will run the business alone. I suppose I worry, too, I just never want to admit it. I also look at Di and Will, and Alex and Malcolm, and I feel—sad.'

They stared at each other for a long, tense moment, not speaking, but sharing so much only in that look. So much understanding. So many things beyond words. Chris kissed her hand, inhaling the sweetness of her perfume, wishing that moment could last for ever.

She pressed a gentle kiss to his forehead and moved away. 'You should get some rest, Chris. You need your sleep. I'll stay here for a while, but no more talking, yes?' She tucked the blankets close around him, looking rather sad, rather far away.

He took her hand again, just for a moment. 'Em— don't worry about Hertford any longer. He will never bother you again.'

She shook her head, her brow creased with a worried frown. 'Chris, if you think…'

'No, I won't hurt him. Just—let me help you, Em. For once in your life, just let someone help you. Let someone care about you.'

She said nothing, but she gave him a gentle smile. 'Only if you will do the same. Now, get some sleep. You must heal and rest will help. I will stay with you.'

He didn't want to close his eyes, didn't want to lose her, but he was indeed feeling very tired. Everything that had happened, the doctor's medicines, it was all catching up to him. He nodded, and closed his eyes, holding on to Emily as he drifted into the darkness.

Emily sat and watched Chris as he slept, not even noticing the light turning pink and pale beyond the window, hearing the voices and clatter of carriage wheels from the street below. She only saw Chris, how young he looked while asleep, how free from the cares he had borne all alone for so long. Like a carefree, golden god, resting in his bower.

She smoothed the blankets around him and felt an overwhelming wave of something she would never have thought to feel for Chris. Tenderness. It was the sweetest, saddest, most astounding thing she could ever have imagined.

She had always prided herself on her independence. She had to be. She had no mother, no siblings, she had to find her own way in the world. She had never felt quite like other girls, except for Di and Alex. It was one reason she had rejected every suitor who presented himself to her, who her father suggested. None of them understood her. None of them had what she imagined she would need in a partner. What she dreamed of. Someone who knew and accepted her for who she really was.

Now she saw that, in truth, none of the men had been Christopher.

Even when Chris seemed so light-hearted, flirtatious, careless, hardly a man she could make a proper life with—there had always been something about him. Something she couldn't quite forget, let go of.

Now she knew why that was. Chris was an actor, a consummate actor, but her business training, her dealings with men of every sort, negotiating contracts, reading the market, had given her her own instincts for people. For when they would make a deal and when they wouldn't. The way Chris would sometimes look at her—watchful, serious. The conversations they would have, his quick wit, his power of observation. The way he could fight when attacked. None of it had quite added up and that had always fascinated Emily as much as it puzzled her.

It was all because Chris was a spy.

He muttered in his sleep, and she whispered softly to him until he quieted again. He looked so angelic in his sleep. No wonder he could fool people into trusting him with dangerous secrets.

He had been willing to sacrifice so much for his country. Society loved him for his fun ways, but they didn't respect him as they did his brother. She understood the feeling of being underestimated. Many men didn't want to make business deals with a woman. But Chris was brave in a way she could barely imagine.

Emily suddenly realised something horrible, wonderful, terrifying. She loved Chris Blakely. Loved his fun, his laughter, his courage, his discretion. Everything about him. And maybe she had ever since the first time she saw him in the garden at Miss Grantley's, so long ago. Who would have imagined it when her father proposed a false courtship in Paris?

But what good could it ever do either of them? Their lives were so very different. Yet there it was. Her most secret heart. And she feared that would never change. She would never love anyone but him.

'Em?' she heard him whisper hoarsely.

She looked down at him with a gentle smile, hoping he would never see her secret. 'I'm right here. Don't worry about a thing.'

He smiled back. 'That should be my line to *you*.'

'Oh, Chris.' She kissed his forehead. 'I think that is for both of us...'

Chapter Nineteen

'Oh, yes, he is still here,' the concierge of James Hertford's lodgings told Chris when he enquired at her grilled window. 'Though he owes me for the rest of the month, that was the agreement, and he won't pay up. He says he is going to fetch his lady friend and leave today!'

Chris handed her a pile of bank notes, afraid that the 'lady friend' the villain was going to fetch was Em. He thought of her sweet tenderness as she nursed him back to health, the sadness and fear he had seen in her eyes even as she tried to hide it, and that made him even more angry. 'I hope this will cover his rent, *madame*. And any damages.'

'Damages!' she cried, but Chris had already started up the stairs. The door at the top of the building was open.

'I'm surprised you haven't already decamped to England, Hertford,' Chris said, watching the man creep towards the stairs with his valise. It felt strangely as if he watched the scene from a distance. His anger at Hertford had been burning so hot as he waited to recover enough to confront him, as he turned over and over in his mind the thought of how Hertford had treated Emily. Now that anger had turned icy cold and that made it burn even more.

Hertford spun around, his case clattering to the floor. In the dim light of the corridor, Chris could see the wild shock on the man's face, his pale, clammy skin and the dilated, frightened pupils of his eyes. Like most bullies, it seemed Hertford was a rank coward. It seemed he knew Ellersmere's office was on to him and now he was fleeing like a rat. But not before he had terrified Emily.

'Surprised to see me, are you?' Chris said, leaning against the railing with his old, insouciant carelessness. 'Or perhaps you were expecting someone else?'

James's eyes narrowed and he seemed to collect himself, standing up straighter. 'What are you doing here, Blakely? Visiting a paramour? I'm not surprised. Some people have no appreciation for the better things in the world.'

Chris remembered how Hertford had seen him with Emily at the Moulin de la Galette. Had it set off his jealousy? 'You never did deserve her. Your behaviour could only ever have driven her away.'

Hertford's face twisted in fury. 'She never even saw me! I, who loved her, who would have cherished her. I would have given her everything…'

'Except what she needs. Love, security, freedom. When were you going to tell her you had lost everything to bad debts? Lost even your honour? Were you going to live off the Fortescue money, once your German pay-off was gone?'

'What do you know of that?' Hertford cried furiously.

Chris realised he had done the cardinal sin in his work—revealing too much to his target. But he did not care. 'I am not the fool you take me for. Leave her alone, for good and all—or we will be having a very different conversation.'

Hertford dropped his case, glancing back as if desperate to find a way out. But they were on the top floor and there was no escape. 'What are you going to do, Blakely? I demand to know!'

Chris was disgusted by the man's desperation, disgusted by what that and his unrequited passion for Emily had driven him to—and Chris feared he might once have been the same. But no longer. He couldn't even look at the man for another moment, couldn't stand what he had done, what he was. He would be gone soon, no longer a threat to Emily or anyone else. Chris would make sure of that.

He half-turned away, but Hertford suddenly lunged at him, catching him on the jaw with an unexpected blow. Though Chris ducked, and the punch only clipped him, it sent him reeling back against the wall. The blow released all the burning, barely leashed fury, and he let it all fly free. He reached out and grabbed Hertford by his coat, slamming him back against the door. He held him pinned there with all the strength he possessed, all the strength his anger gave him. He didn't feel the wound in his shoulder.

'You frightened a lady, stalked her, and you declare it is because you *love* her?' Chris said coldly, merely tightening his hold as Hertford tried to twist away. 'That is nothing but being a damnable villain. You aren't fit to touch her fingertips.'

'And *you* are worthy of her? You're nothing but a brawler, a rogue, Blakely, a nobody!' Hertford kicked Chris, driving him back, but only for a moment. Chris remembered all his training, the moves he had tried to teach Emily in their country inn and came back with a right uppercut that sent Hertford crashing to the floor.

All the fury came pouring out of him as the corridor rang with shouts, curses. All his longing for Emily, his need to be a good man, that raw anger when he learned she was being threatened, his yearning to protect her, came out in the primitive rush of a good fight.

This man would never be allowed to hurt Emily again. Nothing would ever hurt her again. Not even Chris himself.

'Christopher! Stop this,' a woman suddenly shouted.

Through the red, misty haze of anger, he heard the pounding of footsteps up the stairs, shouts and cries, the landlady sobbing about the blood on her floors. Two pairs of fists seized him and pulled him off Hertford, who collapsed to the floor with a rough sob.

Chris spun around, ready to fight even more opponents—only to fall back when he saw it was Ellersmere and two of his men, obviously come to seize Hertford. Laura stood behind them, watching the scene with a gleeful smile, as if she was at the Comédie-Française.

'Oh, I saw, Christopher, well done,' she said. 'You stopped him fleeing! I'm sure he would have been gone before we arrived. But I am afraid you are rather bleeding all over the floor.'

Chris looked down and saw that his shoulder wound had indeed opened and was bleeding through his shirt and coat. The pain he hadn't noticed at all in the heat of the moment rushed back on to him, and he laughed. There seemed nothing else to be done.

'Here, m'boy, hold this against it good and tight and you'll feel back to new in no time,' Lord Ellersmere said, handing Chris a block of ice wrapped in towelling, along with a large glass of brandy. 'It always helped me in my younger days.'

Chris nodded and pressed the towel to his bruised jaw. It was evening now, Ellersmere's office bathed in the golden light of a Parisian sunset. Laura had left for an evening at the opera, after rebandaging his wound and lecturing him on not trying to recreate a *Musketeers* novel, and now Chris was alone with Ellersmere in the dimly lit velvet splendour of the office. He felt aching, sore—and triumphant. Em was safe.

'Well done on preventing Hertford from taking a runner,' Ellersmere said, sitting down behind his desk. 'Now we can ask him more about the German mess. William has gone to fetch Friedland, as well, we shall soon know all, and the ambassador in Berlin is to call on Princess Victoria and warn her. Couldn't have finished it all up so neatly without you.'

'I don't think that is true, Lord Ellersmere.' His work

had only put Emily in more danger. He didn't think it was so 'neatly' done.

'Of course it's true. You have always done a fine job for us, Blakely, better all the time.' Ellesmere poured out more brandy. 'Have you thought any more about what we spoke of in London? Changing your career direction?'

'St Petersburg, you mean?'

'Yes. The embassy there needs a man like you. And a change could be good for you. Lots of quarrels in drawing rooms, of course, but few brawls.'

Chris thought about it. A post, a real post, in an important embassy like St Petersburg would indeed make him look rather different in society's eyes. Maybe make him seem worthy of a serious lady like Emily. And he had shown himself that the world without her was a bleak place. Did he dare hope at all? 'I confess something more—overt might suit me now.'

Ellersmere nodded. 'We aren't as young as we once were, eh? The place is yours, if you want it. Give it some thought.' He took a thoughtful sip of his drink. 'Laura tells me there is a young lady you have been seen about with lately.'

'I admit I am fond of someone.'

'Good, good. If she is the *right* sort of lady, that is. A man in a place like St Petersburg needs a wife. Someone like my own Lady E., with style and good sense. Someone to make contacts, entertain for you. Hear things, as only ladies in an embassy can do. Is she like that?'

Chris thought of Emily, her poise, her elegance, her

smile, her business sense. But would she ever give up what she had to be an embassy lady? 'She is most certainly like that.'

'Excellent! Now, have some more of this brandy, it's good stuff, and then go home and get some rest. You are going to need it.'

As Chris stepped out on to the street, he saw to his astonishment that the day was going on just as any normal day would. The sun shone, a rare, bright gold in a lapis sky that shimmered on the grey roofs of Paris. Windows were open to the fresh breeze that rippled through the window boxes of red, bright pink and yellow flowers that matched the passing ladies' hats. Children dashed past with their hoops and skipping ropes, laughing, making him want to smile, too.

He was sure he floated in the clouds above the whole city, the whole world. Everything had changed.

Once, he had been sure that the only thing to do, the strong thing to do, would be to let Emily go. Once the danger to her had passed, that her stalker had been found, she would not need him any longer. And he would spend his life missing her. Their false courtship would be at an end.

Everything was so different now. He would have a proper career, a place to offer her in the real world. And he would not have to face how empty and useless that career, that life, would be without her.

He had to make her happy. He knew he could make her happy, if she would just give him a chance. If she would just let him try.

Chris turned a corner and suddenly caught sight of

himself reflected in a shop window. His hair stood on end, his clothes were disordered, his shoulder stained with blood. He laughed ruefully. One thing was for certain. He could never go truly courting if he looked like *that*.

Chapter Twenty

'I'm not sure there is room for all of these, Miss Emily,' Mary said, as she tried to stuff hats into their boxes.

'I know, I bought far too many of them,' Emily said with a sigh. 'I'm sure we can find room in some of the trunks for them.'

Mary studied the rows of travel trunks, layered with new Worth gowns in tissue paper, with a frown. 'I hope so. It will be nice to be home, won't it, miss?'

'Yes, of course,' Emily answered, but she wasn't at all sure. Her usual energy seemed to have deserted her over the last few days. She'd finished her business for her father satisfactorily and profitably, but in the end it had not interested her as it usually did. She spent time with Alex at her villa in Versailles, rode in the park with Diana, laughed and smiled, went to the shops, but it all felt so—distant. So strange. Not like her own life at all.

She had heard from Lady Smythe-Tomas that Chris was recovering well and that relieved her mind very much. Yet she hadn't seen him, hadn't received a letter from him, and missing him was an ache that never seemed to leave her.

Chris had been part of her life for so long, part of her thoughts and emotions. Someone who always made her laugh. Who understood her as no one else ever had. Now he was just—not there. And it was too quiet and dull without him. The work that had sustained her for so long was simply not enough to fill that void.

When she was alone at night, she couldn't sleep at all. She sat in the window, staring out at the lights of Paris, turning it all over and over in her mind. Dancing under the stars; walking the streets and parks with Chris; making love as the rain fell beyond their cosy sanctuary, and they were the only two people in the world. Those moments had been so beautiful, so perfect. And now it was all over.

Now he had sent her away.

Emily reached for a box on the table, then put it down without really seeing it. She could only see Chris's face as he told her they couldn't see each other again. The way his eyes looked…

Something about it all was not right. Emily knew now what a good actor Chris really was, what had always lain behind his careless ways. He had even fooled her for so long, as well as his parents. Had he been fooling her in that moment, too? But why?

There was only one thing for it, only one way she could move forward. She would just have to find him, *make* him talk to her. Tell her the truth. Surely he owed her that much? Surely she meant *something* to him, after everything that had happened?

She wished she knew for sure. Nothing had ever made her feel so full of life as being with Chris had and nothing felt so empty now that he was gone. She hated that feeling.

There was a knock at the suite door. 'That's probably the porters, finally,' Mary said irritably. 'And we aren't even finished yet!' She hurried out to the sitting room.

Emily heard the low murmur of voices and after a moment Mary returned, a puzzled look on her face.

'Will they come back later, then?' Emily asked.

'It's not the porters, Miss Emily,' Mary said. 'It's Mr Blakely. Mr *Christopher* Blakely. And he says it's urgent.'

Emily felt a surge of hope, of happiness, as if her longing had summoned Chris to her. 'Thank you, Mary,' she said, surprised she could keep her voice steady. 'Tell him I will be there in a moment.'

She glanced in the mirror and smoothed her hair. She wished she wore something more elaborate, more fashionable, than her lavender morning dress, but what would be the right attire for demanding answers? How should she look, behave? What could she say?

She half-wanted to refuse to see him, to hide behind her trunks like a coward. But she knew she could never do that. Hadn't she just determined she had to find him, talk to him, settle things between them before she could move forward? And now here he was. Yet she had no idea what to say.

It wouldn't get any easier, she knew that. So she smoothed her skirt, patted her hair into place and marched out into the sitting room.

Chris wore an immaculate grey morning suit, his gloves and silk hat in hand, his golden hair brushed to a sunny shine, but a bruise still marred his cheek. His eyes were very blue, unreadable as they sky, as he looked at her and bowed.

'You're getting ready to leave?' he said, gesturing to the boxes piled around.

'Yes,' Emily answered. 'My business is finished here, so it's time to go home. I'm sure that will be true for you, as well, now that your business has been concluded.'

'Soon enough. Hertford is being sent back to London under guard. I'm sure you'll be glad to know he won't be stalking anyone else. The Foreign Office has many questions for him, especially about the Friedland business. It seems he was in the pay of the German on top of everything else.'

Emily twisted her hands in her skirt, hesitating, but then she plunged ahead. 'Chris, why didn't you tell me the truth sooner, about your work? I thought we were friends.'

'Oh, we are, Em. The best of friends.' He put his hat down on the table, taking a step towards her. His hand raised as if he would reach for her. 'I couldn't tell you. It was my job and I never wanted to put you in danger. Of course, none of it ended up as I intended.'

'Put me in danger?' Something dawned inside of her, some glimmer of truth. 'Oh, Chris. That is why you sent me away, isn't it? That is just like you! Trying to protect everyone.'

Chris gave her crooked little smile. 'I only wanted

to do what was best for you. Take care of you. But I've been so miserable. I haven't the strength to stay away any longer.'

'You—don't?' she whispered.

'No.' He reached out and took her hand, gently, warmly, almost as if he was afraid she would pull away. 'Em, I can never say I am sorry enough for the way I behaved, telling you to go away. I thought it was for the best, but now I know it can't be. I can't stop thinking about you, can't stop missing you.'

'Oh, Chris,' Emily sobbed. Relief and wonder washed over her, overwhelming her. 'I have missed you, too, you ridiculously gallant man!'

'You have?'

'Of course!' To prove it, Emily threw her arms around him and went up on tiptoe to press her lips to his, in a sweet, wild, wonderful kiss she wished would never end. And, the best part of all, he kissed her back, as if he would never let her go.

When at last they parted, laughing, holding hands, he drew her down to sit beside him on the chaise. 'I'm being sent off to a diplomatic post in St Petersburg— an official one, this time. I'm told I should find a suitable wife to help me.'

'Is that why you've come here, then? Because you need a presentable wife to make your way in the diplomatic world?' Emily teased.

He laughed, his whole face lit up like a summer's day. It was a wonder to see it, after the last time she was with him and had been so fearful for his life. 'Because I need *you*, Em. If you will have me. I know you have your own work, but surely St Petersburg would be full of useful contacts for your father's business?'

'And Russian ladies who want to hear about women's rights? I am sure you are right. Embassy tea parties and all.'

He stared deeply, earnestly into her eyes. 'So—you will marry me?'

'You haven't asked me yet. Not for real, that is.'

Chris laughed, and slid off the *chaise* to kneel at her feet, her hands held tightly between his. 'Emily Fortescue. Will you do me the very, very great honour of forgetting my foolishness and agreeing to be my wife?'

Emily laughed, yet she knew she was crying all at the same time. She had never dreamed such a moment could come and now it was there, real. Her own, real life. 'Oh, yes! Yes, I will.'

Chris took her in his arms again and the Parisian sun shone on them, promising a bright and fair future, no matter where the world took them.

Epilogue

A few months later

'Oh, Em. You look absolutely beautiful.' Alex finished adjusting Emily's lace-edged tulle veil, anchored with a tiara of diamonds and pearls, smoothed the sleeve of her ecru satin and lace gown from Worth. She stepped back with a satisfied smile at her handiwork, as florists, hairdressers and caterers rushed around outside the dressing room, all intent on their urgent errands.

Baby Florence Emily Diana Gordston slept in her little pink basket, oblivious to the grandeur of the day.

'Surely the most beautiful bride ever,' Alex added, twitching at the diagonal swathe of tulle across the fashionably narrow satin skirt.

Emily laughed, feeling positively giddy at all the excitement of her wedding day. 'I doubt that. *You* were like an angel at your wedding.'

Alex shook her head. 'No. I know I am right. You are glowing like the sun. Go and look in the glass.'

Alex, the hairdresser and the dressmaker who made

sure her hem was straight had forbidden Emily to examine herself before that moment. She spun towards the looking glass and peeked cautiously, hoping she did look worthy of the handsome groom who waited for her.

'Oh, Alex,' she whispered. 'You have worked wonders.' She had ordered many gowns from Worth before, of course, yet never quite like this one. The creamy satin gleamed like her mother's triple strand of pearls at her throat, and the tulle and lace trim made it look like a cloud. Her hair, done by the French hairdresser from Gordston's own salon, was curled and piled high, covered with her lacy veil and the sparkle of the tiara that was her father's wedding gift. The tulle-edged train swirled behind her. It was like a dream dress.

'I found the bouquet!' came a triumphant cry and Diana hurried in, bearing a fragrant creation of white roses and gardenias. With all the towering arrangements in silver vases to set up around the house, the smaller bridal bouquet had gone missing. The florist had been nearly in hysterics, but sensible, organised Di had saved the day.

'Wherever was it?' Alex asked.

'Behind the crab cakes on the wedding breakfast buffet, if you can believe it.' Diana paused to coo down at baby Florence, holding the flowers away from grasping little fingers. Di had confided her own happy secret only that morning—she was at last expecting a baby and the pregnancy seemed healthy. The precious bump was barely visible under her rose-pink silk gown.

She handed the bouquet to Emily and gave her a

hug, a careful one when Alex cried out a protest against crushing all the satin and tulle. 'Oh, Em, I can't believe it,' Diana cried. 'Now we will be truly Blakely sisters together. I shall have an ally at dinners with the in-laws!'

'What about me?' Alex protested with a laugh. 'Am I not a sister just because I am a Gordston?'

'Of course you are,' Diana declared stoutly. 'You are just lucky to have no in-laws at all.'

Emily had to giggle as she buried her nose in the summertime scent of her bouquet. Fortunately, there would be few Blakely family dinners in the near future. She and Chris were soon to leave for St Petersburg, where he would take up his new, official post—no more hiding his work. She would expand her father's business in the new, eastern markets, and one day she and Chris would return to London to take over all the firm's work. Her father would join them in Russia for a long visit, after his own sojourn in Switzerland. Everything seemed to be falling into place for her family.

She drew Alex and Diana closer to her sides and studied the three of them in the mirror. Di, with her vivid red hair, angelic Alex in her pistachio-green taffeta, her own bridal finery. How far they had come since their school days! How lucky they were to have each other.

'Sisters for ever,' she said and blinked hard to keep from bursting into tears. She could never have imagined such happiness as that washing over her now. Her dearest friends all together; her love waiting for her downstairs. All the deception, all the danger, past and gone. A bright new day waiting for all of them.

'We should go now, or we'll be quite late,' Diana said. 'You should have seen all the guests crowding in while I was downstairs!'

'And you can't keep your handsome bridegroom waiting.' Alex laughed.

'Yes, let's hurry,' Emily said. She could hardly wait for that bright new day to begin.

Alex straightened Emily's train and made sure the nanny was with Florence before she and Diana led Emily towards the staircase. A special licence had been obtained to allow Chris and Emily to marry at her father's home and the whole house was filled with the fragrance of flowers. Garlands of white roses and silver satin bows wound along the staircase banisters and silver vases filled with more roses and gardenias made pathways through the hall towards the open drawing-room doors.

Emily could hear music, the sweet strains of a string quartet and the laughter of the guests gathered there. Lady Smythe-Tomas was one of the last going inside, her pink-feathered hat bright against the pale flowers. She waved merrily up at Emily before taking the arm of her handsome young escort and sweeping away.

Emily's father waited at the foot of the stairs for her. He had gained some weight recently and his eyes were brighter, healthier. And there was no mistaking the happiness and pride in his smile. 'My dearest girl,' he said, his voice thick with tears as he took her hand. 'How beautiful you are. Just like your mother.'

Emily tried not to start crying herself. 'I am sure she watches us today.'

'She is always with us. She walks with us right now.'

The drawing-room doors opened one last time and a fanfare of music burst out. Alex and Diana hurried to their seats with their own husbands near the front of the room, waving at the distinguished guests—a prince, some dukes and Lord and Lady Ellersmere from Chris's office. The room was crowded with colour and flowers.

But the only person Emily could see waited for her at the rose-bedecked altar. Surely Chris had never looked as handsome, as wonderful, as he did in that moment. Her golden god in his brocade waistcoat, his bright hair shining, tears shimmering in his eyes as he saw her entrance. The man who had opened the whole world to her, a world of fun and hope and brightness, of making a difference in the world. They would never be alone again. They would see new countries together, make a whole new family.

And she was quite sure that life with Chris would never, ever be boring.

Her father gently placed her hand in Chris's and the archbishop stepped forward to begin the service. Chris raised her fingers to his lips for a gentle kiss, making her giggle.

'A lovely day for a wedding, don't you think?' he whispered.

'Oh, yes,' she answered. 'The loveliest of lovely days.'

* * * * *

Author Note

I've had the most fun working on this series and visiting my favourite place in the world: Paris! Even if it is only vicariously, on the page. I also love the Belle Époque period, a time of such beauty and innovation and optimism. It seemed like the perfect place for my three vivacious debutante heroines and their handsome heroes.

The Exposition Universelle had run from May the sixth to October the thirty-first in 1889, celebrating the one hundredth anniversary of the Bastille, and was a high-water mark in modern Europe. It also gave us one of my very favourite spots, the Eiffel Tower! Covering two hundred and thirty-seven acres, the Exposition featured pavilions and villages from countries all over the world, including Java, Egypt, Mexico, Senegal, and Cambodia, introducing Europeans to a wide array of music, food, art, and languages. There was a railroad to carry fair-goers between exhibits, the Galerie des Machines featuring modern inventions—including a visit by Thomas Edison to show off his newfangled light-bulb and gramophone—Buffalo Bill's *Wild West Show* with Annie Oakley, and the art pavilion with works by Whistler, Munch, Bonheur and Gaugin.

Another popular exhibit was the Imperial Diamond, also known as the Jacob Diamond, in the French pavilion. It was one of the largest stones in the world, previously owned by the Nizam of Hyderabad and then by the government of India. I used it as inspiration for the Eastern Star.

The fair's main symbol, of course, was the Eiffel Tower, the entrance arch to the fair. By the time the Exposition opened, workers were still putting on the finishing touches and the lifts weren't quite working, but people swarmed up its stairs to take in the dizzying views and shop at the souvenir counters and eat at the cafés. It wasn't entirely loved, though. A petition sent to the paper *Le Temps* read, 'We writers, painters, sculptors, and passionate devotees of the hitherto untouched beauty of Paris, protest with all our strength… in the name of slighted French taste, against the erection of this useless and monstrous Eiffel Tower.' The tower was meant to be temporary, but grew on the population of the city, and now is one of the most visited and beloved landmarks in the world, a symbol of the beautiful city itself.

One of my favourite aspects of researching historical background for my stories is looking into the fashions of the day! The end of the nineteenth century and the beginning of the twentieth seems like a particularly elegant period to me and the most famous of all the purveyors of fashions of the day was the House of Worth. Opened in 1858 by an Englishman, the house on the Rue de la Paix was soon The Place for ladies of fashion to shop. Empress Eugénie, Sarah Bernhardt, Lillie Langtry, Jenny Lind, Princess Alexandra and a variety of royalty and American millionaires patronised the elegant, comfortable salon, ordering their wardrobes for each season. The lush fabrics, unique designs, and impeccable service made it famous, and its designs are still well known.

I also had a lot of fun using the real-life visit of Edward VII, then the Prince of Wales, in my story! On June the tenth Bertie, Alexandra and their five children arrived at the Eiffel Tower. It was a 'private' visit—Queen Victoria couldn't countenance a celebration of a country throwing off their monarchy!—but Paris was Bertie's lifelong favourite city and he wasn't about to miss a look at something as grand as the Exposition.

They arrived at the Tower at ten-thirty in the morning, entourage and press in tow, with the Princess wearing a 'simple' blue and white silk gown and a bonnet trimmed with lilies of the valley, and were conducted on a tour by Monsieur Eiffel himself. I expanded the trip with a few more parties and excursions for the royal group, but I'm sure the fun-loving Prince wouldn't have minded!

I hope you enjoy exploring the beauties of Paris as much as I loved writing about it!

The following are a few sources I used in researching the period:

Jill Jonnes, *Eiffel's Tower* (2009)
Amy de la Haye and Valerie D. Mendes, *House of Worth: Portrait of an Archive* (2014)
Claire Rose, *Art Nouveau Fashion* (2014)
Jane Ridley, *Heir Apparent: A Life of Edward VII* (2013)
Richard Hough, *Edward and Alexandra: Their Private and Public Lives* (1992)